# DECAY

# Also By Brad Mathews

**Thousand Branches Series**
The Thousand Branches
The Venom Storm
The Satyr of Fulton Manor
Tomb of the Phoenix

**Era Sinistra Trilogy**
Era Sinistra
Era Sinistra-The Shadow
Era Sinistra-Skyglow

Decay
The Girl from South Track
Revelation

# DECAY

Brad Mathews

Unity Star Books

Mike, thank you for introducing me to the hidden world of semiconductor plants.

"I have noticed that even those who assert that everything is predestined and that we can change nothing about it still look both ways before they cross the street."

Stephen Hawking

# 1

# The Future was Yesterday

*The whole world is dead. Our reality has been reduced to a dystopian landscape that even the fires of hell dare not burn.*

Jalen paused and looked out the window where spring was ripe with hope and the flowers on the locust trees fluttered like waves of confetti on a dazzling stage. Out there was life. In here...everything but. He wrung his wrist, cracked a knuckle, and continued to type.

*Everything is gone. The monolith we created for communication has enslaved us. Humanity is obsolete. We have successfully removed our ability to act, to react, to make decisions, to communicate. Our basic necessities are foolish desires, and our luxuries are bars in the prison that contains us.*

A knock on his office door broke his chain of thought. He closed his laptop and concluded he'd finish it later if he could summon the will to further pursue such a gaunt subject. She had a blank look on her face. She said nothing, only slid a simmering cup of coffee onto the desk in front of him. It was almost as if she'd armed herself purposefully with such an indignant weapon. It wasn't that the coffee was too strong, too sweet, or too black; it was simply not a stimulant worthy of his existence. A better medicine would be a stolen sip of vodka or two. But that had to wait.

He had a life to live. In a different state of mind and in a different era, he might have even enjoyed life rather than endure its curses. Everyday brought turmoil. The frown on his face only spread as he leaned back in his chair admiring the empty world that surrounded him. How did it get like this? He wished he knew the answer to that, but life spun its own cycle, which seemed more and more beyond his control.

A long sigh did little to prepare him for the day. At least it was Friday. That recognition momentarily erased the frown. He let it return before standing up.

The bathroom mirror revealed what should have been a simpler Jalen. He stared at himself as if to ask the all-important question, *who are you?* "What do you want?" He asked, half expecting a detailed answer.

*Progress.* Hadn't that always been the plan? Since the first day of this year—the first day of his life, even—the unspoken priority defined his every move. Everything was learning, growing, failing, exposing weakness, recovering, thriving, and relapse. Those main themes of life surrounded him and constructed his very existence. Without one of those elements, he was nothing but the bare atoms that comprised his body.

He slowly stepped back to his desk, sipped the coffee, and carried it into the dining room. Marie shuffled across the floor in dainty white ankle socks and her cut-off pajama pants that seemed as if they were as old as he was. Her hair was wiry and tangled. She spun to face him, at first communicating joy, but then letting it relax into something resembling confusion.

"Nice day," she said without even looking out the window.

Jalen nodded. He'd already looked out the window but glanced again for some reason. "Could be."

"Friday."

"Like every other day, only I don't have to work tomorrow."

"Going to get drinks tonight?" she asked with a half-hearted lurch of her shoulders.

She wasn't even trying. It seemed they'd both waken on the proverbial wrong side of the bed. He bit his lip and looked away. "Better not."

"What do you have going on today?" she asked, raising her eyebrows, and only halfway communicating concern. He suspected the other half of the expression contained an underlying hint of disgust or even scorn.

"Top secret stuff."

"Per usual," she said, shrugging and glancing away. "Which basically boils down to you don't want to tell me."

"Sometimes there's nothing to tell. Job's not that interesting or glamorous, but someone's gotta do it."

"If you don't like it, why do you bother?"

He relaxed his shoulders and exhaled, which was the expression he most often used when he had nothing verbal to add. "Pays the bills."

"You're good at it."

"Good?" He glanced at her with a skewed expression on his eyebrows as if she'd just said the craziest thing he'd ever heard. *There's only bad and adequate in this job.*

He considered telling her what he really thought, but what was the point? He turned quickly and strode toward the door. He didn't get far before she stopped him.

"Where's my kiss?"

*Must have left it in the car,* Jalen thought. Instead, he lowered his eyebrows as she walked toward him. He planted a quick, dry one on her lips, and let it sink in that his passion for the relationship had dimmed over the past year. Like a trait that slithered through his personality, it had simply become an accepted part of his life.

He released her, frowned and looked at the bowl of fruit on the counter behind her shoulder. He narrowed his eyes but said nothing more.

"You know, sometimes I don't get you," Marie said.

He stared at her.

"Went to bed fine last night. Now it's all doom and gloom. Where's the sunshine? Don't think I don't remember what today is. Time to cut yourself a break."

"You don't know all of it," Jalen said, waving one hand as if to cut off her pleas. "So don't lecture me."

"Been a long time. Maybe it wasn't all your fault to begin with."

His frown deepened. "Gotta go," he said.

"Whatever. Have a good day. Don't get attacked."

He slung the door closed behind him and quickly walked to his car, which sat quietly in the driveway with mist covering its windows. A chill in the air suggested that spring wasn't quite ready to relent for summer. "Good one," he said to himself. Her dry humor had never ruined a day, but often lent itself to more introspection than he could handle. What did she really mean?

Then again, he knew her well enough by now to understand that her short last sentence contained three unspoken words. They repeated themselves in his mind once for clarity and finality. *Don't get attacked for being you.*

He frowned again, climbed into his car, started it, and pulled out of the driveway. He noticed the lack of traffic immediately after turning onto the busy thoroughfare connecting his neighborhood to the rest of the city. The morning radio traffic guy liked to call this phenomenon the 'Friday lights' as if half the people in the city didn't have to work on Friday.

He blankly eyed the overcast sky and tried to coerce a tune to jingle in his mind, but he couldn't think of anything positive. The deep blue clouds, yellowed at the edges from the rising sun, soaked the desert landscape around the city in shadow. He stopped at a red light and closed his eyes in attempt to will the humanity away and to 'dress professionally.'

Marie probably had a point. But the way she made her point seemed insane. It seemed to dodge the very notion that, not only was he her boyfriend, but a real living, breathing human. Basic courtesy could have done her well.

He found it interesting how his own perception of the events that unfolded in his life drove the final outcomes of every circumstance. It seemed almost as if he already knew what the situation meant, and by seeing it the way he did, unintentionally wrought a different end than the one that might have come naturally.

In a timeline that represented each individual event, a precursor was positioned at the front of the line, followed by the main event and then his perception of the event. The conclusion was placed at the end. But what if the whole line was read from right to left? What if time itself were an aberration of logic that could be twisted, molded, and manipulated like clay? In some ways, time was simply another perception that sometimes ruined decent conversations.

This thought made him think about Einstein, which then devolved into the thought of a book he'd read about physics several years ago. The author postulated that, no matter how it was measured, time always moved forward and could not be reversed. It had a definite beginning and an uncertain end. The linear logic at the time seemed rewarding, but later on, concerning. Whatever higher power many others believed in couldn't have been a slave to that one simple rule or else the very idea of that power would be a myth.

Then again, Jalen longed for simpler days with simpler problems, before life spread out into a series of increasingly complicated tragedies. He shook his head when he thought of it. From his own perspective, what he'd written this morning—what he planned to continue later, sparked with terrifying truth. He cursed under his breath. "God, I need a drink."

In the distance, a traffic signal turned red and then green again as if a child were playing with the controls. He hoped he wasn't seeing it wrong. He inadvertently sped up. Behind him, a patrol car appeared and flashed its lights.

Jalen swore and pulled to the side of the street. Driving much too fast, the cop car ripped past him, probably in pursuit of yet another lost cause of justice. For the cop, like Jalen, everyday life dropped these kinds of bombs.

It was nothing out of the ordinary, nothing to run home and tell the girlfriend about while her biting sarcasm somehow drilled holes in every word. He would have to talk to her about that later, but by that time the thought and the emotion of the moment would have vanished and there would be nothing to talk about anyway. Marie liked to talk, but her definition of the event deviated from his in striking fashion.

The spoken admission that he needed a drink bored into his brain for the remainder of the drive. What did it mean, if anything? Could it be another one of those twelve steps? He shrugged, sped up, and bit his lip. "I'm fine," he muttered.

*Nothing like lying to yourself.*

In order to chase that demon away, he mentally attempted to construct the next few lines of his prose. *The world and the life we built are nothing. Nothing but specks of dust in an eternal universe where mankind displays the traits of not even an afterthought. What we long for is nothing more than a sequence of synapses in the brain. Not even a speck of dust.*

# 2

# Between Two Worlds

The world headquarters for Lynx Technologies stood atop a wide bluff flanking the southern edge of the city. The fifty-eight buildings comprising the complex served as the offices of the corporate officials and the base of nearly half of the company's worldwide production facilities. Daily, 26,000 employees commuted to this somewhat isolated desert plateau.

The campus was constructed like a city unto itself. On the north stood the most architecturally interesting structures that housed most of the high-ranking corporate officials while the central avenues served as the transportation and shipping hub. Surrounding the wide urban thoroughfare in the center of the campus, a network of fabrication and research and development buildings interconnected. When viewed from the nearby streets, this complex appeared as one giant building. Beyond the group of fabrication buildings lied most of the company's recreation facilities, which included a baseball diamond, a soccer pitch, a track, and a state-of-the-art gym.

Jalen entered the main south gate as he normally did, thinking about the day's work while conveniently bypassing the security checkpoint that most incoming vehicles were required to stop at. Both surveillance cameras and lightly armed guards patrolled the booths. Jalen's car displayed a level three security ID, which was easily identifiable and could only be obtained with proper clearance at the main security hub off the lobby of Building 27. The security office at times seemed like Jalen's second home, where he could somehow erase the troubles that pervaded life at his house with Marie.

He pulled into his dedicated parking stall and stared at the prefabbed concrete panels making up the building's walls. After exhaling, he took one more moment to think about Marie. The way they'd said goodbye had certainly left a sour taste, which had somehow wormed its way into his mood.

The job description displayed the hallmarks of an easy, stress-free environment, yet reality played a different tune. While a rewarding sense of accomplishment rarely punctuated a work day, occasionally a feeling of gratitude flashed over him. This morning, a departing janitor eyed Jalen through the car's windshield, smiled and raised a palm to wave at him. He halfheartedly returned the gesture before slowly opening his door.

True enough, Jalen didn't initially want this job. Skilled IT technicians who were knowledgeable in physical security were treated like gold at Lynx. While the thought of being little more than a glorified security cop seemed beneath him, the salary was nothing to sneeze at. It allowed him to live comfortably within his lifestyle as long as he didn't try to one-up his neighbor, who seemed to bring home increasingly expensive sets of wheels on a monthly basis.

Jalen sunk his chin to his chest before opening the door. A quick burst of cold wind greeted him. On instinct, he quickly made his way across the small plaza, clutching his security badge as he went. Almost sprinting, he darted inside, where an ambient, sterile warmth replaced the cold outside. A flurry of employees dressed for duty silently swiped their badges across the readers, ascended the steps, and made their way down the halls. Jalen carefully watched a younger woman rifle through her bag in search of her card. She seemed flustered, but Jalen didn't think to offer assistance. Instead, he skirted a broad seating and reception area and entered a narrow corridor at the end of the room.

He swiped his badge across the reader and entered the office. Amongst his fellow employees, an uproarious conversation seemed to switch gears entirely. One of them went so far as to stand up as if Jalen were a court justice.

"Jalen," a skinny blonde woman shouted. The cheer in her demeanor, while most often appreciated, bothered him more than it should have.

"Morning, Sandy."

The conversation went silent. He had fourteen people working under his supervision and he didn't believe he'd ever seen the group behave this way.

"Drew," he said, stepping toward his desk. "Put that away."

He didn't even have to look to know that Drew wielded a powerful rubber-band gun that was accurate to a range of sixty feet.

A tall woman with black hair and glasses sat across from him. She reached for a stapler as she regarded Jalen with a simpler gesture, a cool smile, and a subtle shift of her eyebrows. If he had a friend in the office, she was as reliable as they came.

Instead of returning to her work, Kalee leaned back in her chair and seemed to study Jalen. He pretended like he didn't notice and busied himself opening several programs simultaneously. A frown must have bathed his face in a murky gray, because Kalee's expression shifted. She turned and punched a few keys on her keyboard before facing Jalen again.

"Another fight with the missus?"

Jalen intentionally looked confused.

"It's written all over your face."

"Not so much a fight, "Jalen lied. "Sort of a misinterpretation in communication."

She relaxed, flipped her hair over her shoulder, pressed a few more buttons, and then stared at him some more. "At least you got one thing."

"You?"

"It's Friday."

She suddenly looked up when the office door opened. Mark "Brawn" Larson proudly strutted into the office sporting a huge grin and fanning out a fistful of papers, which he began to hand out to each of Jalen's employees.

A tuft of brown, unkempt hair crowned Brawn's head which seemed to highlight the sharp edges of his jaw. He was built on a slender frame, but displayed sleek muscles that sometimes made him look like the jock type. Of course, he *was* the jock type, but that didn't stop Jalen from judging him. He watched Brawn flip his tie up while he slammed a paper down on Sandy's desk.

"Don't forget to join the pool by three this afternoon," he said, raising his voice.

Brawn turned to face Jalen and grinned. "Be advised, we're going to kick your butts and take some names on Saturday."

"I'm not playing, Brawny. Remember?" He referred to the ankle he'd injured in the first soccer game of the 'season' a 4-1 thumping of the defending champion Corporate Bulldogs. Even though the injury was just about healed enough to play, Jalen didn't exude the passion for the game he had in previous years. These days, he used it as an excuse to be away from home.

"You're still team captain. Be sure to pass along my complements to the Alphas."

"Sure," Jalen said. "Give them some fresh meat to gnaw on."

Brawn and most of the Building 43 Falcons displayed the sort of arrogance that could have chapped the hide of most normal players. They were good at talking. Sometimes, they even trash talked their way to victory on the field, but the attitude didn't intimidate Jalen, and he wouldn't allow his fellow players to fall victim to the charade, either.

Puffing out his chest, Brawn laughed and exited the office.

"Five-to-one," somebody said.

"Gotta take those odds," Decker said. He scribbled something on the paper, then crossed it out and grinned.

"I don't know," Sandy said. "I think I like the points."

Jalen shook his head, then acted alarmed all at once. "Hey, what's that on Camera 64?"

The three of them turned their heads and immediately immersed themselves in work. Jalen offered a cool smile and glanced across at Kalee. "What do you think?"

She stared at one of her monitors before casually marking something on the pool sheet. "I think you're going to win."

"If I don't get stuck working," he said. He saw what she'd written out of the corner of his eye. "And to the tune of a hundred bucks? I don't think even Brawn would be that crazy."

Kalee offered no comment other than a mischievous smile during which she bit her lip. To say that she had her quirks would have been an understatement. She was a curious woman with a real personality, which may have been a rare trait amongst security officers, but which Jalen appreciated.

Instead of saying anything, she fixed her gaze on one of her monitors, leaned closer, punched some keys, and continued to watch. After a perplexed look, she muttered, "Uh-oh."

Jalen stared at her.

"Got a couple of 'access denied' reports, same room within seconds of each other."

"Probably a mistake," Jalen said. "Details on the badge?"

She stared. "Contractor number 1734C. Looks like a tour guide."

Instead of offering assistance, Jalen slightly leaned back and stroked his chin. He imagined his expression to look just like the one he'd given to Marie this morning, only slightly less disgusted.

"What's a tour guide doing trying to access secure areas?"

"Room number?" Jalen said, rising to his feet.

"Contaminant Iso Room 27A113."

Jalen forced a dry smile, and with a simple, single nod, said, "I'll go check it out. Make sure this office doesn't blow up."

"Of course," she said.

"And keep an eye on that badge. Any more strange activity, radio me."

She watched him stroll towards the door. "Good luck."

Jalen strode quickly across the lobby, waved his badge across the reader, and darted up the steps two at a time. The usual assortment of chaos filled the main corridor. A pair of janitors worked at opposite ends of the corridor, pushing carts full of chemicals of which Jalen didn't want to know the contents. Nothing looked out of the ordinary. No tour guides roamed the halls attempting to gain access to secure rooms.

After two steps into the left end of the corridor, Jalen turned around. "Room A113," he muttered to himself.

The room was on the right about two thirds of the way down the main corridor before it doglegged left to join a connecting corridor from the adjacent building. It came as little surprise that no one was there.

Spinning in a circle and trying to gain understanding of why a tour guide wanted to access a contaminant isolation room, Jalen perched a sour look on his face. Should anyone see him, he subconsciously wanted them to know he was nettled.

Before his mind could form the beginnings of a story, chaos erupted down the hall. Towards the opposite end of the corridor, a worker clad in a basic non-clean white jump suit lifted a tray of materials and placed it on a counter. She shrieked, stepped away, and covered her mouth. It was obvious that she was staring at something horrifying on the floor.

Without thinking, Jalen sprinted in that direction. Lack of training and practice had wearied his knees somewhat, but the adrenaline surge powered his muscles sufficiently enough to complete the 400-something foot sprint with ease. When he reached the halfway point, his radio crackled.

"Kalee to Jalen. Chem Lab Process Room 27C143. Access granted, but that also seems a strange room to access."

Jalen connected the dots so fast that it would have made a chemical engineer flush. The contaminant isolation room was used to quickly store materials that were not safe to bring into a clean room. Jalen had seen the inside of the room only once but recalled it quickly. Cleanroom contaminant particles that the room's filtration room caught were sent via duct to this room. A machine separated the dust and static particles before exhausting up to the scrubber units above the fab rooms. Items considered contaminants, which were not permitted in cleanrooms, were delivered to a storage bin. After a shift, workers could request access to this room to collect personal belongings. The system was probably not without its flaws, but problems seemed so rare and isolated that Jalen could not remember a single issue where a fab had to be shut down.

The chemical lab room was even more puzzling. Kalee was right that it was a room that a tour guide should not attempt to access. Exactly how his badge had been cleared for this room was worthy of a shrug, but no system of security was perfect. Jalen made a mental note to bring this to the attention of the badge access department.

He reached the site of the commotion before his thoughts could conclude. He eyed the worker for explanation, but she simply pointed to the floor, where a trail of blood led down a side corridor toward a section of small rooms between cleanrooms. Each cleanroom was equipped with a materials pass-through, which featured a window into a small, negative-pressure chamber. When a worker needed to supply the cleanroom with materials, he or she would scan his or her badge, lift the glass, and place the material in the chamber. After closing the window a small light would flash, alerting workers in the cleanroom to open the glass from the inside to collect the materials. The worker stood frozen near her cart as if she'd just witnessed a gruesome murder.

"What happened here?"

"I-I don't know," she said.

"You didn't see anything?"

The worker shook her head and stepped away.

"Stay here," he said. "Kalee, send armed assistance to the chem lab."

"Affirmative."

The woman didn't move. Her expression slowly morphed from one communicating shock to something representing agitation. He looked at her for several seconds before he said anything. "What's your name?"

"Uh, Cartwright," she said, shaking her head. "Melinda."

"Not a fun way to start, is it?"

"My shift is almost over. For a minute, I thought I'd stepped into an alternate dimension."

Jalen studied her for a few more seconds. He didn't become aware that his expression was slackening before it was too late. *You don't show emotion on this job,* he remembered his boss telling him several years ago. "Skeleton, huh? Graveyard shifts can be hell."

"Tell me about it."

He quietly cleared his throat. "So you were handing wafers through the glass? And then you just noticed this?"

"Walking up and down these halls, you start to not even notice the floor anymore." She explained with an air of patience Jalen found remarkable.

"Until you notice something that shouldn't be there," he finished for her. He'd somehow been in her shoes. Scanning for security issues on the company's servers had become habit much faster than he'd imagined. After a while, he'd trained himself to look past the badge numbers, the code, and the logic to never notice it until something had begun to look out of place.

She nodded slowly.

"I think the cops might have some questions to ask you when they get here."

"You haven't called them yet," she said.

"Protocol," Jalen said casually, looking at a point down the corridor over her shoulder. "When we find where the blood trail ends, we'll call for emergency help if the situation warrants it. We don't know what we're looking at yet."

Three people rounded the corner into the main corridor just as he finished his last sentence. They looked eager, yet lacking the attitude to handle an actual investigation. Jalen had a bad feeling about this turn of events, but it was clear that his subordinates didn't.

"Aren't you going to look in that room?" Melinda asked hesitantly.

"That's what these guys are for. Just in case." He waited for a moment for her to say something, but when it was clear she had nothing else to offer, he continued. "Will you be around here a while?"

"Half an hour," she said, glancing at her watch.

"Why don't you wait in the lobby while we look at the situation and call the cops if we have to? If they don't need to talk to you, you can go home and enjoy your weekend."

"I'll be back tomorrow," she said.

He could sense a node of sorrow behind her words, which he understood. He hoped this situation wouldn't force him to work during the weekend.

Jalen looked back and forth from the witness to the blood trail. His job came with a healthy salary and almost no risk. Being a security guard at first didn't sound appealing to him, but being armed with only a taser gun and a pair of handcuffs had been even less interesting. It didn't seem that safe a position now. His heart began to race. If there had been a murder there was a good chance he would come face to face with the suspect and would be forced to apprehend him. With or without backup, such a prospect would come with peril beyond anything he'd seen.

Already, the memory of the morning was beginning to fade. The disagreement with Marie seemed old news by now. The passion and memory behind the encounter had evaporated into entrails of memory only leaking traces of regret. Even his conversation with Kalee seemed unimportant. Then again, betting on an upcoming soccer match entailed no importance whatsoever, unless one counted the monetary aspect. A person never enters a fun bet with the notion of making money.

Today was a Friday, but this event began to make it feel like a Monday. The spirit of revelry remained, but Jalen sensed a heavier mood filtering in, which darkened the aura. Somehow, joy still lurked, but appeared as nothing more than an aperture conjoining two realms. Catastrophe awaited just a few steps away.

# 3

# Fragments of Infinity

Melinda slowly walked away without looking back, her body language communicating shock and a certain air of sadness. A pang of wanting to know more about this woman, her history, and what drove her forced its way into his head but did not linger.

Marcus, Thom, and Barry served as his backups. They arrived a little too eagerly, each with a crisp stride and a cozy smile.

"What do we got?" Barry asked.

Jalen pointed to the blood trail.

Thom tilted his head, eyeing the room name next to the door. His expression seemed casual, which made Jalen want to slap him. "That's no infirmary."

Jalen led the way, carefully stepping around the spots of blood while keeping his eyes trained on the door. The door's handle was clean. This suggested that whoever had opened the door had not sustained a cut, or worse yet, was not injured at all. Jalen silently assumed the latter. He put an index finger against his lips, drew his taser gun, and swiped his badge across the reader.

The door issued a faint clicking sound. With a fury he had not exercised in weeks, he slung the door open. Breathing heavily, he pointed the gun in every direction. The other three followed in the same manner.

The room seemed to be unoccupied. The main room was essentially a lobby, which served as a common space for the other operations. A small kitchen space consisting of a sink, a microwave oven, and a coffee machine adorned the center of the wall behind the room's front door. Jalen guessed that this room hadn't been used for several hours.

Behind a door with a small window stood the room's main purpose area. The blood trail disappeared under that door. No square of light brightened the door. He scanned his badge to enter, but still did not lower his weapon. Most of the side labs within Lynx's campus were lit with motion-sensing lights to conserve power. After ten minutes detecting no movement, the lights shut off.

After forcefully shoving the door open, Jalen again pointed his weapon in all directions. He had never been in this room, but it seemed to be some sort of a 'think' room to promote development ideas. Soft lighting via manual lamps were carefully arranged around a table with a slate top and a trio of comfortable-looking lounge chairs. Two coasters sat idle in the center of the table. This room was also vacant. The main intention for the room resided behind one more door to a small lab space. The door handle was replaced by a number pad and a laser scanning device that measured handprints. For a moment, Jalen couldn't discern how to open the door.

More importantly, he didn't see how someone obviously not cleared to use this room could have opened it. He almost decided it wasn't worth it, but the blood trail led directly to the door. The blood's owner hadn't stopped to look out the window or to sketch ideas on the table.

He pointed to the other three. "Guard this door," he instructed.

Barry nodded and kept his taser at the ready.

As quickly as Jalen could walk while remaining quiet, he found a corner as far away from the door as he could get. "Kalee," he said, pressing his radio button. "Can you get me an access code for the Chem Lab 27C143-C?"

"Sure thing," she said.

Jalen listened to the sound of her typing on her keyboard. The keystrokes paused and then intensified as she got closer to the information.

"It has a palm reader?" she asked.

"Yes," Jalen whispered.

"I'll give you the emergency security access code, which is the only one authorized to let you bypass the palm reader. You ready for it?"

Jalen strode quickly back to the door and shoved Marcus out of the way. "Give it to me."

"Pound sign seven-four-six-eight. Then pound again."

"Thanks, Kalee," he whispered.

Before entering the code, he eyed each of his associates carefully. "If there is anyone in this room, I want you to shoot on sight, got that?"

As quickly as his fingers could move, Jalen punched in the code. He became consciously aware that his fingers were trembling for some unexplainable reason. Probably a result of not getting that drink. That desire was like a dank shadow that followed him around.

The door unlocked itself and Jalen pushed it open with a little too much force. Before he had much of a chance to look around, one of his associates fired his weapon.

Jalen spun to scan the room. The stainless steel tables were laid out perfectly and were so clean it seemed likely that they hadn't been used today. A row of chemical washing sinks filled a cubby behind the door. The victim stood hunched over with his head buried in one of the sinks and a pool of blood had accumulated on the concrete floor.

"Jesus," Jalen shouted. "A little warning might have been nice."

The three of them stood silently staring at the body and shrugged. Their expressions seemed too stale and ugly for the situation.

"Which one of you tased him?"

Barry looked up. A trail of disbelief and guilt paved a meandering path through the remnants of his previous expression. He somehow appeared older and wiser, as if years had taught him a life's worth of lessons in only a few seconds.

"Was he moving?" Jalen asked, already certain of the answer.

Barry shook his head and looked back toward the body. "I don't...shit."

"Looks like you've got a mountain of paperwork to file, days of interviews with the cops, and probably a psych evaluation. We'll probably have to suspend you." Jalen explained in chopped-up sentences that indicated that his blood pressure had risen.

He stepped closer to the body to examine it. By his guess this man had been in the room for a little over ten minutes because the lights only turned themselves on when Jalen swung open the door. The sink was filled with some clear liquid and the man's face was scarred and burned as if scorched with years of decomposition in only a few minutes. Jalen knew of only one chemical compound that could destroy human flesh so thoroughly in such a short amount of time. Though he possessed a limited knowledge of chemical properties, Jalen suspected the compound to be hydrochloric acid. The police would have to do a week's worth of tests on the solution, its makeup and its potency, as well as whether it had been the chemical that had killed him.

"Kalee," Jalen said after pressing the button on his radio.

"Jalen? Is everything alright?"

"Call nine-one-one. Paramedics won't be necessary. We'll escort the cops to this room when they arrive."

"Jalen, what happened?"

"Can't explain right now." He ended the conversation too abruptly, which recalled emotions wrought from his disagreement with Marie. It had been less than two hours, yet it seemed like an eternity had passed.

His perception of time had changed remarkably in the last ten minutes. In retrospect, it didn't make any sense how one short string of events could stretch out the day as if time itself contained elastic properties that could be molded like clay. Then again, like everything else, time itself seemed to have shattered into billions of pieces that simply floated away into nothingness. He felt the erosion of time take its toll on him while he inspected the room for other clues.

"Jalen, how the hell did the killer gain access to this room?" Thom asked quietly. He had his chin rested on his forehand as if he were a casually interested college intern studying a case which held little emotional relevance to him.

A pang of regret shrouded his heart in a thick blanket that somehow prevented Jalen from breathing. A sense of hopelessness crept up inside of him to take residence in a dark corner of his mind that was littered with the carcasses of dormant thoughts laid silent for years. His eyes darted back and forth and his heartbeat intensified.

"Barry," he said. "You're going to be in lots of trouble."

"I didn't kill him," Barry said. His expression was glum and his voice was purposely sturdy and low as if to prevent emotion from carving his statement into shreds.

"You didn't have to tase the poor bastard."

Barry stepped toward him. Anger poured into his eyes like a viscous compound meant to torch Jalen's brains. "I thought I saw him move, but you told us to shoot first and think later."

Resigned, Jalen nodded and lowered his eyes.

"Next question is," Thom started, "Who is this guy?"

Barry shrugged. "Cops will get to the bottom of that." He knelt down next to the sink and reached for a box of latex gloves on the bottom shelf of the adjacent cabinet. He seemed to know what he was doing. Barry had been on the job since just before Jalen started. He was the oldest in the security office. Jalen seemed to remember a rumor from two years ago that he had retired from the police force, but he couldn't remember why. That detail was unimportant for now, but Barry clearly had accumulated some crime scene experience.

"It's a tour guide," Jalen said. "Kalee and I have been tracking his badge this morning since he attempted to access a room he wasn't cleared to enter. Didn't think he'd turn up like this."

"In another room he shouldn't have been able to access," Thom finished.

"Speaking of which," Barry said slowly. "Where the hell is his badge?" He had ducked his head under the sink so that he could see the man's chest.

"Excuse me?" Jalen said.

"He doesn't have his badge on him. Contractors are required to have it visible at all times. If they don't comply, they lose the privilege to use it. You know that."

"So it might not have been this guy that tried to use his badge down the hall this morning." Jalen spoke with a curious strain, but keeping his voice even and strong. "If that's true, we have a killer on the loose."

He punched his radio button again. "Kalee."

She answered, but not as promptly as he'd expected her to. "What?"

"Shut off that tour guide's badge. I doubt he'd try to use it again under the circumstances, but we need to force him into areas with video surveillance."

"Already done," she said.

"Thank you." He said it as though the sentence's meaning was muddled, but he was sincere.

Waiting on the police required tapping feet and twiddling thumbs to retain sanity. While Jalen had come face-to-face with death once or twice, he had never witnessed a murder or been called on to investigate one. Now that he had control, he wanted to cede it. Besides, in a situation like this, no one had control. Only destiny guided the way, whether to a promising destination or not.

Jalen closed his eyes and shielded them with his palm. He didn't really want to hear it, but his guess was that he'd be working the weekend. The prospect of freedom for two precious days, while sometimes elusive, would promise to be unreachable this week.

After waving off Marcus and Thom, Jalen turned to Barry, whose face seemed shrouded in a simple shade of misery. His look wasn't of shock. He'd seen bodies before. Disbelief. Regret. Jalen relaxed his muscles and steadied his gaze. Barry displayed those traits of humanity, but would not succumb.

"Where's he at with that badge, Boss?"

Jalen shook his head. "Don't know. And don't call me Boss."

"Sorry, Master."

He said nothing. The wait exceeded ten minutes. A weathered security guard trying to make small talk with a retired cop seemed like a lesson from which the only thing learned was futility.

Jalen didn't want to admit it, but too many loose ends remained. The cops would want to follow Jalen wherever he went, and by so doing, pressure him to break. Inflicting stress was part of a cop's job description.

"They're gonna do a crime scene sketch, try to recreate what happened. Then they'll obtain physical evidence, talk to any witnesses—"

"Yeah," Jalen cut him off. "I've watched a few cop shows. In that order?"

"Sometimes. When complex sequences are in question, they'll try to view cam footage and maybe they'll get lucky."

Jalen didn't want to admit it, but luck would play a larger part than Barry surmised. Though the campus's security measures were good enough to suffice, it would not be possible to cover every inch of every corridor with the camera views. In truth, less than ten percent of the complex enjoyed that luxury.

Inside of cleanrooms, research and development labs in particular, camera footage was strictly forbidden, even if used for security. The potential loss from hacking far outweighed the need to see everything that went on. In some ways, this job relied on a certain faith, which Jalen found to be waning.

Jalen's heart sank as he leaned against a wall next to a bulletin board. He folded his arms and tapped his head against the wall. The possibilities seemed as expansive as the bounds of space, yet shattered into billions of fragments that could never be reassembled.

# 4

# The Speed of Life

The vicious circles life spun Jalen in were sometimes too much for him to cope with in a rational manner. Taking his own actions—those required to retain any sense of sanity—often meant sacrificing the needs of others. When that happened, disaster seemed to lurk behind every corner.

One of the four police officers that arrived in the chemical lab volunteered to follow Jalen to the security office, where they would pursue a different avenue of investigation. While true that Jalen was skilled in analyzing behavior and trends, his first objective was to give the officer what he wanted. In truth, Jalen didn't believe he could offer what Officer Lawrence wanted.

"Security footage," the officer said just after walking into the room. He scanned the office.

Jalen pretended he didn't notice the three chatty employees grouped at a desk sipping coffee while sharing small talk. Instead, he ignored them. "Our video security team," Jalen said, showing Lawrence to a grouping of desks that sat behind an array of large computer monitors. The company leadership had been contemplating upgrading this department to its own state-of-the-art video center where employees would watch footage all day long. They'd repeatedly scrapped the plan due to the near adequate security situation and the comfort of knowing they'd never had the need for a system so grand. It wasn't a front-of-the line priority, at least not to the degree of developing a new line of ultra-flash memory that could power the latest and greatest devices.

"Show me the corridor outside the lab thirty minutes ago," Lawrence said.

Jalen nodded to Laurie who searched for it. "I doubt we'll be able to see much," Jalen offered. "Even if there is a camera in the vicinity."

"There is," Laurie said, leaning closer to one of the screens. "Luckily."

"Let me get this straight," Officer Lawrence said. "You guys are protecting the assets and property of a multi-billion dollar worldwide tech company and you lack some of the most basic means of security? Seems counter-productive."

Jalen snorted, but held back. "I'm not in charge of funding or engineering."

"But part of your job should be to tell those in charge what your department does need, so that doesn't say much about your leadership."

The confrontational tone Lawrence used stirred the demons in his brain. He shook his head and closed his eyes. "They are well aware of what they need. Video surveillance is not at the top of the list and never has been. If you didn't notice when you arrived, our campus access system is second to none. It isn't like we've got our hands tied around here."

"Just show me the video," the officer said. The sturdiness of his voice momentarily caught Jalen off guard. He stepped back, rubbed his eyes, and clenched a fist with his right hand.

Laurie quickly opened the file and started playback. Lawrence wore a quizzical look that suggested a certain degree of confidence that Jalen didn't ever want to approach. The smug arrogance in the look could only be rivaled by Brawn.

The video started fuzzy, but with a few keystrokes, Laurie was able to sharpen the image, zoom in, and replay the segment of footage.

The footage seemed inconclusive. From watching, one could certainly ascertain that something had happened, but it would be impossible to bring any new leads to light. The event was halfway out of frame and distorted due to the curvature of the lens. Laurie attempted to sharpen the image again, but couldn't make its case more appealing. The perpetrator's face never showed up.

Lawrence sighed and demanded her to replay it.

Whatever had taken place seemed to be both quick and violent. He could see the cock of an elbow and the hunch of a back followed by nothing. A few seconds passed and the perpetrator almost stepped into frame. He slung something over his shoulder like a small bag and then forcefully shoved the victim forward. They both disappeared out of frame and nothing else happened.

"Fast forward to before the discovery of the blood trail," Lawrence said.

Laurie nodded. The time stamp on the camera showed that about five minutes had elapsed. She zoomed in as far as possible, cleaned up the image, adjusted the artificial lighting, and watched. Someone emerged from the door to the lab, which was halfway out of frame. The man quickly turned and disappeared from view before his face became visible.

"Play it again," the officer demanded.

"Take it easy," Jalen suggested.

"A man was murdered on your watch. Perhaps not taking it easy would have prevented it."

Jalen's face flushed. He pounded his fist into his left hand and grimaced. He looked away for any sign of hope. From her desk, Kalee was watching the drama unfold with a sympathetic expression. When she noticed Jalen glance, she forced a smile, which he let pass.

"Zoom in on the window," Lawrence said. "Good shot, now pause there."

Laurie punched a button.

"Save me a gif."

"We'll need to check protocol," Laurie said.

"You don't—"

"I'll approve it, Laurie. If corporate has any problem with the transfer, I'll take it." Jalen didn't need to add anything further. He clenched his teeth. Useful questions and ideas seemed beyond Lawrence. *Just leave. I'll track the bastard my own way.*

"True leadership."

Jalen stepped away from the video desk and quickly strode down the aisle while Lawrence followed.

"Pardon my approach," Officer Lawrence said. "You know how it is in this business. Just doing my job, and at the end of the day we both go home with a paycheck if we're lucky."

"Don't ever treat my employees like that again," Jalen said. "I run this place and have a pretty good handle on the system. I'll see to it you never set foot on campus again."

"Really?" Lawrence scoffed. "Let's just cut the attitude and get the job done, how does that sound? Don't want to get fired for not cooperating."

Jalen bit his lip, attempting to massage the anger away before he pressed on. Without speaking, he entered a group of files and brought up a screen showing a relevant list of badge numbers. He narrowed the list down by security access and then selected contractor clearance. A list of several hundred showed up. When he entered the date, only a dozen badges of similar clearance level were in use. He entered each one and scanned it. None of them showed any questionable use, except for one.

"I take it all that activity is legit," Lawrence said, watching in anticipation.

Jalen nodded and glanced up. Kalee was staring and looking silently concerned for his well-being. Perhaps she could see the turmoil on his face, but she was skilled at being a friend to the point where she didn't even have to speak to communicate.

"Got you," Lawrence said when Jalen brought up the tour guide's badge.

"This is Carl Kazinsky, the tour guide," Jalen said.

"You give tour guides contractor badges?"

"Rules of protocol," Jalen shrugged. "I didn't set them up. A tour guide is only really on campus four or five times a month. He has good knowledge as to what goes on but has to sign a strict confidentiality agreement that basically allows him to be prosecuted for divulging company secrets. To date, it seems he's complied."

"Except for the part about trying to gain access to rooms he has no business using," the officer said.

Jalen said nothing and stared at the monitor for fifteen seconds. The photograph began to fade as he stared at the red text reading 'active' on the bottom of the badge scan.

"Kalee, you said you shut down that badge, didn't you?"

"I did," she said.

"It's still showing as active."

She nodded and dropped a pencil in a cup. She didn't look concerned. "And it will until he scans his badge to leave. After that, he won't have access."

"Doesn't it shut down his ability to use the badge anywhere else on campus? Jalen glanced at her and then stared back at the screen.

"Of course."

"So how is this guy logged into Cleanroom 27C104?"

"Let me check," she said.

Kalee busied herself typing for a few moments and then stared at the badge. She sighed. "Looks like he scanned the badge for access less than a minute before I deactivated it."

"Smart criminal," Lawrence said.

"Or lucky," Jalen replied. "It's impossible for anyone to know how we do things in this office. We always follow protocol, but we don't always employ the same methods."

"We gotta get to that cleanroom," Lawrence said.

Jalen nodded but didn't move for several seconds. Instead, he stared at the badge and contemplated why a tour guide would suddenly decide to try using his badge where he had no clearance. Reason accompanied every act, whether or not Jalen or mankind as a whole wished to admit it.

"Does the guy need to scan his badge to leave that room?"

"Yes," Jalen said. "They added that feature three years ago as a means to monitor employee productivity and for better security. According to some of the big wigs, it's paid off in spades."

"That so?"

"Downturn on the economy," Jalen said. "When the bottom line's hurting you look for ways to make your money more efficient, and you do that by training efficiency. Workers get enough breaks for lunch, smoking, etc. Just that extra layer of accountability saved the company millions in the first year alone."

Officer Lawrence paced to the door without saying much, but Jalen spun to face him for further instruction.

"Gotta go talk to our team leader," the officer said. "You stay right here and keep an eye on that room. Don't let anyone leave."

"We can't do that," Jalen said.

"Do it anyway."

"You don't understand, leaving cleanrooms is completely voluntary. Our system will not let us stop anyone from leaving."

"Deactivate all of the badges, then."

"Are you out of your mind?"

"Do it, or I'll come back and arrest you."

Jalen slammed his fist down on the table, causing Kalee and everyone else to jump. Kalee subtly shook her head and glued her eyes to her screen. She typed away without saying anything.

Instead of showing remorse, Jalen studied her. She never seemed like the type of woman who could mask what she really felt no matter how hard she tried. For her, telling a white lie was impossible. If she tried to conceal what she felt, her emotion would give her away and her entire lie would be blown. This time, her expression communicated shame. It was fair to say that she didn't like to be around Jalen when his temper got out of hand, which had its way of happening from time to time. As a matter of fact, these little outbursts seemed to be happening with more regularity. Jalen, of course, attempted to pass it off as the demands of a stressful job and a stressful situation, but that didn't tell the whole story.

Three years ago, life began to take its toll. Her disappearance was not his fault, and no one had ever blamed him for it, except for himself, If only things would have been different or he'd handled conflict better or been open-minded. After that, he asked himself, how does one attempt to reassemble the pieces of what could have been considered a successful life? The short of it was that he could not. No force of nature could mend something broken—not even a heart.

A long exhale managed to express Jalen's true feelings to Kalee.

"Three years," she said. "And it's still haunting you."

Jalen ignored her.

He knew her well enough to understand that she wasn't going to use the 'tough friendship' route. She wasn't going to tell him to suck it up and to move on, just that he could access her shoulder anytime he wanted.

It wasn't only her understanding that turned her into such a valuable friend. An ingrained tendency to change the subject when circumstances seemed impassable Jalen deemed to be one of her greatest strengths.

"You're going to win tomorrow," she said. "At least you'd better. I've got a hundred bucks riding on it."

"Don't remind me," he said. "Now we have the pressure of expectations to deal with."

She stared at him. "You don't believe you'll win?"

Jalen sat back and sighed with his fingers laced behind his head. He didn't want to answer her question, but he liked the fact that she was talking to him.

"Will you be there tomorrow?"

He leaned forward and sat up without saying anything. Allowing himself a moment to think about the crime scene, he managed to mutter some nonsense in a low tone. "We'll see."

She nodded and looked at her keyboard, positioning her fingers over the home row. Jalen stood up and took a few steps toward the door. He stopped and turned around, trying to smile, which probably didn't work. "Will you be there?

Kalee didn't look up from her screen. "Of course." She typed something quickly and called after him. "Twenty-four people are signed into the cleanroom, including the bad guy. Be careful."

"I'll call you if I need anything," he grunted while swinging open the door. "Barry. I'll need some backup."

Barry quickly joined him. They made the short walk to the cleanroom without saying much.

"I think live weapons would be a good idea this time," Barry said, not so subtly suggesting that the office obtain some for emergencies.

"We'll have at least one," Jalen said.

"Oh, sure, let me get some of my favorite put-downs ready."

Jalen and Barry approached the clean room to find officer Lawrence waiting for them. He stood tall in the corridor reading some small note that was haphazardly affixed to a cork board across the hall.

"Let's get in there," Lawrence said.

Jalen waved his badge in front of the reader. The door slid open, revealing a rectangular room with cabinets, short benches and lockers. The cabinets lined the walls and their cubbies were stuffed with various items. Jalen and Barry knew what to do. They drew white jumpsuits from one of the cubbies and started to put them on.

Lawrence stared as if in disbelief. "We've got an investigation to conduct."

"Sorry, company policy," Jalen said. He pointed toward the jumpsuits, non-verbally instructing him to get dressed.

Lawrence grunted.

"We're not going to shut down operations," Jalen said. "Could cost this company tens of millions of dollars."

The officer watched them get ready and slowly mimicked them. After his jumpsuit was snapped up, he took out a hairnet and an orange hood from a bin labelled 'contractors.' He slipped them on and grabbed a pair of booties, which were never easy to put on. This time, taming those beasts didn't seem so difficult. He snapped them up, grabbed a pair of cloth glove liners and a pair of latex gloves.

They waited for Officer Lawrence to get ready. Barry pretended to be impatient simply to amuse Jalen. Lawrence took at least five more minutes fumbling with all of the items needed to smock up.

"Phones and radios aren't allowed," Jalen said. "You store them in the lockers. In this case, we're going to have to bring our weapons. There's a protocol for that, too."

He motioned the officer to follow them to a short metal stand next to a waste can. He grabbed a lint-free cloth and a bottle filled with approved saline solution. He sprayed the cloth lightly with the solution and then picked up his taser and thoroughly rid it of contaminants.

"I can't believe you go through all this to protect a few chips," Lawrence said, shaking his head and visibly trying not to look ridiculous. He followed Jalen and Barry's lead and cleaned his gun, before turning and placing his radio in an open locker.

Jalen silently counted the number of closed lockers. He counted twenty-seven, but understood that some employees could have left for a break and not bothered to take their belongings with them.

He deposited his radio while Barry observed himself in a small mirror.

"You know something?" Barry said. "I'm probably the only person that looks sexy in this get-up."

"Dashing," Jalen said.

Seconds later, Jalen swiped his card and waited for the door to slide open. The three of them entered a tiny entry room, which showered them with a blast of warm air from above. The next door slid open and they stepped into the cleanroom. The floor was made of vented carbon fiber poly tiles that were removable. Jalen glanced through the tiny holes at his feet. The underfloor lighting was on, but these were not motion sensing lights, and even if they were, they could likely detect the movement above. The loud humming was always hard to hear over. Communication required speaking loudly.

After a head count revealed the presence of twenty-three workers, Jalen decided to individually isolate them and ask them questions. With everyone dressed the same, it was impossible to single out a person that did not belong.

Jalen talked to twelve employees while Barry handled the rest. Officer Lawrence accompanied Jalen and inserted his own questions from time to time. None of the employees reported having seen anything out of the ordinary. After Jalen and Barry shared their results, Lawrence stared at them.

"And we're sure they didn't have any chance to leave the room?"

"None," Jalen said.

"Which means he must still be in here," Barry added.

Jalen stepped into an open area with a defined walkway while Barry fetched a hook that hung on the wall near the entry. Jalen selected a tile and used the hook to pull it out. He slowly lowered his head into the two foot square hole and looked around. Equipment bases and banks of cable baskets obscured his vision through most of the room. Hundreds of metal pedestals supported the tile floor and were bolted to the concrete slab below.

He looked up and regarded Officer Lawrence, "How are those knees?"

Lawrence cursed. He clearly didn't want to do it, but he had to. Jalen looked back and forth from him to the hole in the floor as Lawrence stepped toward them. He cleared his throat and tried to grin. "After you."

# 5

# Butterfly Effect

Officer Lawrence lowered himself into the hole by resting his palms on the floor tiles. The last foot or so to the concrete slab had to be made up in freefall because the subfloor depth was too great for his arms to handle. Lawrence possessed a height advantage over Jalen and Barry, so the drop would be almost enough to cause pain, especially if he landed wrong.

Jalen followed the officer, and Barry descended as soon as Jalen could get himself out of the way. Artificial light the same color and feel of the lighting in the cleanroom spread through the underfloor more sparsely than anticipated. Jalen took a moment to adjust his vision before pivoting on his knees to scan the space. The array of support pedestals spread in all directions but seemed to stop well short of the walls. The bases of the fab equipment too heavy for the floor system to support created a simple maze of corridors that seemed to meet at a single point. Jalen led the way straight ahead towards a wall. Crawling on hard concrete seemed to do a number on his knees. He imagined that kneepads should be a necessity when traversing under clean room floors.

"Doesn't seem to be anyone down here," Lawrence suggested.

Barry shrugged. "We should check out the whole room before saying something like that."

Lawrence fought back. "If there were anyone here, he'd be aware of our presence. A guy doesn't commit a heinous crime like that, armed with god-knows-what, and then hide."

Jalen sighed and turned his head so that he faced Lawrence. The hood was beginning to cover his eyes and the booties bathed his feet in an itchy pool of sweat. The soles had slid off of his booties so that only a thin layer of cloth separated his shoes from the concrete. "He's right. Still want to check every corner just in case he left us anything. Right, officer?"

The cop nodded and peered straight ahead past Jalen. They crawled down the central corridor single file for about thirty feet until they met the wall. Two darker aisles jutted off the main corridor in both directions. A flashlight would not have illuminated much more detail than the orange lighting provided, but Jalen wished he'd brought one. Normally, a flashlight was part of his uniform, but he didn't carry it everywhere. This time, he'd left the office without thinking to grab it.

The side aisles dead-ended between the black iron equipment bases and the wall with a row of filtration panels designed to collect the air pumped into the fab space from above as part of the circulation system. Each cleanroom was equipped with a similar system. The filters above the ceiling push cool air into the room and the air then falls down through the tile vents while cooling the equipment. The filtration collectors extract the air at the walls and push it up through plenums in the walls back above the ceiling where the filters clean and cool the air again.

Jalen could see nothing. He turned and peered down the opposite aisle, which appeared to be a mirror image of the other.

Barry uttered a dull '*humph*,' turned around, and then lurched forward. Lawrence followed him while Jalen brought up the rear. For some reason, Jalen feared coming face to face with the maniac before the search was finished. He mentally prepared himself for a fight that may or may not come. He couldn't shake the feeling that whoever committed the crime still lurked somewhere in this room. After all, how could he get out? The doors cold only be opened by scanning a valid badge, and Kalee had ensured that only Jalen's badge could open the door from the inside.

Another narrow aisle jutted off to the right and offset around a metal box served by a single stainless-steel pipe. The area behind the equipment was mostly visible. Jalen crawled a few feet down that aisle, took a moment to scan for evidence, and then turned around to join Barry and Lawrence. Barry checked out a shorter corridor that took off from the left.

He proceeded before he'd spent any time looking. At the end of that corridor stood a long plastic object labeled 'chem tray' and a wire mesh basket containing dozens of wires that powered the equipment and connected it to

Lynx's huge server center. The last of the floor plan was more open and only required a quick scan to reveal nothing of importance.

The officer swore. "I guess we can send a forensic investigation team down here if necessary, but I don't see that leading anywhere."

"You are right about that," Jalen said, "These jumpsuits are sort of designed to not leave any kind of forensic evidence behind. You won't find fingerprints or even distinctive glove prints because all the gloves come from the same place anyway. Your only chance would have been something the criminal carried. Nothing like that down here."

"Let's go back to your command center and find him a different way," Lawrence demanded.

"Green," Barry said.

"Excuse me?"

"Just saying, we gotta get in all the lockers. I'd bet he left something he'd touched in there."

"Absolutely," Jalen said. "That's our next task. Besides, if this guy is smart enough to ditch the badge, we'll never find him with computers."

"Only good police work," Lawrence suggested.

The three of them climbed out of the floor space through the tile Jalen had removed. He looked around again and tried to count how many people were in the room. Before he got to twenty he stopped. Frustration flushed through him. "Can't have just disappeared into thin air, damn it."

"We'll find him," Barry assured him.

Jalen swore and stomped a foot on the tile. "Damnit!"

The three of them made their way back to the entrance and into the smock and bootie room. Two people were waiting, fully dressed to enter the room. Jalen approached them and studied their faces for a few seconds each.

"IDs please," he said.

They showed him their badges, which confirmed that they were authorized employees of Lynx Technologies. Had they been contractors Jalen would have turned them away both for safety and for other security reasons. If the killer wasn't operating solo, any person with a contractor badge could be helping him, which Jalen didn't want to risk.

For Lawrence, removing the smock consumed far less time than he'd used to put it on. Jalen observed him while he took off the jumpsuit. It had almost become habit for Jalen, even though so many smock rooms had a slightly different setup that threw him off initially. Today marked only the second or third time he'd been in this particular cleanroom. He silently wondered why some cleanrooms were equipped with orange lights, while others were bathed in the more traditional white lighting. Orange had its way of making everything appear foreign—even alien. It was like Jalen walked the earth alone. Those other people dressed in the same sterile garment, seemed like sentient species of a race not native to earth.

When Barry tossed his latex gloves and hairnet in the trash, he stood to face Jalen as if asking for further instruction. Jalen tried not to stare. "Should I go get the master key?"

Jalen carefully glanced at him. Something seemed off about his eagerness, but Jalen couldn't quite place the burden on him. The string of events lacked a certain sense of reality that shrouded his emotion in sour thoughts. "Run. Tell Kalee to keep the room locked down. No one exits without personal authority. Tell her to temporarily shut down contractor access to the room until we have this all sorted out."

"Ten-four."

Barry darted for the exit. Through the window Jalen witnessed Barry break into a sprint. It almost made him want to smile.

"Ex-cop," Lawrence said. "When did he leave the job?"

"Retired four or five years ago," Jalen guessed. Barry was one of the first to greet Jalen on his first day at Lynx. He seemed to recall his professional demeanor and instant spirit. Jalen liked him from the start.

"The department needs guys like him."

Jalen consciously noticed that Lawrence hadn't said 'guys like you', as in him and Barry. It didn't come as a surprise that Lawrence lacked the basic skills of trust. He understood that for safety reasons, the police academy strictly trained trust out of cadets. In some ways the sense of awareness that prevailed caused them to do their jobs better, but Jalen wondered if an air of humanity could be prescribed as a method of preventing unnecessary violence. That unnecessary violence was an unfortunate side-effect of keeping a greater peace. He appreciated cops more than he admitted but chose to question their methods at times.

A grunt signaled that Jalen didn't wish to engage in small talk.

"Think this guy left any evidence for us?"

Jalen slowly nodded, which was a deliberate way of injecting an uneasy feeling into the conversation. "Bet he did."

"What makes you think he left the badge?" Lawrence studied his dark expression with a stale blankness spanning his face.

"I don't know, maybe an understanding that this guy is trying to get off campus, and the only realistic way to do that is to ditch the badge and hop a fence. He just didn't realize we'd be on to him so quickly."

"At least your department is good at one thing," Lawrence smirked.

A cold glare replaced the dreary mood he displayed. "Cops," he muttered. "Total disregard for everyone else, think they need to control everything."

Officer Lawrence didn't hint at surprise. Instead, he shifted his stance and squared his shoulders. "What's your point?"

"Maybe you should let trained security personnel do their jobs instead of forcing your ideology down everyone's throat."

"You feel threatened," Lawrence said. "I've been in a few interrogations, and I've seen this behavior before."

Jalen groaned. "What does that have to do with anything?"

"This is a matter of law. It is my duty to uphold that law, no matter what."

A skewed glance suggested to Jalen that Lawrence neared a point at which he could relent. He pressed. "You really want to start a turf war with a security officer for one of the world's largest memory producers?"

"I don't need to start a war. We have the authority to investigate this to its conclusion."

"And we have the authority to act autonomously under the international and site-specific rules of this organization."

The officer backed down unexpectedly. He didn't press his ideals any further. Instead, he stared at Jalen with a cool frown etched across his lips and a piercing stare shooting from his eyes. He stood toe to toe with Jalen as if this wasn't the last breath of the battle.

Barry returned with the key right on time and didn't seem to be short on breath. "Let's see what we got."

Jalen approached behind him and watched him insert the key into the locker. The metal made a loud crash when it collided with another open locker door.

Still wearing the latex gloves, Jalen reached in and extracted three items from the locker one by one.

"We'll get prints off these," the officer said.

Jalen first inspected the tour guide's badge. Finding this item didn't surprise him, although from his standpoint, it didn't provide any further clue as to who had taken it. He mentally reminded himself to find out how the killer got onto the campus in the first place. Was he an employee or a contractor?

He handed the badge to Lawrence. "You can take this. The prints on the two devices will match anyway, and I'm betting we're going to have our work cut out for us on them."

"We should probably give them up to the cops as well," Barry said.

"No. They're going to want us to run diagnostics on them, figure out if they were running off Lynx's wireless system and what they're doing here."

"They're personal artifacts," Barry argued.

"And evidence," the cop suggested.

"We've got a capable set of hands with IT specialty on staff," Jalen said. "We'll get him working on it right away and report back to the police department with our findings, at which point we will turn the devices over."

"A skilled IT guy on a security staff?" Lawrence looked amused. "Who might that be?"

"Me."

Jalen withdrew the phone and placed it in his pocket. He doubted whether he would deem any of the information on these devices relevant, but he pledged to look at them anyway.

The third item stored in the locker was a small, high-end tablet that could double as a laptop. He examined the screen and the casing before turning the screen on. What he found caused him to gasp. The screen glowed blue when a complex application appeared. Jalen stared at it and consciously avoided pressing any buttons until he could get its data backed up. What looked like a pie chart adorned the center of the screen and showed a percentage of something. The chart wasn't labeled but a ribbon showing five other buttons lined he top edge of the screen.

He read the buttons without speaking. The buttons were labeled Phase 1, Process, Integration, Variable, and Abort. Instead of pressing any of the buttons, Jalen left the app open and returned to the home screen. He went into the control center and looked at the list of apps. Two other apps were currently running. He brought the first one up and looked at it the same way he'd looked at the first.

Barry and Lawrence were huddled around him like apt students who couldn't wait to get their hands on the latest technology. "The hell?" Barry breathed.

"This one doesn't look so complicated," Jalen said. It didn't have a pie chart, and only two buttons. The app was called *Control,* which seemed to complement the *Variable* button in the other app. The center of the screen displayed a simple yes or no question. *Did the test provide the desired results?*

"No it didn't," Jalen said, again choosing not to answer the question.

The third application seemed to mimic the security home screens Lynx used. Jalen knew the software well, and he decided he would dig into that later. He shrugged.

"What does it mean?" Barry said. His eyes narrowed and his lips creased. He perched one eyebrow higher on his forehead while keeping the other steady.

"It means we've got a big problem," Jalen said. "Seems the police have no choice but to let us further inspect the device."

"What's the big problem?" Lawrence asked.

Jalen spoke to Barry as if he had asked the question. "These first two apps are working in concert, I can tell that without looking closer. It looks like they are running some sort of experiment, possibly having to do with our own security network. This third app is our own control home screen. Lynx's. And it's a working app, not just a screen cap. It looks like it is software purposefully constructed using our model. Do you want to guess how he got this?"

"Downloaded it off our servers?"

"He's an employee," Lawrence surmised.

"I'd assume so," Jalen said. "But what security level? Where does he work? Even with a face, we can't narrow it down because we don't use facial recognition software. Means he has to be one of 26,000 employees. Judging from what he's running on this device, I'm thinking high-level."

"Damn," Barry said.

Jalen clenched his teeth. "We can't just go investigating any official we want. Even if we do manage to keep it on the down-low, we could be in major trouble."

"As in fired?"

Jalen shrugged, glared, and lowered his head. A knot began to work its way through his stomach. An unexpected drowsiness crept over him.

Lawrence wore an inquisitive look that was somehow riddled with subtle shades of contempt. Jalen didn't stop to examine his expression. It wasn't that it mattered at all. It only mattered that Jalen's weekend had been officially flushed to the tank. Fear and rage bound themselves together and snaked their way through his brain, producing a tired feeling Jalen didn't understand. Perhaps he could prescribe more coffee to divert the effects, but coffee could not alter an emotion this deeply embedded within him.

Chaos floated through his mind as he exited the smock room with the tablet in his hands. Whatever he found himself investigating stood on the brink of total disaster. So many possible outcomes presented themselves in his head that it was difficult to predict which would come to pass. For now, Jalen didn't even want to know what this meant. He felt his heart collapsing into despair as Barry and Lawrence walked away. Instead of making the trek back to the office, he leaned against a wall and slid to the floor with his face buried in his hands as panic rolled through his veins.

# 6

# Critical Mass

Within five minutes, Jalen witnessed several pairs of shoes stroll by, some with and some without little blue lab booties on. He'd greeted each with his own style of disregard, somewhere between casual noticing and apathy. His posture wrought an ache akin to the agony he endured following that fateful day three years ago. That time could have been described as the moment his life took a wrong turn. Rather than that, Jalen reflected on it as the day when the destruction began.

He lifted his head slightly when a pair of broad heel shoes approached from the corridor entrance and stopped five feet in front of him. The woman wore black business slacks with a tidy blue button down shirt. He didn't need to look at her face to realize who she was.

Instead of speaking, she waited for him to warm his expression. Such patience, though a virtue, didn't strike Jalen as a quality without its faults. Sometimes action, rather than patience, was required.

He shook his head and pretended to clear his throat.

"You okay?"

"Just taking a time out," Jalen said. "Thought I'd examine these tiles."

She attempted a smile, but instead of showing her teeth, her lips simply parted, which made her look surprised. Her look was perhaps too simplistic, but the fact she cared in the first place spoke volumes. "Walk with me."

Jalen struggled against the wall while trying to push himself up with his hands. It probably made him look silly, but he wasn't about to ask Kalee for help.

Still wearing the same expression, she extended her hand. Jalen reached for it and, pushing off the wall with his foot, lurched to a standing position. "Where to?"

"Cafeteria. I think we could both use a cup of coffee."

"We got a coffee machine in the office," Jalen said with a straight face. He knew what was coming and didn't feel in the playful mood.

"You know that doesn't count."

"But we've got work to do," Jalen protested.

"I know."

Her expression changed. Jalen regarded it with a stroke of interest, but let the emotion fade away before allowing his eyes to droop back toward the floor. She slowly lifted one eyebrow as if questioning, but a simple knowing gesture fluttered across her eyes. She tightened her lips and slackened her jaw.

"I don't think it's that time sensitive," she said. "Besides, the cops are talking with...what's her...Melinda while setting up for the CSI team. A few minutes won't hurt."

"It might," he said.

She flushed but remained steady. She gradually slowed her pace, but didn't fully stop. His reaction certainly would play a part, especially to a woman as observant as Kalee. "This doesn't have to be about our investigation. It has to be about you."

"God," Jalen groaned.

That he didn't want to talk about it didn't seem lost on her. Instead of relenting, however, she pressed on. "Take me to three years ago."

"No," he said, veering a step further away from her. "I'm never going back there."

She drew closer to him by altering her course and angling her trajectory towards the corridor wall. "I think," she started, "that in some ways you're still there. Like you choose to live there. And you fail to realize that there is still life. You just have to reach out and seek it."

"I've moved on," Jalen said.

"You're lying. You don't think I can see it on your face, especially today, but it's there lurking somewhere beneath the surface like a predator looking for the right moment to strike."

Thinking he was little more than prey to an imaginary construct of emotion seemed like a good tactic. He should have known she would try it on him, but it didn't matter. "Something I can't control," he said.

"I know." She nodded and looked down. "That's something you gotta learn again. You take charge around the office, which is good. That's your job. And I think you'll catch this bad guy with your perseverance. It's just that it works against you from time to time."

"What do you suggest?"

"Roll with the punches," she said. "Don't think I don't know anything about what happened. About how it affected you."

"You know?"

"I've read, I've listened. I've been a friend."

"I'm okay," he said.

"Then why the long face? Why are you sitting in the hallway with your face buried in your hands like you've just lost the Super Bowl?"

"It isn't about her," Jalen said. It was no lie. Again, his perception of the events was beginning to clash with what would have been the historical account. Instead of dwelling on it, he shrugged it off. "It's about the case. How does a guy just completely disappear?"

"How indeed?" she said.

As they rounded a corner and entered Building 22, Jalen stared at her. Her expression had become warm, but he looked away and pretended not to notice. "You don't seem so startled."

"Startled? Why would I be?"

"There was no way out of that cleanroom."

She tilted her head to the side and flipped a strand of hair over her shoulder. "I'm just as perplexed as you are. But we'll find him."

"Inspiring confidence," Jalen remarked. "Only problem is that badge is our only way of tracking him."

"I think we've got other leads," she said.

"Such as?"

"What about his car? We can match any badge with any parking permit. Plus, I keep thinking there is more to this tour guide than we know about right now. I'd say we bring up every detail we can find about him and go from there."

Jalen nodded slowly. Outstanding charm or not, Kalee displayed the sort of intelligence that Jalen valued. Then again, he believed this was about more than the tour guide. The tablet provided more than enough evidence to suggest that. And the killer was smart enough not to let details from his victim give him away.

Instead of saying anything, Jalen offered a quiet grunt. They turned into another corridor and descended a carpeted ramp that connected Building 22 with the complex of Buildings 4, 6, 9, 11, and 12. Building 11 served as a central gathering place for those employees who chose not to leave campus for lunch. In addition to a full-service cafeteria, the building housed several fast food outlets with trimmed menus. The seating area provided ample space for more than a thousand people. Aside from the kitchens and the main campus access, no area in this building required a badge to enter.

Kalee led him to the counter, where a gentleman in a suit was swiping his credit card to pay for a cup of soup and a drink. "What do you want? My treat."

"You don't have to buy me coffee."

"I want to."

Jalen didn't argue. He selected a cheap cinnamon latte and waited. A pervasive sense of serenity inexplicably spread over him. Whether the ambiance of the room or Kalee's demeanor instigated the feeling Jalen could not be certain. Rather than question it, however, he temporarily allowed its warmth to swallow him. He stowed away his frown and tried to look more upbeat, with startling success.

Kalee caught his reflection in a mirror and flashed a smile.

Neither of them spoke again until they departed Building 11 for the trek back to 27. Jalen sipped his latte and clutched it in his right hand.

"Can I ask you something?" She asked.

Jalen waited.

"What was your fight with Marie about?"

"No idea," Jalen said.

"That's odd."

Jalen sipped his drink and tried to act cool, but the question agitated him for some reason. His leg twitched in mid-step, which suggested he'd become restless.

"You don't have to pity me," he said.

She stared at him and curled her lip with innocence. Her step quickened momentarily. Her body language suggested she was attempting to hide something, and Jalen always caught on quickly. She was a terrible liar.

"You know what I'm talking about. Don't get me wrong, I appreciate the sentiment and all that, just don't go around wasting pity on me. Isn't worth it."

"Friends don't pity," she said. "I'm just providing an avenue for you to express what's eating you. I'm listening."

Jalen let the comment go and strolled through Building 22 in silence. In a situation like this, moments of reflection shone like stolen seconds where solace and desperation flooded through him in waves. He sipped his drink again, attempting to wash away the symptoms, but regret constructed a monolith in his mind. Ignoring it was like meditating during a firestorm.

Kalee offered bits of her own mood for the remainder of the walk. She smiled at a passerby, casually glanced at a bulletin, and took keen interest in a pair of chemists in a hearty discussion. For her everything around sparked with the electricity of life. It all seemed so mystifying, but given the circumstances, off-putting.

He didn't share this thought with her. Instead, he allowed it to pass until they turned into the Building 27 corridor and the mood of business flushed back into his brain.

They slowed as they passed the cleanroom. Officer Lawrence was conversing with another officer, nodding, and jotting down notes. Part of their team wheeled a gurney into the lab. A janitor had arrived with a mop bucket and began to carefully clean up the blood. Jalen hoped they'd taken a sample, but then again, they probably wouldn't need it because they had the body. They'd run a full autopsy and conclude that the cause of death was either stabbing or ingesting acid. Jalen didn't care about that. He cared that somewhere on campus lurked a murderer and Jalen had no idea where to look.

"It's disturbing," Kalee said.

Jalen silently agreed. He watched until keeping his gaze upon the scene required him to turn his head. Jalen sensed that Lawrence followed them. His frown deepened and his pace quickened. Otherwise he pretended not to notice until he opened the office door. Kalee entered first and Jalen held the door for Lawrence.

He took mental note that Melinda had gone. The officers likely questioned her and then quickly dismissed her because she hadn't actually seen anything.

Chaos greeted them as they entered. One or two had left the office on patrol or to check into security issues in other areas. The video desk was abuzz with three people standing around it talking about a new crisis.

"What's going on?" Jalen asked.

"A lab tech just punched out a chemist. You gotta see this." Marcus looked up and laid eyes on Officer Lawrence, who had already caused several people to dislike him. "When you get a chance," he added.

"He's being escorted off campus as we speak," Laurie said.

"What happens in a situation like this?" Lawrence asked.

"Disciplinary action, obviously," Jalen said. "As a precaution, we remove him from campus and put a temporary lock on his badge for the rest of the day while a review is made among his superiors. If they decide to fire him, it goes on his record and he won't be able to get any kind of badge for three years. Least, that's how it's worked in the past."

"Mostly," Marcus added, "We just do what the big wigs tell us to do. We don't actually have any HR or management powers here."

"Just security," Lawrence said.

"Physical and cyber," Jalen said.

"How does the protocol work when issuing badges?" The officer asked. "Just anyone can come in a get a badge?"

Jalen cleared his throat and looked down while Marcus attempted to explain the process. "Badge request is done by paper application, with the approval of a host. It isn't hard to get a contractor badge, but denial can and does happen."

"We don't require background checks," Jalen said, his voice lower than he'd intended. He paused as a way to inject more urgency into what he was saying. "But a screening process goes into effect each time. Takes us about twenty-four hours for the badge issuance office to verify employment status and review their assignment with their host."

"What kind of questions are on the application?" Lawrence asked.

"Employment status, how long, history with Lynx Technologies, have you ever been denied or had your badge revoked for any reason? There's a section about medical condition, but answering those questions is not mandatory. If they give an honest answer and we don't think they're fit to have a badge, we'll deny it."

"That isn't legal."

Jalen shook his head, bit his lip and continued. "You'd think not. But this isn't an application for employment, merely security. By law, applicants don't have to disclose medical info if they choose not to. If they do, that's on them and we have no liability because having a contractor's badge doesn't constitute employment."

"What other steps are taken? If they pass the application, they get a badge?" Lawrence looked like he didn't believe it. He gradually raised his eyebrows as he spoke. His eyes narrowed and he clasped his hands together.

"Once a week, they have a sort of seminar," Marcus said. "Security personnel are not invited."

"Each week, the pool of applicants is required to attend an orientation class, which consists of an hour long video detailing the proper use of equipment tags, safety protocol, you name it. I think they include a brief section on sexual harassment. There's also an overview of dress code and conduct for cleanrooms and other areas."

Kalee flipped her hair over her shoulder and looked up from her monitors. "Jalen, you might want to look at this."

Surprised, Jalen turned to her. "Show me."

She motioned him to join her at her desk rather than simply turn her monitor around. Jalen stretched his legs and circled the end of the desk. He examined her screen for several moments without saying anything. Her findings didn't elicit much enthusiasm.

The contractor's badge issued to Carl Kazinsky, the tour guide, had been in use for just over a month. Jalen reviewed the brief history of the badge. His feet twitched and his knees seemed weak. Kazinsky had only used his badge to enter campus five times during that span, which seemed to indicate a once-a-week pattern. Jalen shook his head and decided he'd look up how often third-party tours were allowed. To his knowledge, Lynx didn't offer any such tours. The company's operations were intentionally kept secret, so Jalen doubted an interested person would actually learn anything from a tour. He seemed to remember a few middle school classes being shown around once in a while, but never thought anything of it.

"What are you looking at?" Lawrence asked.

Jalen didn't answer.

"It's a rundown of past badge uses by the tour guide," Kalee said.

"Not very revealing," Jalen admitted.

"This is the first time he's ever tried to access rooms he's not allowed in," Kalee said. "Although it probably wouldn't be too hard to jump the scanning gates."

"Video security covers those pretty well, though," Jalen said. "He'd have to be a genius to make it through that without being seen."

"Then again," Lawrence said, squaring his shoulders and tensing his jaw muscles, "You might have to be a genius to escape a locked down room with cop and two security guards inside. Somehow, he managed."

Jalen flushed. He clutched a pencil on Kalee's desk so tightly that it snapped in his fist. He slanted his eyebrows downward while his other emotions simply retreated into the corners of his mind where they gathered dust and withered in the dark.

"And that makes you really ticked off," Lawrence prodded.

"Get out," Jalen said slowly, pointing to the door.

"I can't do that. We're investigating a murder here, not some kid who stole a five cent piece of candy from a vending machine."

"Stop it," Kalee said, maintaining her cool. She leaned toward Jalen and looked up at him with concern rippling across her face. "Just drop it and try to cooperate." She shifted her glance to Lawrence and finished, "Both of you."

"She's right," Lawrence said.

"Always is," Jalen whispered. He glanced at Kalee with a guilty expression flashing across his face. It seemed amazing how she always seemed to reduce him to the weaker position in any setting. Being the boss, Jalen had grown accustomed to having the dominant edge.

After allowing a few moments for tempers to subside, Kalee brought up Kazinsky's parking pass. Jalen examined it closely. Security never recorded vehicular access to campus except for processing deliveries and watching first-timers. At the security gates, the officers simply verified the identity and make and model of the car to allow access. If a person arrived without parking permission, he or she would be escorted to the badge office to apply for a parking permit. Depending on the urgency of the matter, they would either be turned away and required to wait twenty-four hours or be granted a temporary pass for the day.

"It's a Lincoln," Kalee said.

"Nice car. Probably set him back fifty or sixty Gs."

"Is his car on campus?" Lawrence asked.

"Maybe," Jalen said. "Can't be sure without going out and looking for it."

Lawrence glanced at Laurie, who remained busy checking into the assault incident. Jalen saw a perplexed look flash across her face and then resolve itself before more than a second or two had passed. "Or we could look it up on the security cameras."

"Or that," Jalen said. "But we don't know which gate he used or where he parked."

"Does that report have a license plate number on it?"

Jalen nodded and resumed staring at the screen. "Of course it does. And driver's license number."

"The security tapes would show the license plate," Lawrence said.

"Or you could go search the parking lot yourselves. Whatever you do, just having us verify whether the car is in one of the parking lots doesn't determine a whole lot. You'll probably want to search the vehicle. I think your time would be better spent doing that."

"All of the lots are interconnected," Kalee said. "You can get to any lot from any of the four entrances to campus."

"So we'd have to drive around looking for a silver Lincoln and then stop to check the license plate? Among how many cars?"

Kalee looked surprised. She leaned back in her chair and studied Lawrence's expression. "Most people park pretty close to the building they intend to access, so I'd start in our own Building 27 lot."

Lawrence displayed a blank look for a second or two while he visualized how many cars seemed to be parked in the lot.

"Then again," Jalen started, "if the 27 lot was too crowded, he could have decided to park in the 24 lot and hoof it because that lot is closer to our entrance than the back of the 27 lot is."

Lawrence swore and clenched a fist.

"Not an easy job," Jalen said quietly.

"You're coming with me," the officer said.

"We got other leads to pursue. We'll continue to do it without your...*interference* and report back to you if we find anything significant.

From the expression that Lawrence showed, he clearly meant to counterattack for the little jab Jalen inserted into his comment. Instead, he offered a soulless nod and walked away with his arms loosely dangling at his sides. When he left, the room went quiet for several minutes. Jalen stared at Kalee's screen in awe of how good she was.

"I thought I'd get rid of him for you," she said with a mischievous smile.

"Well done."

"Can we all get props?" Marcus asked.

Jalen shot him an icy glare, stood up, and flexed his wrist. A weak frown carved his face with a shade of frustration. "Not until the job is done."

Instead of speaking more, Kalee immersed herself in work and paid no attention to Jalen. He quietly returned to his desk to resume digging. A dark aura shrouded his inner mind while a headache began to form. *I really need a drink.* But the clouds of reality painted a bleak portrait of everything underneath their spell. Reality began to gather into a potent storm that brewed within the confines of Jalen's brain. Desperation invaded. Events were beginning to coalesce into a perfect storm that promised far more misery than victory. Jalen frowned and punched the keys harder than he'd intended. The harrowing admission that he wanted to drink set up an unconquerable fortress in his mind. He cursed under his breath and decided to wait it out. Still, weathering this kind of storm invited the inner demons to attack from all sides. It was a battle Jalen couldn't win.

# 7

# Wormholes

The late morning sun punched a hole in the canopy of cloud cover, casting a dominant feeling of hope over the campus of Lynx Technologies. Glittering from the roofs and windows of thousands of cars, the sun's rays seemed to partake in an intimate waltz over the city's skyline.

A team of police officers had assembled near the rear end of a silver Lincoln luxury car that, surprisingly, didn't look all that out of place. Lawrence instructed the men but also took part in the scene.

The car's interior was so clean it looked as though it had never been driven. The owner had taken meticulous care in removing dust, lint, and other pollutants that could pile up and make the car seem old. Lawrence tried to guess how long the contractor had owned the car, but for now the parking pass told him all he needed to know.

The windshield displayed the parking pass sticker in the bottom right side of the window, tucked in just above the VIN, but not visible from the driver's seat. A pair of officers swept the vicinity of the car in search of some kind of evidence, but nothing suggested this man had any idea what was coming.

"So what kind of job does a tour guide have to have to come up with enough cash to buy one of these?" Officer Leonard asked.

"Probably runs his own company," Carson said. "Pretty good gig if you got the chops."

"So Lynx hires the guy to run ten-year-olds through the halls, and pays him enough coin to feed a small island for six years, all to show a few curious future job seekers the details they don't want anyone to see?"

Officer Lawrence sighed. He scooted his feet across the pavement and considered the conversation.

"Why are they so secretive to begin with? It isn't like they're designing nukes or anything."

"Fiercely competitive business," Lawrence said, shrugging. He strode back to the car and popped open the trunk.

"They're probably worried about spies," Leonard agreed.

"Ten-year-old Bonds." Carson knelt down on the pavement next to the hood of the car and peered into the shadow beneath the car.

Lawrence cleared his throat and raised his voice. "All it takes is one seemingly innocent social media post and the kid just let Lynx's biggest competitors in on secrets. It doesn't take much to ruin a company's bottom line these days.

"No bodies, no blinking red lights indicating a bomb, no homing beacons," Carson said. "Hell of an espresso machine, though."

Leonard smiled but didn't offer a chuckle.

"Who needs a homing beacon when you've got GPS?" Lawrence asked. He withdrew a metal stick from the trunk and slammed it shut. Walking quickly, he approached the driver's front door. He'd helped out old ladies locked out of their cars in this way before but had never used this method to break into a car that could be treated as evidence.

The other two officers watched as Lawrence wedged the narrow end of the device between the weather stripping and the glass. When he'd lifted the seal enough, he inched the metal end downward towards the door locks. Power locks made this task so much simpler. Then again, this car was likely equipped with some sort of antitheft system.

The horn started honking and the lights started flashing before Lawrence was able to depress the unlock button. He smiled and thought about what a waste the system was when it only decided to work when the process of breaking in was all but complete.

"Leonard, I want you to get into the car's GPS system and find out where he's been and don't tell me the supermarket and the local brothel."

"Actually," Carson said. "Brothel might be an interesting destination. Could lead us to some kind of motive."

"Yeah," Lawrence said. "But if it isn't central to our case, based on what we know, we leave it alone. We have too many other avenues to follow."

"Guy could have been killed for cutting in line at the store for all we know," Carson argued.

"There's no chance that was the case and you know it," Lawrence said. "Use your imagination, but don't go overboard."

"What's that security cop up to?" Leonard asked, kneeling down and attempting to plug into the car's computer.

"You think we can track the signal to the key?" Lawrence said.

"Nope," Carson said, straining his voice. "If we've got the key's signal, we could find the car, but I've never heard of a method of using a car to find the keys."

"Worth a shot."

Leonard plugged into the car's computer. "It's just going to be data until we plug it in to a terminal. How far back do we want to go?' Because I think this might just give us the entire driving history of the car, which is a lot of data to comb through."

"A month," Lawrence suggested. "Just as long as he's had the parking pass."

"Why are we going into this kind of detail investigating the victim?" Carson asked.

Lawrence brought up mental images of the security officer frowning at his very existence. The spat had been fun to take part in, mostly because he didn't trust Jalen, but also because Jalen displayed the same personality traits that Lawrence despised. His head was too big and his mental space too exposed. Still, a certain air of emotional incompatibility with everyone around him seemed to single him out. Lawrence wouldn't have been surprised if the man's virtues were twisted around a moral compass that didn't always point true north. A compass that doesn't work well, Lawrence was once told, is about as useful as a spinning top. Good enough for a little entertainment, but nothing to navigate the difficult waters of life by. Instead of continuing the thought, Lawrence shrugged and watched Leonard.

"Okay, I think we got it. Let's plug it into the car and see what we get."

"I'll do that," Lawrence said. "You two see if you can find me something we can justify your pay on."

Lawrence took the small USB drive from Leonard and took his seat in the patrol car. He plugged the device in the car's computer and had an idea. If he could track the GPS data from the car, chances seemed high that they could do the same thing with the phone. He mentally vowed he'd have Jalen look into that later.

The computer brought up a series of charts that mapped the course of every route he'd taken. A common stopping point was on the outskirts of downtown near the river and the university. He figured it must be either the contractor's residence or his office. Another common stopping point was nestled on the west side of town, where seemingly endless subdivisions marred the landscape.

He found the Lynx campus after little searching. True to his badge's history, the tour guide had only taken five trips to Lynx in this vehicle. They all started from the same place, which had to be the place of business on Myrtle Street.

Nothing peculiar stood out to him. He grunted and searched through random maps, finding nothing. He'd enjoyed the park once or twice and seemed to frequent the same convenience store on an almost daily basis. The next idea would be to find out where the tour guide had been spending his money by bringing up is credit card records. That would have to wait, but he guessed it would only lead to another dead end.

He clenched his teeth and stood up beside the door, leaving the device plugged in and the computer on. "What do you guys got?"

"Not a damn thing," Carson said. "It's like this guy's a ghost."

*A ghost indeed, just like his killer,* Lawrence thought. The only problem was that ghosts were not supposed to haunt semiconductor plants and use technology like yesterday's news. Instead of wallowing in his failure, Lawrence conjured up thoughts of Jalen going crazy, which proved oddly cathartic. Truly, he didn't hate the man. He had no reason to. But it was entertaining to watch him suffer.

***

Jalen sat quietly at his desk, contemplating the meaning of the latest chain of events. Watching them unfold ached like the memory of some long-ago pain. He surrendered to time and history as though it held him hostage. Then again, what better way could he describe it?

Kalee looked thoughtful as she worked away. She peered through her glasses with seemingly unending curiosity. She would pause once or twice to glance up at Jalen, but she didn't say anything.

"How can we figure out where this guy is going without a badge? Without one, he can't get anywhere unless he is an employee and has his own badge." He was talking to himself but Marcus seemed to be listening. Tracking more than 20,000 badges would be futile.

"Mechanical spaces," Marcus mused.

Jalen stopped, frowned and looked up. Marcus wheeled his chair closer to him but spoke normally.

"Most buildings have mechanical rooms for the HVAC and stuff. It might be a good place to hide out."

"Where is the closest one?" Jalen asked.

"Good question. I think I saw one labelled around the junction of Building 29 once. Down a side corridor. We could look there."

"Go," Jalen said. "Take Li with you."

They hurried out of the office, leaving Jalen, Kalee, Barry, and Laurie isolated.

"That's what they call a wild goose chase," Kalee said without looking up from her monitors. Jalen glanced at her and then returned his gaze to his computer.

"You know, I heard a rumor," Barry said. "Legend has it that this whole campus is honeycombed with a bunch of hidden chambers and tunnels where you could theoretically pass from building to building and fab to fab without so much as scanning an access badge."

"Any truth to the rumor?" Jalen asked.

"Your guess is as good as mine. But at least it gives us something else to do. I think Kalee can handle the place for a while."

"Sure I can," Kalee said as if she weren't even paying attention. She shrugged. The reflection from her monitors flickered across her glasses, which seemed to inject her face with an unexpected flair and tenacity, not to mention youth. "Be careful."

"How are we going to find out?" Jalen asked, walking quickly towards the office door.

"Engineering, over in Building 21."

Building 21 stood across the central drive used for deliveries and other mechanical uses. There was a way to reach that building without going outside, but such a route would have required making a huge horseshoe loop through the cafeteria, Building 22, and the corporate offices. Cutting across the drive was a worthwhile shortcut.

The walk was uneventful. Jalen and Barry suffered the inane small talk before reaching the steps leading to the engineering department.

"Where did you and Kalee go earlier?" Barry asked.

"On an adventure to the magical world of the cafeteria, for coffee."

"Sounds like a hot date." Barry chuckled. "Not that you two could ever hit it off like that. Just saying. Well..."

Listing to Barry stumble over his own words could have proven humorous on any other day, but today his antics agitated him. Jalen deepened his frown and furrowed his eyebrows. "Well, what?"

"Hey, is it true that they have better coffee there than we do?"

"Everyone has better coffee than we do." Jalen shook his head, looked sideways at Barry as if in disbelief, and then refocused his gaze straight ahead. "What else do you know about mechanical rooms?"

"Not much. I guess they house furnaces and pumps for plumbing. Maybe water heaters."

"For a place like Lynx, I'd wager there's far more to it than that," Jalen said. "In fact, I doubt there's just one. Is sure hope this isn't one of those unproven urban legends where they claim there's a guy with a chainsaw and a hook down there murdering people."

"They say urban legends are loosely based around a true story most of the time."

"Right," Jalen said. "Heard some of them and they're all outrageous. If they have any resemblance to a true event, it's remote, imaginative, and assumed. Like Jane sleeps with a mask over her face and wears heavy coats and sunglasses everywhere she goes, therefore Jane is a vampire."

"You need to write fantasy stories." Barry joked. He had no idea Jalen had ever written anything, let alone a story. His journal might have been a good start and most of the time it was fiction, so perhaps Barry had a point.

*Our cities look brand new, but they've been destroyed from within by a virus called progress.* Jalen's heart seemed shrouded in the cold, murky shadow of a hopeless future, a place he feared almost as much as he feared his fragmented past. He looked down as he walked and closed his eyes more than once while trudging through the first floor corridors of Building 21.

One of the two main stairways in Building 21 rose in the northeast corner of the building, while the other climbed in the southwest quadrant. Since Jalen and Barry had entered from the southeast, they had approximately 250 feet of corridor to navigate before reaching the stairs. Building 21 certainly had an elevator. All buildings were required to have one. Jalen had no idea where the elevator in 21 was located and as a general rule, no signs provided directions to the elevators.

The stairwell jutted off the southwest corner of the building behind a metal door with a window. Huge windows lined the corners of the stairwell opposite from the exposed piping. Structural steel members crisscrossed the window and formed a giant X in front of the stairwell, which cast interesting shadows. The design seemed industrially efficient if anything. Few of the buildings were aesthetically pleasing and not even the engineering building was immune to the blandness.

After climbing two flights of stairs, Jalen pushed open the door and entered a large open office sectioned off in hundreds of cubicles in the center. The perimeter of the floor included the offices of engineers and other high-ranking personnel. Since Lynx Technologies often provided their own designs for expansion and new construction to avoid the expense of third-party professionals, the company had a large drafting area. Due to design development and research, new projects, most of them low-profile, took place constantly.

Barry led Jalen down a central aisle and then took a left toward what looked like a large printing area. Two cubicles away from the printing area, Barry stopped and greeted the man Jalen wanted to talk to. Ted Sanders dressed in business casual attire. With neatly pressed slacks and a pin-striped button-down shirt, he looked like an engineer. Barry introduced Ted to Jalen without diving into small talk.

"What can I do for you?"

Jalen decided not to delay by acting cordial or even conversational. His head hurt far too much for that nonsense. "Does this campus have a rumored underground system?"

"Which one?" Ted asked.

"Which campus?"

"Which system?" Ted looked amused at the question. "I suppose you're looking for a map."

Jalen straightened his knees and peered across the labyrinth of cubicle walls. A cute secretary strolled the perimeter and disappeared into an office. "That would be helpful."

"Well, you won't find one."

Jalen stared at him with a hint of annoyance on his face.

"See, since each building out here was constructed at a different time with a different budget and different engineering requirements, there never was a cohesive underground map built. Outside of the main tunnels there are dozens of little side trenches where you can easily get lost if you don't know where you're going. I can't give you a map, but I'll see if I can pull up an as-built layout of the mains."

Jalen rolled his eyes at Barry, who shrugged.

Ted spun his chair toward the computer and searched for files relating to what Jalen needed. The search lasted the better part of five minutes, after which he turned and stood up. Ted's shadow hung above Jalen like the shadows of spring clouds interrupting a pleasant day. His face erupted in a stiff smile, which for some reason made Jalen want to punch him.

"Follow me," he said.

Without speaking, Jalen and Barry followed him toward the printing area. In the center of the area, a large stainless-steel table stretched across the floor at least twenty feet. Shelving below the surface of the table contained somewhat unkempt stacks of plans printed on huge sheets. An impressive array of racks, each supporting numerous volumes of plans, surrounded the table.

Ted flipped through one of the racks, keeping a close eye on the set titles as he went. Before long, he removed a thick set of plans and hefted them to the table. He thumbed through twenty or thirty pages until he found what he sought. The smile flashed across his face again. "I believe this suits your interest."

Jalen gazed at the white page, which contained surprisingly few notes and details. What he stared at seemed nothing more than a jumble of awkward shapes flung together across a snowy expanse of paper. A legible north arrow sat next to a brief description of the drawing. In some respects, it resembled the layout of the campus, but it was like nothing he'd ever seen.

"This is the main arterial," Ted explained while running his fingers along what appeared to be a hidden corridor that increased in width from north to south. The corridor doglegged left and right in a few spots where the layout of the buildings suggested a slight shift in direction. Multiple junction areas connected smaller side tunnels that fed off the main to connect to other buildings.

"Can you walk in there?" Jalen asked.

Ted offered a lifeless chuckle, but retained the smile. "You could drive a truck in there, although transportation options are limited. Your best bet is walking."

"How long are they?

"Combined?" Ted's smile had vanished. He fixed his eyes on the plans. "I'd say six or eight miles, but there are plenty of uncharted areas down there that probably only a small handful of people even know about."

"How do you get down there?"

Ted looked up. "In the corporate offices there is a library. You go to a certain section, pull out a Hemingway book and a secret passageway appears. You take the long spiral staircase down into the secret lair, which contains the skeletons of scores of men who could never find a way out of the dark."

"This is serious," Jalen snapped. "Dispense with the sarcasm."

Ted nodded and looked down without focusing on the plan. "There are a number of entrances from each building, the vast majority of them unmarked. In some of the old buildings, you enter an old boiler room and descend down a narrow hatch with a ladder. The newer buildings have stairs."

"Do you have to use your badge to access these tunnels?"

"You have to scan a badge to get down there," Ted said. "But it isn't going to deny access unless your badge isn't active. Ask and it shall be opened."

"Bible," Jalen said. "Don't start with that."

"People get lost down there. Cell phone service only works some of the time, and you won't find any maps or signs. If you have good knowledge of the campus, you could go from Building 59 to Building 1 with a stopover in Building 22 without so much as setting foot above ground."

"Why would they design a network of tunnels like that under an industrial campus?" Jalen asked.

"Because it's an industrial campus," Ted said. He didn't appear to be joking, as his smile no longer lightened his face. He still appeared familiar, but like an old friend rather than a passing acquaintance.

"What's a good way down there from 27?"

"Use the stairs. Going from memory, I'd say they're in the southwest area of 27. You go down a narrow corridor, hang a left, pass a mechanical room and a few closets, and there is an unmarked door at the end. That should get you down to the main tunnel. After that, it's up to you where you want to go. But do be careful, because when you don't know what to expect and you don't pay attention to where you're going, that's when injuries happen."

"Thanks for the info," Jalen said without meaning it. He turned to Barry and constructed a mourning expression of pained curiosity. He shifted his eyebrows and simply stared.

Barry stared back, but his mood was less somber. "Your guess is as good as mine."

"One more question," Jalen said. "Could you access the tunnels from inside a cleanroom? If you wanted to?"

Ted shrugged but didn't appear entirely committed to his answer. He tilted his head, raised his eyebrows and said, "It's possible, but unlikely. They keep clean space isolated from mechanical space for good reasons. If they just had a door from one to the other, it would contaminate the cleanroom in a hurry."

Processing all of this information eroded the frailty in his mind. The irony was that no one could escape that cleanroom. It was as unlikely as there being another point of access to the tunnel, yet where he went, it was impossible to track him. The killer could do anything and get away with it.

"Shit," Jalen whispered. The pain expanded in his head. He spun to face Barry without uttering another word to Ted. He walked away so quickly that a sprint wouldn't have been much faster. A feeling of stark urgency crept up inside him as panic welled in his veins. He had to tell somebody something. It was a matter of life and death.

Without doing much, Ted had exposed a gaping hole in the campus's security systems. Mechanical areas never included security cameras. If traversing from building to building was as easy as Ted suggested, then other attacks, potentially much larger could occur at any time. It wouldn't be hard to get away with murder in a place like this.

The desire to drink enveloped his soul as he thundered down the steps. He erupted from the door at the bottom of the stairs in a sweat, punched a wall and sprinted toward the entrance he and Barry had used. An unquenchable terror spread through his veins, sparking confusion and illusion in every memory. The stairway Ted pointed out—the tunnels—seemed like a parallel universe where life and death teetered ever closer to chaos. The stairway marked the gateway to oblivion and the tunnels constructed a nightmare where a simple purpose prowled and nothing else mattered.

# 8

# Pillars of Creation

Jalen's sprint down the main corridor of Building 27 displayed as much recklessness as he'd ever shown. Without caring who got in the way or what injuries could result, Jalen ran as fast as his legs would allow before his legs and his heart could not keep up. This particular sprint lasted about three hundred yards, only briefly interrupted by an encounter with stairs. It was much further than he'd ever run non-stop on a soccer field.

Without warning, a cop emerged from the narrow hallway leading to the chem lab and managed to spin facing Jalen. Jalen had little time to react. He willed his leg muscles in a little twitch to alter his direction, but instead of changing course, Jalen's leg buckled. His momentum carried him forward into painful, headfirst dive. He collided with the floor first, bounced, and rolled straight into the legs of the officer.

The officer collapsed and rolled around in obvious pain. Jalen clutched his knee, and winced. Jabbing splinters of agony clawed at his joint. The ache reminded him of the injury he claimed prevented him from playing soccer. It was in the same leg. If he kept up this nonsense, he might be unable to walk before long.

"What the hell is the matter with you?" the officer shouted.

Jalen gasped in panicked gulps of fresh air that could somehow not ease the pressure in his lungs. "The clean...cleanroom. Tunnel access."

"What?"

"Tunnel access. Get backup...Officer Lawrence. We have to...search. He's armed."

The cop, whose nametag just became visible, appeared to be the leader of the group. He and one other officer lagged to finish up the initial crime scene investigation. "You found him?"

After a second of silence, Jalen gasped while clutching his knee. His heart rate seemed to have doubled since the collision. There was no time, not even to think. He shook his head.

Lieutenant Marlon extended a hand to Jalen and offered a perplexed but understanding look. Jalen grasped his hand and used Marlon's aid to pull himself up. "Try to relax," Marlon said. "Tell me from the top."

Though breathing gradually became easier, Jalen found that he still could not form cohesive sentences but at least his speech wasn't limited to single words. "Went to engineering. Looked at plans. Lynx has lots of tunnels underground." A wheezing gasp interrupted him, but he pressed on. "You can get anywhere. We have to search the tunnels."

Marlon didn't look surprised, but an edge of urgency surfaced in his actions that Jalen found lessened the sting of his findings. "Do you have the manpower for this?"

Jalen shook his head and narrowed his eyes. "Get Lawrence and the others to search. We'll spread out. Meantime, I'll get Kalee to help."

Without so much as nodding in agreement, Marlon turned around and pressed his radio to bring in all of the other officers. Time marched away as relentlessly as the northern jet stream brought spring winds. The success of the search would rely on coordination and speed.

Jalen limped down the corridor toward the office, not noticing the sweat that had started to pour down his face. Pain rocked his knee with every step, but he found it necessary and even relished its throbbing.

He burst through the office door without speaking and made a B-line to her desk.

Kalee looked horrified. "Jalen you look...what happened?"

"Lock down campus. No one gets out the gates. Put out a level three alert to all buildings. Killer could be anywhere."

"We knew that already," she started to say.

"He can do anything he wants. Just now realized what damage he can do."

"I thought we assumed he was an employee," Kalee said, furiously typing on her keyboard. A pale frown engulfed her face in a kind of stress that she could not conceal.

Jalen attempted to watch her but continued rattling off jarring, yet somehow uninspiring sentence fragments. "Get everyone to patrol the corridors."

*Get me a drink.*

Speaking up, he added, "No one breaks from this case. Not for any reason. Kalee, I'm...going underground. You're in command. Till I get back, if I get back."

"Jalen."

"I know you can do it."

She shook her head and glanced up long enough to give him a contemplative gesture with her eyes. "It's not whether I can do it, but whether you can. Be careful and keep me updated."

With a quick nod, Jalen departed the office and retraced his steps. Lawrence and two other officers bolted through the front doors and ran full speed to where Marlon awaited at the top of the steps. They vaulted the badge scanners and met him like a pack of hungry wolves looking to please the alpha male. Jalen followed behind them, still limping. Adrenaline surged through his veins, which helped to numb the pain in his knee. Knowing morning would be brutal, Jalen pressed on. He led them down the right end of the main corridor toward the dogleg that separated Building 27 from the adjacent building.

The narrow corridor Ted had described jutted off to the right, changed directions in a series of bends, and then dead-ended at the unmarked door.

As Jalen made his way toward the door, his radio crackled. "Jalen, come in." He recognized the caller as Barry. "Marcus and I will join you in the tunnel."

"Negative," Jalen shouted. "Stay above ground. You know what to do."

He thought he heard a curse word before the radio fell silent.

With their guns ready and at firing position, the four cops followed Jalen toward the door. Their silence wrought a sudden chill Jalen couldn't begin to explain, but the hammering of his heart told him all he needed to know.

He momentarily closed his eyes, readied his taser, and swung open the door with his left hand.

A hot gust blasted him the second the door opened. Behind the door lied a different world. A shaft of large and small piping lined and concealed a concrete wall that shielded a metal grate stairway from realms he thought only his nightmares could produce.

The stairway descended three flights and the air progressively got warmer. For one reason or another, Jalen assumed it would be cooler underground, but understood that mechanical spaces were seldom cooler in industrial facilities than conditioned spaces were. A howl gradually became audible and then suddenly drowned away in a punishing cacophony of roars. Machines hummed and grinded, buzzed and chugged. Motors plugged away at consistent RPMs.

Down here the lighting was inconsistent and somehow paralyzed the scene in murky shades of yellow and orange that morphed into deep shadow at the edges of the tunnel. Jalen guessed that the tunnel stretched to fifty feet wide and up to twenty feet high at this location. Banks of piping and ductwork serving god-knew-what hid every wall and the ceiling, running in parallel, organized racks and dispersing into spaghetti at the intersection where another corridor jutted off.

Jalen stopped to look both ways. To his right, the tunnel opened up to a wider avenue. A couple of hydraulic lifts indicated a work site a hundred feet away. The tunnel doglegged to the left to serve the buildings at the south end of campus. To the north, the chamber narrowed significantly but remained straight. He peered in that direction. Rows of black, white, and silver piping seemingly stretched into infinity.

The corridor seemed mesmerizing and dark. He decided to wander that direction without speaking.

Marlon spoke up. "Lynx security will take the far-left end. Until the tunnel runs out."

"It could be miles," Jalen said.

"Lawrence, you go straight ahead down the side corridor. Officer Carson, go in the opposite direction. Leonard and I will go right and explore that end. I assume there is more to it than that."

"Don't get lost," Jalen warned. "Be careful, because there are plenty of ways to get hurt down here."

"Stay alert," Marlon commanded. "You know what to do."

"There are too many people down here to assume they're all the bad guy. Question everyone you meet and don't shoot unless you have to." Jalen had begun to sweat through his shirt. He wiped beads of it off his forehead.

"You have our channel," Lawrence noted to Jalen. "Communicate."

"Be careful," Marlon said.

Without another word, the group dispersed. Jalen plunged into the darker, narrower corridor with a hesitant, painful step. A small, corrugated ramp containing exposed cables crossed the floor in front of him. Jalen carefully stepped over it while keeping his gaze straight ahead. With every step, more of the long chamber revealed itself. The heat seemed unbearable, but the dimmer lighting seemed to evoke a certain humid chill in the air. He didn't remember seeing this avenue on the plans, but then again, he hadn't paid attention that closely. He hadn't known enough about the plans to make any specific judgment regarding the length or destination of the tunnel.

The tunnel seemed to morph into an industrial wasteland littered with dust, steel and torn insulation devoid of life. A sensation of foulness accompanied a dank odor reminiscent of a residential crawl space.

The dark mesmerized him. The spacing of the lights could never hope to clearly illuminate everything a person needed to see. Jalen began to wonder how often engineers or mechanics truly needed to access this tunnel. On a daily basis? Weekly? A black char on a large, insulated pipe seemed to indicate that welding had been done recently. Jalen looked at the walls and the ceiling.

Hundreds of pipes of various sizes joined in racks above, darted below large overhead ducts, and disappeared in shadow. On both sides of the tunnel, larger pipes up to two feet in diameter followed the walls. Each pipe displayed a strategically placed, yellow identification sticker that indicated what service flowed through the pipe as well as the direction of flow.

Jalen studied them. A thump that sounded like something wooden colliding with a corrugated metal barrel interrupted the hums and vibration of the pumps and other equipment. This corridor seemed to insulate the worst of the noise, but never fell totally silent.

He pressed onward until he encountered a pair of metal grate steps that ascended over some black piping. The steps led to a tiny corridor no more than a foot wide. The floor of the walkway remained metal grating before ending abruptly. Jalen followed the corridor and stared down into a thirty-foot-deep pit containing a number of large tanks. He gazed through the dimly lit room, scanning it, before he saw motion.

A stocky man in a dark blue jumpsuit seemed to be working on replacing a valve or something. Jalen eyed him curiously before shouting down to him. He believed that at this angle, his taser had the range to reach him, but instinct prevented him from drawing it. "Security," he yelled. "Hold up your badge."

The man did as he was told. Of course Jalen could not make out any badge details, but the fact that the man actually had a badge and was not opposed to showing it, told Jalen that he couldn't assume the mechanic a suspect.

"You seen anyone else down here?"

"No. Not in this area. I'm repairing a pump motor on this solvent line. Didn't hear anyone, either."

Jalen didn't consider thanking him. He backed down the elevated walkway and descended the steps backwards into the tunnel. He peered in both directions. A chill vaulted through his spine and shattered in a dazzling array of tingles across his back. Beads of sweat worked their way down his face and humidified the air around him.

No one was there. He considered backtracking to check for other interruptions in the piping, but instead limped onward. His adrenaline still surged, but allowed isolated bursts of pain to twist in his knee. It might be worth a trip to the doctor's office, he thought. The tunnel's end appeared three hundred feet in front of him.

Jalen kept his weapon ready and quietly marched onward, looking back at the corridor behind him at certain intervals. Just before the tunnel's end, a narrow ladder scaled eight feet up the side of an exposed concrete wall. The ladder led to darkened void that could house mysterious monsters for all he knew. A memory of a movie scene from nearly a decade ago flashed through his mind. A lonesome man explored the darkened corridors of a fallen hospital with an inefficient flashlight. Quiet ruled, and then zombies roared, pouncing on him from all sides to devour him.

The sweat on his back felt like ice that somehow penetrated his skin, causing further discomfort. Jalen removed his flashlight from its holster, flipped it on, and then climbed the ladder. The elevated portion of the tunnel was just high enough for an average-sized man to crawl through. Jalen scanned the nearby walls for a light switch after aimlessly flipping the cone of light through the darkness. When his flashlight finally illuminated a switch, Jalen reached for it.

He half expected something or someone to jump out at him, causing him to fall to certain paralysis eight feet below. The tunnel contained nothing more than lonesome black piping along both walls. There was surprisingly less piping, but Jalen crawled into the chamber anyway. It was long and angled left after about fifty feet. Beyond that, only darkness prevailed.

His knee ached against the hard, warm concrete. In the scant light, the black pipes seemed to be phantoms following each move Jalen made and instilled a faint spark of the macabre. Another chill shot through him as he made his way toward the darkness beyond the bend.

Jalen poked his head around the corner and then, half-expecting a zombie to come at him wailing like a tortured ghoul, flipped on the light. The darkness seemed surreal and the black pipes were not helping. He spun the light in all directions before a glimmer of white stopped him. Ahead, two large pipes with an intricate assembly of valves terminated. Jalen crawled a few feet toward them when his flashlight fell on a heap of something dark.

"Hands up!" Jalen shouted into the darkness.

The heap didn't move. Jalen painfully scraped his knee against the floor as he crawled toward the figure, attempting to maintain enough light to see the person.

A pang of horror struck him. A second murder on his watch on a Friday? He swore under his breath as a fresh batch of chills bathed him in what seemed like a sea of icy water. "Marlon, BPD come in!" he yelled into his radio.

"BPD," Marlon answered. "Murray."

"Get down here right away, we got a dead guy!"

"A...Shit, copy. We'll keep up the search with two while Lawrence and I join you."

"Run," Jalen said. "You'll come to the end of the narrow tunnel and there will be a ladder on your left. Climb the ladder, crawl until you find me. I'll be waving the flashlight."

Jalen waited. After a minute or two, he decided his time would be better spent examining the body but without touching. He scooted toward it, mentally attempting to shove the terror toward a dark corner.

The first thing he did was look for a badge. He didn't see one. "You gotta be damn kidding," he said.

The man appeared as though his face had been smashed in with something blunt and a scabbing, blistering burn boiled his face around the wound. He scanned the tunnel in search of a weapon, but didn't find it. After a moment, the cone of light fell upon something galvanized and painted. At the end of the large, white, insulated pipes, A sparkle of still water puddled on the floor. When he pointed the light at it, he noticed dripping. On instinct, he shone the light up to the ceiling. The dripping seemed to originate from both the pipe and the concrete ceiling, for the concrete was wetted.

There should have been more water, Jalen thought. He followed the large lines further into the tunnel with his light to find the yellow labels. The labels appeared approximately ten feet away from the body. The upper pipe was labelled as a steam line and the lower one as a steam condensate. The pipes appeared to be slightly graded downward away from the body.

"Murray!"

"I'm here," he said, crawling away from the body and spinning the light. Within a few moments, Officer Lawrence and Lieutenant Marlon rounded the bend and crawled to a stop next to the body.

"Gloves," Marlon said, removing a pair from a small pouch in his pocket and tossing them to Jalen. "Don't tell me you touched anything."

Jalen slipped the gloves over his fingers, noticing that the tingling chills had subsided. He focused on the body, wondering what would happen next. The killer remained on campus, but where? Had he already killed again?"

"Take enough pictures before we send the forensic team down here to collect the body and other material evidence," Marlon instructed Lawrence.

The flash of the camera became dizzying and pain-inducing too quickly. 'No badge," Jalen said quietly, staring at the steam piping.

Marlon rested his larger flashlight on the floor so that it illuminated much of the crime scene. He glanced at the piping Jalen stared at.

"Steam," Jalen said. He pointed at the galvanized chunk of metal on the floor. Splotches of blood painted a portion of the threaded end of the metal. "Looks like part of a valve or something. Hit him in the face."

"Clever murder weapon," Marlon said.

"Or an accident," Lawrence said, ceasing the photography long enough to answer.

"It can't be an accident," Jalen said. "Too much coincidence. A guy shows up dead with his badge stolen, and then another guy turns up dead in a tunnel and we assume it to be an accident?"

"I don't see any evidence that shows otherwise," Lawrence said.

"You've been looking for three minutes."

Lawrence pointed at the bloody, threaded object and then to a hole in the pipe. "That's part of that valve."

"It can't have fallen with enough force..."

Lawrence cut him off. "It didn't. Looks to me like pressure ejected it at him. Steam pipes carry a lot of pressure, for obvious reasons. So the pressure got too high and the valve failed. This guy was in the wrong place at the wrong time. No other blood except for small drops around the valve, the guy's head, on the floor. Nothing. The forensic crew will verify it."

"Do you recognize him?" Marlon asked.

"No. It doesn't mean he's not an employee. But where's his badge?"

"We'll handle the remainder of the investigation..." Lawrence paused, staring at the body and looking shocked.

"What?" Marlon asked.

"Lieutenant," Lawrence said, lowering his voice and sounding concerned. "I think this is the killer."

Jalen listened while trying not to rest his eyes on the body or the blood.

"He has blood on his hand. His clothes are burned, there on the sleeve. That's no ordinary burn. I know because that's the same sort of burn on the tour guide's collar. Same type of fabric. Chemical burn and, it looks like it tried to cut a hole in his flesh, too."

Jalen cringed when Lawrence spread the burn hole in the fabric and revealed a soupy mass of flesh pooling on the arm.

"Go update your people," Marlon said, looking up at Jalen.

Jalen spoke into his radio. "Kalee. It's Jalen. We've got another body the cops think is the same guy that killed the tour guide. Another killer might be on site. Keep an eye on all contractor's badges and watch for suspicious activity."

"I will," she said.

Jalen shuffled through the corridor and down the ladder, trying to think quickly while his knee shifted and tortured him from the inside. He needed to speak to Ted again but decided to go it alone.

As fast as he could run without subjecting himself to further injury and exhaustion, Jalen sprinted down the corridor back to the stairway they'd descended. From this location, the trip seemed like a journey through several different realms.

Before his eyes had a chance to adjust to the bright light, Jalen sprinted outside toward Building 21. The light morphed with hallucinogenic shades of blue and purple partially shrouded in black. His perception folded like gases from a nebula hundreds of light years away.

Still, he was able to see well enough to find his way. Before he reached the back door, his vision had adjusted. His knee ached with every step he took.

Ted sat silently in his cubicle with a cup of coffee perched next to his keyboard. He held his phone in his hands and read something. Jalen startled him when he entered.

"You again," Ted said. "What can I help you with?"

"What do you know about the steam system?"

Ted rested his device on the desk and stretched his arms. "Quite a bit. I'm a mechanical engineer with solid knowledge of structural construction practices. Years of experience…"

"Let me describe something, see if you can tell me what happened." Jalen didn't care that he'd just cut Ted off. "Imagine a bank of steam and steam condensate piping with a dead end in a tunnel. A smaller branch comes off and stops with a little valve, but something is broken before the pipe size changes. It looks like it just came off."

"It sounds like you're talking about a drip leg," Ted guessed. "Since high pressure steam in a pipe expands, some of the vapor condenses. To keep the condensation from pooling and flowing backward enough to block the pipe, a drip leg is installed at the end of the run. It collects the water and a small valve allows an engineer to drain the water into a floor sink nearby. A similar setup occurs on the steam return line, otherwise known as steam condensate or condensate return. The broken thing sounds like it could be a safety valve."

Jalen waited for further explanation.

"The pressure is monitored closely, but if too much pressure builds up, the safety valve will pop off so that the pipe doesn't burst and ruin everyone's day."

"The valve ruined someone else's day," Jalen said, trying not to divulge too much information.

"The pressure is often monitored and controlled by a large pressure reducing station in an interstitial space above a fab floor. That's up in the trusses. The system is connected to our servers so we can easily check status from any authorized station in this building."

"Are you authorized?"

"Absolutely," Ted said. He quickly logged into his computer and flipped through several files before finding the appropriate one. He shrugged as he leaned closer to the monitor. "You're right. One popped off about forty minutes ago. We'll send a mechanic out to repair the issue promptly."

"Thank you," Jalen said, attempting to walk away.

"Say, what makes you so interested in the steam system and the underground?"

Jalen sighed, looked to his feet and consciously noted that his knee throbbed. An aspirin or two chased by a shot of vodka would help, he thought. After refocusing his attention on Ted and affixing a deep frown to his face, Jalen spoke. "Call it a security issue."

9

# The Black Hole

Afternoon wore on. Seconds sped away into the emptiness of history right before Jalen's eyes. Having seen so much was one thing—perhaps the only thing—but it seemed that his subconscious desire and the pain in his knee conspired to grind him to powder.

Jalen swallowed a pair of aspirin in hopes of washing away the agony and thought about the case while he downed a cup of water. This would probably make him drowsy before the day was out, which wouldn't help.

Recognizing the look on Jalen's face, Kalee pressed a questioning frown to her lips and tilted her head. She stood up and walked around the desk to casually push a chair to Jalen's side. She looked at him for what felt like several minutes before she said anything.

"You're only as strong as you feel," she said.

Jalen didn't answer. Instead, he offered her a sideways glance through cautious, yet curious eyes. He already didn't like the way this had started.

"I'm just saying," she continued, using a pause to gulp and sigh. "You can withstand it if you believe in yourself."

"Little Engine," Jalen said flatly. "Right now I don't have the strength to sit here, let alone investigate a case that gets more and more bizarre the more time goes by."

He pictured a shot glass filled with clear liquid sitting next to his computer at home. The scant light spread shadows through the room as he stared at it. His mind and his heart begged him not to take the leap. He told himself that he didn't even want it but his conscious mind proved particularly adept at constructing believable lies. The shrewdness of the drink, however, was something he couldn't quite match no matter what he tried. *But you do.*

"I believe you." Kalee whispered something while turning her head to look at Laurie, who seemed to have seen something interesting on one of the cameras. "The torture you put yourself through, it's hard to..."

"It has a mind of its own," Jalen said. "Believe it or not, I can't control everything."

"In your state, you can't control anything."

Jalen shot her a glare that she didn't deserve. He sighed, leaned back in the chair, and threaded his fingers together behind his head. The pause weighed on him like lead. He subconsciously decided to use one of her favorite tactics and changed the subject.

"Should be case closed. But I don't think it is. Do you know what the odds are of getting pummeled to death by a steam pressure valve? You'd have a better chance of getting struck by lightning."

"That's something no one can know."

"Ted over in engineering describes it like one of these things rarely pop open. There aren't enough people wandering around in that tunnel for it to be an accident." Jalen shook his head and leaned forward.

"It's odd, she agreed. Are they wrapping up the case now?"

"Not quite," Jalen said, trying not to make eye contact with her. "They're going to exhaust all available leads before they throw in the towel. If they don't find anything, it will officially have been an accident, and we can all go about our lives like nothing happened. And maybe nothing did happen and this is some ugly fantasy we've all built up in our minds to combat the daily grind. That would seem swift justice."

Kalee looked surprised. As if letting an eon pass away without so much as blinking, she looked away with warm, soulful eyes. When she spoke, her voice was soft and caring yet unwilling to part from the facts. "But it did."

Jalen wanted to continue working, but her comment struck him like a shock of electricity. A jolt of pain slammed into his knee, causing his thigh to bounce. He winced. It seemed exactly like what he imagined the shot glass to say to him. "What did you say?"

"You heard me."

"Do you know what middle school kids want to see when they come here on tour? They want to see something flashy. High tech in action. They don't want to see the buckets and buckets of low tech stuff they used to build these buildings. Architecture students wouldn't give a damn about the tensile strength of iron beams or what the flow velocity is on a pipe."

"That seems about right," she said. "Do you think the tour guide had a different agenda?"

They'd spent the last several minutes running down every use the contractor had for his badge. He'd used it to access the mechanical space. Of course, the computer simply said, "Mechanical," which could have referred to the tunnels or any number of other mechanical rooms. Jalen assumed that there were at least fifty-nine mechanical rooms on campus.

"He had to. He wouldn't go out of his way like that if somebody didn't have some interest."

Kalee shifted her attention to Jalen's screen, which displayed one use of the tour guide's badge. "What does the INT in parenthesis mean?"

Jalen looked closer and tilted is head.

"Intermittent. Inter—connected? State?"

An idea blasted Jalen's mind all at once. He'd heard the word earlier in the day. "Interstitial."

She nodded. "That was going to be my next guess."

Kalee didn't have to offer a chuckle for Jalen to know that she was joking. To her, much like to him, it was just a word, and barely even that.

"It's in the roof trusses," he explained. "The emergency shut off valves were monitored and controlled by a station in an interstitial mechanical room."

"The same one the tour guide accessed," Kalee guessed.

"That's too much to be a coincidence. Do you know of a way we can find that room?"

"Could be in 27."

"I have an idea, but I'll need Ted's help. Care to join me?"

"It sounds exciting." She raised her eyebrows to consider, leaned back and examined the office. "I guess this place isn't going anywhere."

An inescapable vortex burned a hole in Jalen's mind until he could only sense a void that seemed to mushroom into something much larger. The singularity in his brain spun and began to draw everything toward it. Kalee and the case seemed to rotate around it as if nothing more than material to be decomposed as they crossed the event horizon, destined to become only matter, and barely even that.

Jalen walked faster than Kalee could manage. Jalen could hardly control his speed. His muscles worked with ease, with or without the pain in his knee. The more he walked, the less it ached. The agony began to evaporate, but its memory persisted.

Ted turned around and stared at Jalen as if in denial. His gaze seemed casual but forced. "Looking for more info on that steam valve?"

He shook his head and frowned. "You mentioned that steam valve's control center was located in an interstitial mechanical room. Where is that room?"

"You'll need engineering or mechanic access."

"Or security access," Jalen said. "My badge should open the door."

"Are you showing her the ropes?" Ted looked pleased with himself. A serpentine smile slithered across his face, but he attempted to hide it when Kalee shot him an icy dagger.

"Kalee's my number two on the cyber side. We're checking into something together."

"Security issue?"

Jalen didn't have to answer the question. He stared as Ted brought up the steam schematics for that building. His fingers danced and bounced off the keys with such fluidity and energy it made Jalen question whether he possessed the heart to do his work anymore.

Finding the schematics proved to be easy. Ted tilted his head sideways to read a note and then nodded. "I don't know how obsolete this is or how much has changed since the last as-built, but the general concept should be the same."

Jalen grunted and glanced at Kalee. She folded her arms in a show of defiance and wrinkled her nose.

"You want the mezzanine level in Building 5. Walk down the main corridor about halfway and you'll see a row of offices on the right. Between the last two office doors is a door labeled 5216 Mezz. Once you open that door, you'll climb a flight of stairs.

"Thanks," Jalen said.

"There aren't flashing lights or anything on the panel and it won't be clearly marked. Your best bet would be to find where the steam main feeds up into the mechanical room. There will be a small port on one side of the pipe with what looks like a wire sticking out of it. The wire will go into a small conduit and travel to the panel."

Jalen nodded and Kalee unfolded her arms. She glanced at Jalen as if ready for an adventure.

"Good and lost?" Ted asked.

"Clear as mud."

"Good luck."

Jalen spun without offering more to the conversation. It was clear that Kalee meant to start another conversation, but she seemed stumped. More than once she looked at Jalen's face, opened her mouth, then curled her lip and looked away.

After several attempts, Jalen looked back at her. He wanted her to say something, just not what he believed she wanted to say. He didn't speak, but maintained his gaze just long enough to make an impression.

"I never thought I'd see a murder here," she said. "I know there's plenty of places and plenty of weapons available with the right imagination, but there's never been any motive, even after the layoffs."

A pair of unattended janitor's carts distracted him as she spoke. Her last sentence managed to snap Jalen's attention back to her. "Layoffs."

She nodded. Indeed, during the most recent economic downturn, thousands of Lynx employees received the pink slip. Jalen never thought of that situation as dangerous, especially since Lynx was more than willing to aid laid-off employees with assistance and benefits in searching for another job. Still, a layoff could have become a motive.

"That's an idea," Jalen said. "And it's a good starting point. The list of laid-off employees may be long, but now that we have body, the police might find an identity. We can match that up with former employees."

"His badge wouldn't work anymore, and his parking pass would be expired. They wouldn't even let him on campus."

"You want to get on campus badly enough, you find a way," Jalen said. "This isn't the Pentagon."

Kalee shrugged as if uncommitted to the process of searching for the killer's identity. Then again, it probably didn't matter as much as Jalen thought it did. After all, a dead killer usually closes a case. Jalen now needed to discover why it happened and what led up to it. If headquarters ever had a reason to up the security budget, a murder would qualify as an excuse. Jalen would then convince his boss to use the added funds to beef up the security of mechanical areas, which would likely result in adding new staff, which would render the main security office obsolete. The new money might have to come in a huge sum.

Building 5 was constructed as a research and development fab back in the mid-1990s. Several areas had been converted to offices since and as a result, fab space had dwindled. The company was locked in a period of aggressive expansion at the time. The increase in demand for product necessitated the construction of more fab space. Buildings 45 and 46 directly resulted from the loss of research and development space due to the conversion of parts of Building 5.

Finding the door to the mechanical room didn't prove difficult. In retrospect, it hadn't even been as difficult as the journey. Jalen scanned his badge and pulled the door open. The stairs were constructed of heavy concrete with blackened patches.

They climbed the stairs quickly and emerged into a room that stretched much larger than he'd envisioned. He rolled his eyes and passed rows of huge equipment he could not identify.

"He didn't say this was going to be a needle in a haystack," Kalee said.

Each of the walls was cluttered with some kind of machinery. The things required to build an industrial building were staggering. Jalen kept his eye on the wall to his left. Kalee had wandered from his side. In the far corner of the room, at least a hundred feet away, a bank of pipes penetrated the floor. Most of them appeared to be black or stainless steel, but some of the larger ones were white. Jalen excitedly walked in that direction, leaving Kalee behind.

As promised, the main steam pipe seemed to terminate at a small piece of equipment that stood in the shadow of a monstrous piece of equipment that allowed access through several man doors. This mechanical room housed several of these units. Due to the huge runs of duct wrapped with silver insulation, Jalen assumed that these room-sized units were part of the main heating and cooling system.

The steam pipe branched off into two smaller runs, which after a huge array of controls equipment, recombined into a larger main. Jalen approached and examined the piping carefully. Just as Ted had described, a silver conduit terminated into the piping. Near this port stood a small gauge that Jalen hadn't the slightest idea how to read. He followed the conduit to a tall metal electrical panel that stood against the wall. The panel was padlocked and didn't appear to have been tampered with. Jalen guessed that only an authorized mechanic could open the panel. He had no idea how to find the key, but it didn't really matter anyway.

Jalen had guessed he wouldn't find much in this room, but a pulse of hot blood poured through his veins. Sweat began to bead on his brow from the heat. His hands began to tremble and he attempted to combat the energy with more energy. "Damnit," he said quietly.

Kalee appeared at his side before he was able to say much more.

Jalen lunged and kicked an abandoned box of screws, which scattered across the floor. "Damnit!"

"So it's a dead end," Kalee said. Her voice didn't intone disappointment. Instead, it offered a faint degree of hope. "It isn't the end of the maze."

"Can't accept it was an accident," Jalen said, his voice still simmering and caustic. "These things don't just happen."

"Let's see where the rest of the paths lead before rushing to judgment," Kalee said.

"Easy thing to say," Jalen fought back.

"Jalen, this means as much to me as it does to you."

"Funny way of showing it."

Instead of firing back another strained reply, she stalked away. Jalen knew this act to be a method of diffusing tension by making him follow her. This time, him physically following her footsteps didn't turn out to be her primary motive. Subconsciously, following meant releasing anger and succumbing to her point of view. When saying it meant little, showing it proved more precise.

Her demeanor seemed to glow as she descended the stairs. Jalen followed with urgency and respect.

Still, a storm brewed in his heart. Moments of emotion churned into infinity as the case drew him nearer and nearer to a single point in time and space where neither thought nor emotion could escape. He steeled his nerves and plunged toward the abyss.

# 10

# Ghost of a Star

Productivity waned as Jalen sat in his chair, leaning forward with his elbows on the desk. He halfheartedly pressed a few keys and moved his mouse once in a while to give the impression he was working on something important, but he felt he could contribute nothing more to the investigation.

Kalee didn't pay much attention to him other than stealing quick glances at him now and then. He wondered what was going on inside her skull but feared that her thoughts dwelt on him and his 'condition.'

Jalen didn't want to admit anything was wrong but understood that he often didn't need to speak to display emotions so deep they were rooted to his soul. More than fifteen minutes had passed since Jalen and Kalee had returned from Building 5. Most of the other security personnel patrolled the corridors at Jalen's request, but Jalen didn't believe they'd find anything, let alone detain a suspect.

Then again, 'condition' didn't seem like the right word. As thoughtful as he could be in a time of distress, Jalen passed the idea through his head several times before concocting an explanation. His condition was merely a state of mind, one he could change if he chose to. There was little use to being cheerful, so he set that idea aside, rested his chin on one fist and massaged his scalp with his left hand.

Kalee glanced at him, wearing a blank expression that somehow communicated more than Jalen believed she wanted to show.

The hammering in his head had also subsided since he'd swallowed the aspirin. Now that the day was nearly over, Jalen used an intense thought to scour the horrors of the investigation from his mind. Marie might have dinner ready when he got home, or she might chose to order in. Whatever her plans, Jalen feared that her mood would further affect his.

He decided he'd use some of the free time sitting at the bar. The prospect of having a drink, while stressful and intimidating offered a sense of relief. It seemed rewarding rather than demanding. These kinds of thoughts didn't serve him well. After years of increasingly using alcohol to numb his senses, Jalen had come to recognize a pattern, not without Marie's help.

Sometimes, the thought of a drink crowded his mind to such an extent that he could scarcely focus on anything else. If the condition were simply a state of mind, it collapsed in on itself until ideas became nothing more than faint, distant glowing orbs that had lost their luster and luminance, spinning faster and faster before extinguishing themselves. Echoes of thoughts became merely memories that would soon become nothing. Just pulsars at the end of existence.

Jalen was still stroking his scalp when Officer Lawrence strode into the room looking as haughty as Brawn before the big game.

Lawrence offered a curt nod to Kalee and then a hapless gesture to Sandy and Laurie, who had been huddled in front of the video monitors for the last ten minutes. He stopped at Jalen's left side and stared at the screen before saying anything.

"Doesn't look like we can rule out homicide yet. In the event that sufficient evidence supports the accident theory, we'll stop investigating it as homicide."

"Came all this way to tell me that?" Jalen raised his head, but spoke softly, which he didn't think Lawrence would take kindly to.

"The lieutenant and I were discussing this and we're going to need your full cooperation from this time forth. You'll execute orders we give like you are part of the force."

"May as well be armed as one," Jalen said, darting his gaze away. "And you'll probably want to bring this up with my superiors. Like it or not, I'm the head of security. Even if we've had a murder, I have duties to perform."

"We thought you might bring that up, so we saved ourselves the trouble and helped you out. You should receive an email from him anytime."

Jalen swore under his breath and shook his head.

"He wasn't opposed to you working Saturday. We will be, so plan on being here. You have a weekend team?"

Campus security required twenty-four hours of continuous operation. As such, even after hours, Building 27 never truly shut down. Most main fab buildings maintained production through the weekends and only occasionally shut down. With about a third of the normal daytime personnel, nights and weekends could be particularly boring. Jalen rarely needed to come to the office, but remained on-call at all times in case of emergency—or murder.

Jalen rolled his eyes and clenched his fist.

"Take six hours for a rest and get back here at five am to help us out. We want you to find out what those apps on that tablet were doing, how long they'd been installed, etc. Search the device's memory for other clues. If this is an accident so be it, and we're probably done."

"I'll be here," Jalen said. "Little reason to be home anyway."

Kalee shot him a worrisome glance from across the desk, but lowered her eyes when Jalen broke his gaze from Officer Lawrence. "I'll be here too," she said quietly.

"Loyal staff," Lawrence smirked.

"Don't you want to watch the game?" Jalen asked. "You promised."

"I promised when I thought you were going to be there leading the team. It isn't that I don't care about 27 overall, I just know you'll need assistance."

"A hundred bucks," Jalen reminded her.

She shook her head and kept her eyes on her monitor. "I don't need to be there to win."

Lawrence glared at her and then shifted his focus to Jalen.

"The identity of the killer," Lawrence started, "is still a mystery. Whoever he is, he has no record. Not that they won't figure it out when an autopsy is performed, but we still want to figure out who he is."

"I have a couple of candidates," Kalee said. "Maybe Laurie can spare a moment to help us out." She looked up and nodded at Laurie, who looked up from her monitors with interest.

"How'd you do that?" Jalen asked.

"It was a little idea I had on the way back from 5. The database automatically keeps a log of all badges being used, both in and out. There are only four badges in use today that have not been used since the incident this morning."

Jalen stood up and took a second to stretch while Lawrence darted behind her with blinding speed.

"These four are still here," she said.

"Three now," Jalen said, staring at the screen. "And I don't think so."

"No?" Lawerence said. "That's a quick decision."

Jalen glanced at Kalee and then leaned closer to the screen. "Face was pretty messed up and it was dark, but none of these belong to the dead guy."

"Are these employees only?" Lawrence said.

"All badges," Kalee repeated.

"Didn't he have to have employee level security access to set up the apps?"

Jalen stood back upright, folded his arms, and stared. "Could have been an app designed to imitate ours, but I won't know until I have a chance to look it over."

"We think the victim knew the killer," Lawrence said. He didn't look away from the computer. "Can we narrow down any people associated with him?"

"Unlikely, even if we had a badge," Jalen said. "Enough people come and go that..."

Lawrence cut him off. "You can do something. How did he get in the building without a badge?"

"I don't think you have to have a badge to get in the building," Jalen said slowly. The admission made his head throb.

"The hell?"

"These underground tunnels are accessible a number of ways."

The memory of Ted's voice echoed in his brain. *You could drive a truck down there.* It was a simple sentence that somehow triggered a surreal reaction. Now, Jalen had been cast into the waters of panic where desperation could never be used as a tool.

"I think...*shit*...There's a ramp."

"What are you getting at?" Kalee said.

"Officer Lawrence, I think I know how to find the identity of the killer."

"Explain."

"Delivery personnel have to check in though a special gate on the north side, where they can then access the main boulevard through campus.

No badge is necessary, but trucks have to stop. When they check in, they escort you to your destination, use their own badges for access, and let you make your delivery. You still need a badge to access all areas above ground, but if you know what you're doing, you can get into a lot of places through the tunnels. And I believe the tunnel has vehicular access."

"It does," Laurie said. "There's a ramp under Building 25 with two roll-up doors. "They mostly deliver construction and maintenance materials there. There's no camera showing that exact spot, but I've had to follow someone there from the back gate before."

"How could you not know such a ramp exists?" Lawrence said.

"Most people don't, even people out here every day. It's something you can pass by repeatedly without even noticing."

"And deliveries are frequent enough that most people don't pay any attention at all." Jalen spoke with an air of confidence that somehow could still not match up with Lawrence's.

Laurie searched for the footage from the north gate before any of them could walk over to her desk. Instead of asking Jalen to join her, she waited, momentarily paying attention to the conversation. She was one of Jalen's most patient workers, which sometimes turned out to be a flaw.

For a moment, Jalen let his eyes wander. He regarded Lawrence with a forced contemptuous look he didn't really mean. If he wasn't going to get along with Lawrence, his body language might as well play the part, he thought. His eyes fell on Kalee's dark, straight hair. He thought he could see his reflection in her glasses. For less than a second their eyes met. She combed a finger through the front strand of her hair, tucking it behind her ear, and promptly looked away. Jalen flinched and stood upright to glance at Laurie.

"You got the tape?" Lawrence asked.

"Ready to roll," Laurie said.

The three of them huddled around the footage desk and stared. She held down rewind until the footage showed darkness. When she pressed the 'play' button, the time stamp on the bottom right corner read 6:06 a.m. She paused when a blue and white delivery truck approached the gate, stopped, and signed in. She was able to get close enough by zooming in to catch the driver's face. They all stared at the face for too long before Jalen uttered a long sigh. He leaned over and rested his fist on the table.

"Doesn't look like the face of a killer."

"Could have been smuggled in," Lawrence said.

Jalen glared at him. He was right of course, but the suggestion seemed callous and off-color to the point of inciting anger.

"Is that a mark on his forehead?" Kalee asked.

Laurie zoomed in as far as possible and allowed the resolution to catch up. She stared at the image and shrugged, but Kalee had seen something none of the rest of them could.

"Good eye," Jalen said. "That's our guy. It didn't register at first because I couldn't get past the severe burn, the blood and the smashed features. Print an image."

Laure did as instructed, and then zoomed out. Allowing the footage to roll more, she relaxed her fingers and watched. The security vehicle escorted the truck off camera. She took less than two minutes to find footage from another camera that showed the same thing. It seemed to be approaching Building 25, but the angle was too wide and the camera was not pointed directly at the bay doors.

"Is there any camera showing that truck leaving?" Lawrence said.

"It will take a few minutes to search," she said. "Stand by."

"No," Jalen said. "That truck is still here. Let's go take a look."

Lawrence stood but didn't act impressed. He squared his shoulders and stared at Jalen. "You think you know that."

"I saw it," Jalen said. "I wasn't paying attention enough to even see the ramp, but now that I've seen the footage, I know I've seen the truck."

"He doesn't trust you," Kalee whispered after Lawrence strode away.

Jalen nodded and followed him.

"I'll stay here and do some research," she said.

Instead of directly answering her, he turned his shoulders and glanced at her. The look indicated sincerity without revealing the thought behind the look. He appreciated her more than she knew. He could have better communicated that but knew she was aware of it.

Jalen radioed Barry and asked him to meet them at the back door of Building 25, which entered into a main corridor. The door was unmarked, but Jalen was certain Barry would be there.

No conversation filled the space between the security office and Building 25, which Jalen managed to notice without fanfare. Instead of personality, Lawrence often seemed filled with an artificial coldness meant to intimidate others. Whether or not Jalen wanted to admit it, the tactic worked with such precision that it was shocking.

The back door of Building 25 stood next to a high concrete wall that jutted out from the building and enclosed something. The wall blocked the view to the other end of the building. Most buildings on campus were designed to make the most efficient use of space and so seemed settled in simple rectangles and squares. For any utility not directly connected with the use of the building, square extensions jutted off the back sides of the buildings. As far as Jalen knew, two buildings didn't follow similar construction patterns. The corporate offices in Building 11 and Building 27 were laid out differently. From this vantagepoint they could not see the ramp, so Jalen guessed that it was tucked against the building somewhere on the other side of the wall.

The square protrusion of the building seemed odd to Jalen. It rose less than the height of the building's other exterior walls and Jalen did not believe such a protrusion existed inside the building. Knowing the Lynx campus, the room had a purpose and was not a waste of space.

Barry swung the door open behind them and emerged onto the small patio ready to go. He offered a curious smile to Lawrence and looked around. Jalen led the way down the steps to the paved causeway in the center of campus, which in this area seemed as wide as a complex of airport runways. Small rails and plated steel sheets were embedded into the concrete in certain areas. Jalen never thought to question the purpose of these items.

A steel ladder to the roof was bolted to the exterior wall of the building protrusion. He wondered what was up there for a moment before they reached the other side. Some two hundred feet of blank concrete wall lined the ramp about eight feet tall. The three of them turned the corner all at once. The truck had been parked at the bottom of the ramp, blocking part of the bay door all day.

"We'll get some fingerprints and run the registration," Lawrence said. "You don't have to have a special pass to make a delivery?"

"No," Jalen said. "Never been a reason for that."

"I don't think he was acting alone," Lawrence said. "Whoever was riding in the back of that truck, find him and bring him in."

"Easier said than done," Jalen said. "If he's camping out in the tunnels, we might never find him, if he even exists."

"Are you disagreeing with me?"

"It's an assumption," Jalen said. "I thought you guys were against that."

"Not speculation. That's our job. We ask questions that we think will have satisfactory answers."

"It's a neat trick," Barry said. "But it's hard to argue with the effectiveness of the strategy."

"The fingerprints will match," Lawrence said. "If there was a passenger, he or she may not be on campus anymore. We'll need your manpower and cooperation to find out."

"Working Saturday," Jalen said, looking to Barry for help.

"What about the game?"

"No more talking about a game on my time," Lawrence barked.

Jalen's heart rate quickened and his face twitched. Somewhere in his brain roamed the beginning of a fiery retort, but instead of fanning its flames, Jalen allowed it to smolder. The heat it emitted seemed to consume Jalen's heart in an inescapable fury. He clenched his teeth and tightened his jaw.

"Not worth it," Barry said, seeing his reaction. "I'll volunteer. We'll man the hallways around the clock."

Jalen stared at Barry long enough for him to catch a glimpse of his face. He pointed his index finger at Barry and then at himself before making a fist, bringing his thumb up to his mouth, and titling his head back.

Barry smiled and nodded. "I'll make sure the night crew know what to do and assess them of the situation."

They stayed and inspected the truck more closely which drove the clock past 5:00. Without much conversation, the inspection lasted less than twenty minutes. Lawrence promised that the police department would take the steps to closely examine the truck for fingerprints and other evidence in due time. The three of them parted ways and Jalen walked back to the office alone. Barry already knew where to meet Jalen.

Barry's company would be greatly appreciated. He was not at all like Kalee. While she made her mark through speaking and open communication, Barry made his by not talking about the trouble spots at all. Both were appreciated, but tonight, only Barry could help him.

Drowning his agony in alcohol seemed a poor way to commemorate the events of three years ago, but in truth Jalen only wished to forget. To wipe the memories away with a cloth and to start over. He could not get her back. She was a piece torn off from the whole and discarded. Maybe her memory would reduce itself to a pale glow in time as the energy that illuminated her face flickered and died.

# 11

# Dark Matter

Reflections danced on pavement as a cold rain swallowed the city and sunk Jalen into a deeper state of chaos. Sleep had been rough and a hollow ache pounded inside his skull, which would make the task of focusing on anything next to impossible. Jalen could only blame himself, true enough. He'd succumbed to the perils of what some people liked to call 'recovery.' It sounded like such a pleasant word when compared to 'rehab,' but Jalen despised both terms so deeply that each time he heard it, he felt his eyes could erupt a concoction of vomit and blood.

What was life without letting loose from time to time? He wasn't about to destroy his weekend by sitting at home with a woman whose moods seemed to shift like the winter fog. Barry, while not possessing the qualities of a strong friend, had one major benefit. Around him, Jalen could simply be himself. With Barry around, no murder investigation and no disagreement with his girlfriend could pervade the mood. Even in the absence of adventure, Barry was fun. If Jalen could not have a little bit of fun, he could have nothing at all.

He leaned his head back and gently rested it on the headrest behind his seat. Turning onto the main street proved difficult and even at the early hour, traffic was a bear. He chose not to think about everything going on until he got to work.

A light smattering of cars sat nestled against the edges of the buildings on the main campus of Lynx Technologies. Jalen parked in his usual spot and watched a woman stroll toward the Building 27 entrance, dressed in a thick black coat and cowering under an umbrella. When she approached the doors, Jalen recognized her as Kalee. He emerged from his car and walked quickly toward the building. He shivered when he pulled open the door and attempted to catch up with her.

"Good morning, boss," she said without turning around.

Boss? Great way to start the weekend. Rain and 'boss' were two things he hated. One of the great benefits of living in this city turned out to be the stunning lack of both. An arid climate and people so friendly they addressed each other by their first names, even in contexts of business.

"Great weather, huh?"

Jalen harbored no deep distaste for small talk, but he wasn't good at it, so he often refrained. That sort of attitude had caused some people to label him as antisocial or even square, a common reaction that annoyed him. Kalee didn't see him like that, but she rarely judged anyone.

"I was thinking about ditching the joint and playing golf," he said.

"Were you? It would be kind of lonely."

"And slippery."

She laughed, folded her umbrella, and unzipped her coat. Her straight, black hair rested on her shoulders and highlighted her rosy cheeks. A glint in her glasses sparkled and faded, leaving a smile in its wake. The smile didn't droop, even when she laid eyes on him.

"Rough night, I take it," she said.

"Not really."

"Word has it you went to the bar with Barry. Did you have fun?" It seemed like she knew what demons plagued him, even though he had never mentioned any of his troubles around the office. He didn't think even Barry knew. Then again, if Barry knew, he probably would have shunned Jalen and told him to stay home so he could wither in agony.

He didn't answer her, at least not vocally. Instead, he pinched a spot of skin above his eyebrow and then stared straight ahead. The corners of his mouth angled downward, which he tried to make up for by uttering a low chuckle.

"Well, it's good to see you," she said. "Are we going to win today?"

"Maybe," Jalen said. "If the weather clears up. I'll talk to the troops and make sure you get your hundred bucks back and then some."

"Please do." Her expression seemed to communicate that she was ready for work.

Six other people were in the office. Abby manned the video desk on her own, while Lester, the most senior security officer on campus, tapped his flashlight against his palm. Madison, David, Louis, and Karl sat reclined in their chairs, only seeming to contemplate getting up.

The speech had to come, whether or not Jalen wanted to give it. "Listen up. Some of you might have heard, we had a major breach of security yesterday. We need continuous corridor patrols and make sure everyone has a badge clearly displayed. If not, you ask them to show it. Abby, keep a close eye on the north gate. If any vehicle with no pass comes in, I want to be the first to know about it."

"I heard the bad guy was dead," Louis said. He frowned and leaned forward slightly before lingering.

"I've heard he same," Jalen explained. "But his death remains suspicious, so we need to be on high alert until we can get this sorted out."

The office door swung open just as Jalen finished his speech. Barry burst in, soaked from head to toe, wearing a huge grin. "Guess who just went for a jog?"

"You're insane," someone said.

"One of the night janitors," Barry started. His grin didn't cease. "Came up in the parking lot where that dip is and I happened to be on the sidewalk. He splashed me."

Louis laughed.

"Why are you so wet, then?" Abby asked.

The grin loosened, but he took it in stride. "I parked by Building 11."

"And the corridors were closed?"

"No, I just wanted to spend a few extra minutes outside."

Kalee shook her head, sat down, and logged into her computer. Tapping resounded from in front of him for several seconds.

"Great," Abby said. "Let me know how that pneumonia is going and I'll send you a card in the hospital. Maybe we'll all sign it."

"I won't," Louis said.

"No one can read your writing anyway."

Jalen clenched a fist and pounded it onto his desk with such force that it surprised him. "Let's get to work." He feigned a friendly attitude by dressing his remark in a casual tone.

Kalee looked up. "What do you think the cops are up to?"

***

Officers Lawrence, Carson, and Leonard huddled around a rectangular table with a slew of notes and pictures strategically spread in front of them. Marlon situated himself at the head of the table and examined a photograph of the body from the tunnel. When the others looked up at him, he grunted and carefully placed the photo back on the table.

"Tunnel guy is also known as Burton Cambridge," Carson explained.

"Like the town?"

Carson nodded and continued. "Came from a small town called Midvale, then migrated to Caldwell where he took up over-the-road truck driving. It suited him for five years, then he added independent transport to his repertoire. He works for himself by leasing the van from a small Caldwell transportation company. The fingerprints in the truck match those taken off of the dead tour guide's badge."

"Which isn't surprising," Lawrence said.

"How does a guy decide to kill a man for no apparent reason and then turn up dead just hours later? That just doesn't happen in real life."

"It's puzzling." Lawrence looked down to a set of notes, crossed his legs beneath the table, and stared. "What we do know is that Cambridge was filming himself, possibly even committing the murder."

"Why would he do that?"

"We found a hidden camera disguised as a button in his jacket," Lawrence continued, feeling bored. He stared at a spot on the wall below a large bulletin board covered with evidence from another case. Before continuing, he tapped the heel of his pen on the table. "We can't know for sure whether it was activated during the killing, but we did not find his fingerprints on the lens."

"Do we know if there's a taping system?" Marlon asked. "Or only live footage?"

Officer Leonard picked up a page full of notes and scanned it momentarily before speaking. His voice suggested intrigue laced with a particular air of smugness that Lawrence keenly relished. "We don't know that at this time."

"Find out," Marlon said. "We need you to track the signal of the device so we can go to the source and talk to someone."

"I've tried that," Leonard said. "Signal was jumping around all over the place, and I lost it in North Korea. You don't make this stuff up."

"What does North Korea have to do with anything?" Marlon asked.

Leonard hurried through a brief response. "I didn't say that, just that's where the signal disappeared."

"But it's internet-capable," Carson said. "Surely you can use the web to track it down."

"When you lose a signal, it's gone. You can't just reach out and grab it. It could have gone into dark web or any number of possibilities, including being rerouted back to the U.S."

"Guy is covering his tracks like he knows someone important will be trying to track him down via this method." Marlon appeared subdued, but not surprised.

"How do you reroute a signal when you're dead?"

"He could have set it up a long time ago," Leonard said.

"What else do we know?"

Lawrence spoke first. He dropped his pen on the table and brushed a more somber look across his face. "The security team at Lynx has no idea this is going on, but they're computer-savvy enough to figure it out, given the right info. We also know that Cambridge was wearing a digital watch with a GPS."

"Smart watch?"

"Definitely not," Lawrence said. "It's more like one of those watches hiking enthusiasts like to wear. It has an altimeter, too."

"Can the watch tell us where he's been?"

"Negative," Leonard said. "It doesn't have that kind of capability and there is no signal we can track. The GPS is rudimentary and shows only coordinates. It doesn't even keep a history."

"No?" Marlon said. "Then why do we have it in our evidence?"

"It had fingerprints too," Lawrence said. He flicked his fingers and glanced down at a photo of the tour guide. "Two sets."

"Who do the other prints belong to? The tour guide?"

"Unknown," Lawrence said. "No record, but..."

They waited for him to speak.

Lawrence hesitated only long enough to strengthen his point and to add a layer of intrigue, lest Marlon pass it off as inconsequential before moving on to more unimportant matters. "The second set of prints on the watch match a partial found on the camera."

"Do you think someone was using the camera and the watch track him?"

"The coordinates go down to seconds, which amounts to maybe a hundred yards. "In a place like Lynx Technologies, that isn't close enough to be entirely reliable." He paused, tapped his pen again, and then continued. "In some of the more high-end cars, the GPS is capable of reading fractions of seconds. But without a signal, you just can't track it."

"But what if the camera is working in concert with the watch?"

"They have no link whatsoever," Carson said.

"We need to know who's watching the camera footage," Marlon said. "That's our next step. Figure out the manufacturer, who it sold to, find the retailer, look at video footage from there. There are more ways to find this person than one.

"I'll lead that," Lawrence said, squaring his shoulders and tilting his head back.

"Talk to Officer Murray at Lynx again," Marlon instructed. "See if he has any more luck."

"I plan to," Lawrence said. He let a wry smile slither across his face and then vanish without saying another word. Jalen acted like he had problems bigger than Lawrence could realize. His overly aggressive attitude towards him, while completely warranted and even expected, proved a disadvantage Lawrence aimed to exploit. Jalen's reactions were amusing.

"Lynx is working other avenues internally," Lawrence said. "I'll check with them later today to see if they've got anything else."

"Good," Marlon said. "No media yet, even though it's already too late."

One by one the officers stood. Lawrence waited until everyone departed the room before picking up a photo of the tour guide and examining it. An idea crawled into his skull and nestled itself there, invading his consciousness like an army of one to pollute every other thought with strains of darkness. Some unknown fabric held this case together and Lawrence was determined to find it. Somehow, it all hinged on Jalen, whether or not he wanted to admit it. There was a good chance Jalen could find out where the hydrogen chloride came from.

He bit his lip, dropped the photo and leaned back in his chair. Jalen didn't present himself as an easy man to figure out. What drove him seemed to differ from the motives of almost everyone he'd ever met. While true that no reaction he'd given seemed extraordinary, the construction of his thoughts seemed to indicate a dark past and a bitter attitude toward the future. Lawrence didn't need to investigate Jalen. Finding out the truth through natural means delivered sweeter rewards. Though he overtly communicated disdain towards Jalen, his own attitude dwelt on deeper interest.

Lawrence sighed, placed the pen on the table, leaned his head back, and closed his eyes. Life could be different in many ways if his motives weren't muddled with cop duties. Then again, his duties as a cop had opened his mind to a wider realm of possibilities and interests. That dark and mysterious history being recounted somewhere behind Jalen's eyes sparked a sense of allure. And not even soon-to-be Detective Lawrence was immune to Jalen's perils.

# 12

# Half Life

*Time is a pervasive enemy. It contorts our realities and preaches its own importance while humanity falls victim. It tears us apart piece by piece until we are rendered but the ashes of a spent nuclear weapon that we invented ourselves.*

Jalen pressed the 'send' button before he even knew what he was doing. If Marie read that, there would be hell to pay. Then again, Marie wasn't the least of his concerns.

He leaned back and thought about his words. Their darkness enriched the fluidity of his heart, but a sinister quality wrought more significance and meaning than Jalen had anticipated. He shook his head, bit his lip, and glanced up at Kalee. When his fingers vomited the sickness trapped in his own brain out onto a blank page, the feeling waxed cathartic. Yet when he saved these words with knowledge he'd be able to peruse them again and again, a feeling of guilt clung to his veins.

Instead of saying anything, Jalen and Kalee stared at each other for more than a second, which was long enough to form a bind, but short enough to evade awkward tension. Jalen looked away first and tapped his foot. Out of the corner of his eye, a faint glimmer of a smile wisped across her face and then vanished.

Jalen punched a few buttons on his keyboard and then turned toward the killer's tablet at the end of his desk. He turned on its screen and further examined the first application that had been running since yesterday morning. Whatever type of analysis the code was running, Jalen had to put a stop to it. He touched a button, which brought up a short menu. He pressed the 'app security' option and waited. The screen that came up displayed some kind of clock, which showed a time far different than the actual time. He attempted to swing the clock's hands to alter what the clock showed, but the app denied him access. Why would the tablet's user be blocked from modifying apps?

On the bottom right corner of the screen, Jalen saw a button that promised safety. He paused for a moment, staring at the word 'abort' until it seemed to dance in his retinas. The moment he pressed the button, the screen on his master monitor flashed. Unlike the continuous flashing monitors always did so fast that the human eye could not detect, this flash caused his screen to go dark for a fraction of a second. He raised his eyebrow and spun his chair toward his computer. He opened up the control panel and checked his monitor connection, but it seemed almost as if the flash were his imagination.

"Did you see that?" He asked loudly enough for only Kalee to hear.

"Huh?" Kalee looked up and glanced over the rims of her glasses.

"My monitor just flashed, like there was a blip in the power."

"I'm sure it did," she said.

While her sentence didn't reflect scorn, her tone indicated a kind of comical ignorance that worked its way into Jalen's consciousness. He allowed a sour expression to flourish on his face before dropping it. "Connection's fine."

"You know Lynx only relies on public power for about half the energy we use," she said.

Jalen was aware of that truth. In fact, Lynx Technologies hardly had an employee who didn't know that. It was one of the first and most impressive things the average employee learned on the job.

In the southeast quadrant of the campus stood the complex's power generators. The generators ensured that Lynx did not need to be subject to the frailties of public utilities. Because production was continuous and precision was vitally required, public power could cause a lot of damage just by failing even for a few seconds. The regional power grids routed over high-capacity transmission lines near campus. From a variety of points, Lynx tapped into this power source by feeding steady amounts of juice into the transformers that allowed Lynx to store energy in a set of generators, each housed in separate outbuildings. The power generation center was purposefully isolated from the majority of campus. The nearest parking lot ended some two hundred yards from the high fence topped with loops of barbed wire. For added security, a steady current of power flowed through the fence without being grounded. Only qualified electricians could get near the system and needed a special code to enter through the only gate. In some ways, the vitality of Lynx Technologies rested behind that fence, yet few people even gave it a second thought when driving by it.

"I guess it's no big deal," Jalen said. "Just caught me off guard."

Kalee nodded and busied herself typing on her keyboard. Traces of boredom showed on her face but didn't linger.

Returning to the tablet, Jalen summoned a node of energy from a locked portion of his internal vault. Pressing the 'abort' button had caused the app to shut down. A quick warning appeared, but vanished before Jalen could read the message. Instead of dwelling on that, he examined the second app. A brief wait allowed another error message to pop up on the screen. The message was from the application itself. "Application PressPro has been terminated. Please restart PressPro to update this application."

Instead of following the instructions, Jalen closed out of the error message and searched for an 'abort' button in the second app. The application seemed to be laid out in similar fashion to the first. He quickly aborted the app, which also caused this one to close. Its closure seemed to wreak havoc on the third app, which mimicked the security program installed on all of the computers in this office. "You gotta be kidding," he said.

"Problem?" Kalee asked.

None Jalen wanted to share. He ignored her and read the first of three error messages. "Security detected that PressPro has been terminated. To continue, please restart PressPro." He closed the message and read the second one. "MaxSoft was using data from Security One, but has been terminated. Pressing OK will return this app to normal conditions." He hesitated, but closed out of this app. With that, the tablet's screen flashed. The app's appearance subtly changed, yet it still looked nearly identical to Lynx's security software.

"Don't know what kind of security this thing is running, but I'm going to find out what it is," Jalen muttered.

He stopped to examine some of the settings in the security software that was set up as a quasi-operating system on his computer. He took mental note of each important setting and turned back to the app. The app's settings were identical.

"Someone has been using our internal software to run some kind of test on this device," Jalen said. "That killer was up to something, and more than just murder."

"I don't follow," Kalee said. She stood up and carefully stepped to his side. She stared down at the screen and allowed a look of disbelief to span her face.

Jalen shrugged and intensified his stare.

"They've duplicated our software," she said. "I didn't think someone would steal it."

Jalen looked up and replaced his frown by raising his eyebrows and entrenching a questioning gaze into his eyes. "What did you do?"

"I backed up our data," Kalee said.

"You did what? Damnit, you know that's against protocol."

"The boss asked me," she said, subtly leaning away and letting her arms dangle at her sides. Contemplation furrowed her brow, but instead of backing away entirely, she squared her jaw and stared at the tablet.

"The boss knows protocol better than I do," Jalen said. "But I don't see any reason to authorize that. Where did you back it up to, the cloud?"

"A portable hard drive," she said. "It looked like it had about a terabyte of storage space. He gave me a release form, had me sign it, and I scanned it into our server so we could have record. Then I gave it to him."

"You personally handed it to Doc?"

She nodded.

"Then what makes you think it was stolen?"

She flinched and pierced him with a solemn shift of her shoulders. "Jalen, our software is secure. The only way it could have been put on this tablet is if someone lifted it from that hard drive and used the coding to duplicate the software. Unless that thing is connected to our servers—"

"Brilliant," Jalen said. He minimized the app and searched the tablet's settings. The wi-fi recognized Lynx's security signal, which didn't come as a surprise. For curiosity, Jalen tapped the Lynx wi-fi network. The security access password didn't seem to be in the memory. A bad feeling crept over him as he contemplated connecting it to Lynx's servers. If this device stored some kind of malware, the whole system could get infected.

"No?"

"Maybe you need to go have a conversation with Doc," Jalen said.

"You do," she said. "But I'll come with you." She paused long enough for a forlorn look to loom over her face like the shadow of an ominous cloud. "I'm sorry, I thought it was legit."

"You did your job," Jalen said, forcefully studying his voice and lowering his tone. He glanced around the room and then returned his gaze to the tablet.

"That makes me so happy." No line of humor resonated in her sarcasm, which Jalen took to be a bad sign.

"Whatever happens," Jalen started, not certain of why he was acting the way he was, "I'll cover for you if Doc is unhappy."

"It isn't your fault," she said, emphasizing the last word. "That tour guide might be still alive if not for me."

"You don't know that," Jalen said. "Be a man about it."

She smiled, though the expression was pained and nullified by the torture that played out in her eyes. "That would serve me well."

"Indeed," A voice behind them said.

Jalen knew the voice. He spun his chair around to face Officer Lawrence, who appeared to be alone. The smug curvature of his jaw suggested victory, but Jalen knew he wouldn't even be here if he didn't have questions. He tilted his head and waited for an explanation.

"What was I here for?" Lawrence said, as if pondering. "Yeah, we're going to need you to track down the signal on that device."

"Already did it," Jalen said.

"And?"

"It's all internal. It isn't connected to our building at all. We think we know why."

"Let's hear it," Lawrence said, acting polite all at once.

Jalen folded his arms and scooted his chair backward until it collided with his desk. "I don't think so."

Lawrence exhaled slowly and clenched his fist. "Stand up."

Jalen spun and grabbed at the tablet, but Lawrence kicked out his foot to stop the chair. He repeated his order impatiently and glared at him. "You're under arrest."

"It's bullshit," Jalen said quietly, without standing. In this situation, it seemed difficult to pay Lawrence much attention, let alone take him seriously. As far as he was concerned, the security breach stood as greater cause for concern. To ensure that such a string of events would not happen again, Jalen had to act within his own jurisdiction and use the rules of Lynx Technology to bring the matter to a close. Lawrence simply got in the way.

"I don't think you understand the severity of the situation," Lawrence said, standing firm and folding his arms loosely.

"I don't think you do," Jalen said. He knew his words were not forceful enough to make an impact before they'd even finished leaving his mouth. To combat the lack of emphasis, he exerted greater strength into the last word, making the whole thing sound like a foreign language.

"Then explain it to me."

Kalee looked up, narrowed her shoulders, and looked apprehensive all at once. Still, she stepped up when she needed to. Watching Jalen almost give in to verbal attack must have caused her alarm. "I backed up the data, and I think it was stolen?"

"What data?"

Jalen clenched the tablet while he spun to return his computer to the main security screen. He held up the two side-by-side long enough for Lawrence to draw a conclusion. "There's only one way this could have happened," he said.

"Who do you think stole it?"

"It's obvious, isn't it?"

"We know who he is," Lawrence said. "There's no way the killer would possess the technical expertise to pull off something like that."

"You think he's being manipulated?" Jalen spoke as if that came as a shock, but after yesterday he didn't think much could surprise him.

"We suspect," Lawrence said. "Unfortunately, we can't back that up, which is where you come in. If you don't think you can do it, work your magic and invent a way. You're smarter than you let on."

Jalen didn't know whether to be insulted of feel gracious. He narrowed his eyes and stared while subtly raising the corner of his mouth.

"For now, we're looking at an accident," Lawrence said, standing upright and glancing at the computer.

"So that's why you're investigating it as a murder," Jalen said.

"Protocol," Lawrence said, rotating his shoulders a few degrees. "You seem to know a thing or two about that."

"Doesn't take a genius to figure it out," Jalen said. "Still too many holes."

"Holes you're going to help us fill in."

"OSHA's going to have a field day if we play it like that," Jalen said. "It's best if this doesn't go public."

"I'm afraid it already has."

Jalen cursed quietly and continued to stare. It had always been a not-so-tacit truth that some of the mechanical areas on campus could prove to be treacherous to those unaccustomed to navigating said areas. The safety seminars all badge applicants had to undergo communicated the danger, but could obviously only highlight a few dangers. Having been down there, Jalen felt that he understood the dangers of the tunnel on an intimate level.

Lawrence addressed Kalee without so much as glancing at her. "I want you to find out how that backup ended up in the wrong hands."

"I give orders here," Jalen said.

"Then give them."

"He doesn't have to, I volunteer," she answered. She returned to her desk, punched a few keys, and walked out the door without saying anything else.

"Doc isn't here today," Jalen said. "Suppose she'll poke around a little. Find out if the hard drive is still there, if the data has been accessed or copied. She's good."

"Better be."

For a moment, probably less than a full second, Lawrence stared into Jalen's eyes as if in search of some lever he could grasp that would change him into a better person. The expression on his face turned blank.

There had always been answers. Life itself teetered on the brink, lost between an expanse of matter and a shadowy realm that plunged all imagination into eternal blackness. How could the killer of the killer not have existed? These things don't just happen, or at least he didn't think so. Yet the more chaotic life became—the more it decayed—the less certain everything grew. Where the past life had been moored in reason, existence began to venture into uncharted territory.

Jalen waited for Lawrence to stand up and to decide he had better things to do with his time. After all, he'd gotten everything he wanted.

Lawrence turned around, walked toward the door, and then paused to glance at Jalen once more. Jalen's frown deepened, but for two or three seconds, Lawrence didn't speak. "Keep it together."

Blinking and leaning forward, Jalen watched Lawrence leave. For some reason, that simple sentence brought him to the edge. Helplessness clawed at the insides of Jalen's brain. He could not stop things from shattering. The more he tried, the more life faded away into futility. He slapped his hand down on the desk, bit his lip, and lurched forward. Life at the bottom had become so familiar Jalen had begun to assume there was no other way. Down here, death lurked in all corners, eager to take him no matter the path on which he embarked.

# 13

# String Theory

The sun poked through a hole in the canopy of clouds long enough to spread warmth to the poor souls deciding to play soccer today. The rain had stopped temporarily, leaving a muddy pitch that, cleats or not, would cause slipping and possibly injury.

Dressed in street clothes, Jalen hurried into the huddle, glancing back to Kalee. She stood next to the track and grinned while twirling the closed umbrella against the turf. Just as the hole in the clouds closed, Jalen caught sight of Lawrence, who stood firmly behind her as if escorted to the pitch.

"I wish I could join you today," he said to his teammates. "Unfortunately the man's got me. We got Brawn and the cockiest group of soccer players Lynx has ever seen. Don't let them rattle you. Let your play do the talking. Win with style."

"Style," the other thirteen players said in unison.

Jalen didn't exactly brim with confidence, but showing humility amongst his teammates could prove disastrous. He jogged back to the sideline and faced Kalee.

"Didn't think you'd come," he said.

"It's my pleasure," Lawrence answered. Kalee had opened her mouth to reply while he spoke. Instead of saying anything, she shrugged and grunted.

"Help you?" Jalen asked, lowering his eyebrows.

"You can come with us."

"No I can't."

Lawrence stepped closer. "It's not what you think. We're searching Burton Cambridge's house, and we recommend you join us."

"Seriously?" He shook his head and walked twenty feet parallel to the sideline while Lawrence followed. "Why do you need my help?"

"Funny you should ask. It seems like you're important to the case, being on the inside. Since Cambridge killed right under your nose, I'd say that makes you obligated."

Jalen exhaled and nodded. He wasn't expecting to watch his team play, but no matter how much he despised the man, Jalen was bound to help Lawrence anyway. A cold sensation crept over his body. For the first time during the investigation, Jalen was about to leave campus. Into the real world, which despite Lynx's recent security lapses, remained a much more dangerous place.

"Yeah," he said. "My mission is to protect Lynx."

He turned back and took several steps toward Kalee.

"Now," Lawrence insisted.

"Gotta hand off the reins."

Kalee offered a polite smile, but Jalen could plainly see the mistrust behind her eyes. She backed away from the sideline while clutching her umbrella more firmly.

"I'm going off-site with the cops," Jalen said. "You're in charge." He lowered his voice. "You've got your radio? Make sure my team doesn't lose."

"The office will contact me if they need to?"

"Of course." Jalen left his weekend crew to handle the day-to-day issues and to watch for any signs of violence in the corridors. They were capable and Jalen trusted them. Kalee had volunteered, but she had been planning on visiting campus all along. That along with her personality made Jalen want to take it easy on her.

Without saying anything else, Jalen followed Lawrence to the west beyond Building 40. The sidewalk paralleled a road connecting parking lots across a ditch and through a narrow chain link gate where it intersected with another small road in front of an enormous parking lot. Lawrence appeared to have driven his own car. They approached it quickly.

"Nice, convenient place to park," Lawrence said.

"Kalee escorted you? She's got a meeting at corporate in an hour and a half."

"Important one?"

Jalen nodded but didn't want to tell him that her assignment was exactly what he'd so forcefully ordered less than an hour ago.

As Officer Lawrence drove through the north gate towards the main boulevard, rain began to sprinkle the window. The skies covered the valley in bleak shadow while the rain obscured the nearby mountain range northeast of the city. A nagging feeling crept up in the back of Jalen's skull and demanded the kind of attention he once believed only the deranged would quench. It had been a day like this three years ago, where heavy rain and wind tore the blossoms from the trees and sent them fluttering like driven snowflakes. The mood had been pervasive and cold...

"You think this is going to take us anywhere?" Lawrence said after they'd driven more than a mile.

"Doubtful."

"You never know. That's why you look into these things. Assume nothing but suspect everything."

"You must be a great cop, believing that," Jalen said. He curled his lip but didn't remove his gaze out the window.

"Can't go wrong that way. And it covers most scenarios on the job."

"Who drilled it into you?"

"It's something you learn along the way. I think your buddy Barry would give the same sentiment if you ask the right question."

"I don't misunderstand you," Jalen said with a quick glance at the dashboard.

"One could say the same about you," Lawrence said as if indicting Jalen's character. He didn't remove his eyes from the road and said nothing more for the remainder of the trip.

The house was constructed around the 1960s out of traditional wood framing with a brick veneer that stretched halfway up the exterior walls. Above the brick, particle wood siding reached the eaves and framed the windows. Years of spotty upkeep had weathered the house into something resembling inner city blight. Cracks scattered across the driveway and the front steps. Giant holes rendered the screen door useless.

A pair of other police cruisers rolled up to the house seconds after they arrived. Jalen moved to open the door, but Lawrence stopped him. Lawrence didn't say anything. He nodded at several of the officers and waited until they kicked the door open to move. He motioned Jalen to get out of the car while he drew his gun and waited for the all-clear.

His radio crackled, and then he closed the door and motioned Jalen to follow him.

The interior of the house was scattered with paper, various food wrappers, and several different types of bottles. Some water, some soda, some beer. Jalen scanned the floor plan while taking interest in how similar the residence seemed to his. One of the qualities of the bench neighborhoods was the variety and density of the housing developments. While many of the houses were small, different materials and floor plans injected the neighborhood with a certain charm.

"Lives alone," one of the officers said. A pair of officers began to dust for fingerprints as Jalen watched.

"Bills, credit card offers...no birthday wishes or Christmas cards," Lieutenant Marlon noted. "Guy's living like a bachelor."

Another officer opened the refrigerator, the cabinets, and all the drawers. He shuffled through junk in one of the drawers, pulled out a piece of paper to read it, and then shoved it back into the drawer.

Lawrence stepped forward to assist Marlon in going through one of the bedrooms. He turned and tossed Jalen a pair of latex gloves before pointing at a laptop sitting on a desk. An empty soda bottle stood next to the monitor while a half-eaten bag of potato chips adorned the desktop next the mouse. A mound of papers caked with approximately four years' worth of dust had been shoved away from the computer into a corner and some pages had fallen off into a network of cobwebs next to the sliding glass door.

This task would require a stiff tonic, Jalen told himself. A small glass of whiskey ought to do the trick.

Jalen managed to bypass the log in screen with little effort. He dove into the list of programs on instinct. The software was a basic, out of the box operating system with no modifications. Jalen wondered how often the webcam had been used. He searched its files and found a self-photograph with nothing notable in the background. No video footage had been recorded, but that didn't mean live footage had not been uploaded to the internet. A quick check of the system's wi-fi confirmed an internet connection. Before trying anything, he scanned through cookies and noted the presence of two different sets of spyware. In this day and age, most websites attempted to download cookies and a handful used spyware to obtain data for advertising purposes. The temporary internet folders looked like they'd never been cleaned out. Jalen's eyes began to droop.

He looked through all of the files behind a particularly nasty spyware that was advanced enough to not only monitor web visits, but also record keystrokes. If the software had that kind of capability, the computer must have kept a log somewhere.

After a search, Jalen found it. The history went back less than three weeks. An internet chat about video games here and there revealed nothing, and the user had posted to two different message boards during the period. Without context, Jalen would have guessed the conversation had been about football. Another message board revealed questions about basic computer code that someone with a rudimentary knowledge should have known how to navigate.

The killer certainly wasn't tech-savvy like Jalen had imagined him. In fact, it seemed like he didn't know what he was doing at all.

The cookies ranged from passwords to large-platform shopping websites, news outlets, and even a blog or two. As with most users, four or five websites garnered most of the web browsing history.

Lawrence stepped up behind him as he typed away on the keyboard looking for other ideas. "Anything?"

"Depends on your definition," Jalen said.

"Just tell me what you found."

Jalen blew through it while leaving out his own speculation, but it became apparent that Lawrence had a key idea he shared with Jalen.

"That doesn't sound like someone who can manipulate and reroute signals. It could be a front."

"It isn't," Jalen said. "Keeping your ideas and thoughts private inside your own head is easier than it is online. Everything posted on the internet stays there for life. Search histories can reveal a lot about a person's personality. There's no way this person is pretending to be a guy who doesn't know much about computers."

"Has he accessed the dark web?"

"I doubt he knows how," Jalen said. "You can't get on dark web sites through search engines or by linking from CNN."

"Check it out," Lawrence said.

Jalen bit his lip and clenched his toes inside his shoes. For this result, searching proved more difficult and consumed more time. Before he even paid attention to the clock on the bottom right side of the screen, more than forty minutes had passed. He attempted to stifle a yawn and got away with it. Lawrence distracted himself by rummaging through the papers gathering dust. Behind him, one of the cops loaded items into small plastic evidence bags.

"This isn't going to be anything," the officer said.

"Couldn't hurt," Marlon said.

The search revealed nothing out of the ordinary. The computer had never been used to access a dark web page as far as Jalen could tell. It was really clean and tidy in how unkempt it was, which gave Jalen an idea. He used the search feature on the software and input the dead tour guide's name. The name had come up twice, both in emails. The emails had been deleted, but their shadow lingered. The spyware had recorded it.

Jalen swore and read it out loud to officer Lawrence. "What about Kazinsky? We can't do anything until he's done. Don't do anything stupid." He paused to indicate that the other person was speaking. "Kazinsky's an idiot. Don't be surprised if he manages to screw up the whole thing. He's been a pain in the ass since day one."

"What was Kazinsky doing that had to be done?" Lawrence asked.

"Done as in dead," Jalen said. "The tone doesn't seem to indicate that Kazinsky was involved. You know what this means?"

"It means Cambridge was murdered," Lawrence said. "Now we have to find out who and the whole damn thing starts over again."

"Son of a bitch!"

Jalen shoved the computer away from him and it toppled backwards. Covering his eyes with his left forearm, he allowed a harrowing sigh to carve out his insides, leaving nothing but dusty entrails of thoughts. Though the case seemed to be unraveling faster than a cheap sweater, threads kept darting off in unexpected directions.

If you investigate something deeply enough, Jalen thought, you could uncover so much more than you bargain for. The hard truth is that with or without the internet, everything connects to everything else in some fashion. The strands could scatter in millions of different directions and when a person attempts to reassemble the pieces, he or she could go mad.

A shiver tingled the back of his spine. He rocked backward in the chair while a headache began to pound at the inside of his skull like a thought begging to be released from its prison. With so many different threads, reason was beginning to lose its grip and Jalen could not combat that loss. It would destroy him, he thought. But then again, he was already destroyed.

# 14

# Eight Light Minutes

The jolting revelation that the tour guide's murder wasn't so simple brought an aura of darkness to Jalen's mind. The dark crowded him from all sides, closing in until only a pinprick of light pierced its shroud. His lip fluttered as he leaned toward his computer, attempting to use the act of work to massage the dark out of his mind.

It had taken about two hours for the rain to recommence. The rain seemed to entomb the city in gray, the type of color that added a sense of foreboding and dread to classic landscape paintings. What came next Jalen almost didn't want to know. He didn't even want to guess. But what happened years ago suddenly sprung to the center of his mind as he tried to forget about everything.

Cold had far outlasted the furthest reaches of winter that year. Its sensation hung in the air like vapor on a windless day. Rainfall came and went as the day progressed. Without knowledge that some premonitions warned of imminent disaster, Jalen had treated it as any other day. He was fresh at Lynx Technologies and fresh at life.

But the cold had its way of ruining serenity. "I don't think you should go," he heard himself saying with a lump in the back of his throat.

"It's just one of those deals," she said. "It's an opportunity."

He'd shrugged and looked away briefly. "Don't know. It's just…"

"I'll be back by eight."

A kiss on the cheek. It had been enough to tear her away from him permanently. The way the simplest of treasures could erupt into the most tragic nightmares brought a frustrated tear to his eye. The world always offered a chance at reconstruction, but rarely assisted in hammering the nails. Faith ran thin as the scars piled up. Days. Weeks. Months passed. But she never came. All told, twenty-six people departed on that bus and twenty-five were cozy in their lounge chairs with loved ones hanging on their arms as Easter approached.

"Be careful," he remembered saying. Even now that simple command echoed over and over in the deep of his soul and each reverberation further enriched a haunting sadness.

He'd pled with someone somewhere he was sure, but to whom he'd spoken had long since been erased from memory. Then again, he wasn't entirely certain he'd spoken the line to anyone in particular or even if he'd ever opened his mouth. *You can't do this to me.*

Jalen growled at his task bar for interfering with his work. Some stupid icon one of the idiot programmers loaded onto his computer before he started with Lynx blinked to warn of some kind of security flaw. The damn thing detected a simple MP3 file as a major worm and attempted to hijack his entire hard drive to eliminate the threat. He'd never witnessed the software correctly identify a bug. It was the most useless pile of programming the world had ever known. Deleting it was a bad memory because it left a stain on everything it touched. Eventually he was forced to reinstall the thing to stop the hate and to appease Doc.

The office door swung open behind him. Jalen spun in his chair as Kalee strode into the office carrying two cups of coffee. She hardly glanced at him. "I brought you something."

"Thanks," Jalen said, as if a simple cup of coffee could somehow reverse the damage in his brain. He eyed the cups with feigned zeal.

She placed the coffee next to him and walked around to her station without saying much more.

"How did it go?"

"I didn't let them lose," she said. "They did that on their own. It was pretty ugly actually. The grass was slick enough from the rain to eliminate all traction."

"Wasn't talking about the game."

"Neither was I," she joked.

"How's the coffee?"

"That's not what I brought you." She dug into her jacket pocket and removed a black memory stick that Lynx Technologies supplied to itself for minor data transfers. Tossing it to him, she said, "I thought you might want to see it."

"Do I even want to know what the score was?"

"Nope."

Jalen plugged the drive into the USB port on the front of his computer and waited for the navigation window to open.

"Doc took the backup hard drive and loaded it into a permanent storage system. I don't know if it changed hands, but Doc wasn't the only one working on his computer."

"IT personnel," Jalen said. "The big wigs might be great at running a company, but they don't know the first thing about computers. Ironic, isn't it?"

"Doc's capable. But I don't know about the IT guys. "They seemed to be poking around in site maintenance fairly recently."

"There was an equipment malfunction in 43 two weeks ago. Seems plausible that Doc would take a look there from time to time."

She tilted her head and stared at him before sitting down. "Doc wasn't logged in."

"Idiot running around pushing buttons, probably just some college grad thinking about causing mayhem. They never lock their doors."

"Maybe," she said. "But there was some encrypted code written in a temporary folder on the company's server. It probably had a Trojan attached to it, so I quarantined it before opening."

Jalen opened a folder labeled 'Code' and scanned through about a dozen plain text files. Digging into the first one, Jalen clenched his teeth.

"That's complex," he said. "Those algorithms look familiar."

"That's what I thought."

"See if any of them bear a signature."

Code writers at Lynx Technologies had gained notoriety through years of writing code. Otherwise meaningless characters that did nothing for the code itself were often placed in a random segment to indicate who wrote the code. Those guys had their quirks, but most of them only lasted a year or two from the early years of the company. One of the board members once wrote code for custom-built tools and had advanced through the ranks rapidly.

"I already did a lot of the legwork," she said. "It was something else I wanted to show you. Open the 'tour guide' folder."

Jalen opened the file and stared at a short list of files. She had downloaded the tour guide's badge information and parking pass, but the file that caught Jalen's eye was simply labeled 'lease terms'. He clicked to open the file and took a sip of the coffee as an air of panic spread through him.

Refocusing his eyes and leaning closer to his screen, Jalen read through the large pdf file. The first page of the file showed the completed application. "Thought you had to be a big wig," Jalen said. "To get one of these units."

"I thought so too."

Another in a seemingly endless line of Lynx secrets, the leasing office oversaw leasing of all available space in Lynx Technologies. While the majority of campus was used for corporate purposes, some extra space was available to lease. Lynx owned several office buildings in the vicinity, which technically did not reside on the main campus. This space existed to be leased and was mostly used for light industrial and retail uses. Still, one building on campus often drew question. While Building 40 had never stood vacant, few people knew what it housed. The building served as a sort of miniature long-stay hotel, which did not include any typical hotel services. Units were typically leased by the week, though some units included a day-to-day option.

Building 40 stood adjacent to the outdoor athletic facilities. Typical large square windows punctured its long, white walls. While Jalen had never set foot in the building, he understood its primary use. The idea behind the concept of the building surmised that out-of-area visitors would need a nearby place to stay without having to drive from the nearest hotel, which was approximately four miles away. In time, leasing was opened up to more common uses. To qualify, applicants needed to meet a number of strict requirements to lease a unit. Without paying much attention to the application itself, Jalen scanned through the four pages of leasing terms, careful not to miss key points.

Applicants were not allowed to pursue any damaging pastimes, usage of internet was to be personal and not linked to Lynx's wi-fi systems at any time, and noise and other vibrations were strictly forbidden. The terms could seem heavy-handed to some, but Jalen understood the reasons for the restrictions.

The application was dated just under three weeks ago, and the leasing office issued a key three days later.

"Why would he need a residence unit?" Jalen asked.

Kalee shrugged without looking away from her screen. "Your guess is as good as mine."

"Can you open that door for me?'

She shook her head and searched for something in her coat pocket. Before Jalen had a chance to speak, she continued. "That's why I brought you something else."

She slid the key across the desk to him. "Lifesaver," he said.

"You know me."

Jalen didn't need to think twice before standing up and making his way to the door, but he allowed himself a quick moment to examine the key. The keys to the residential units could have been plastic access cards that could offer a certain level of privacy, but the leasing department went with a magnetic keying system instead. An emergency trigger designed to open all doors in case of fire linked the building to the Lynx network, but the trigger had never been used.

The opportunity to search the unit presented itself with a subtle simplicity that was not altogether unexpected. Jalen saw it as a chance to escape the office for a while and knew such a trip would be productive. Chances seemed high that Kazinsky stored a laptop, cellphone or other device in the room, which Jalen could search for evidence of a relationship between him and Cambridge.

"Be careful," Kalee said in a simple tone.

Her voice seemed to echo in ethereal waves stretched into time. *Be careful. Careful. Care...* His heart sunk into a dark trench somewhere in an aphotic portion of his body as coldness swept over him.

The trek to Building 40 or "Hotel 40' as he'd heard it called, led him through Building 25 across the central boulevard. The rain intensified as he bypassed the engineering building down a drive that cut a narrow passage between two buildings. A drainage ditch and a row of hedges separated the athletic facilities from the remainder of campus. Building 40 included an underground walkway into the nearest building, which Jalen hoped would not give access to the tunnel system.

Getting into the building did not prove difficult. He was able to simply walk in. Kazinsky's unit stood on the second floor about two thirds of the way down the hall. The second-floor corridor followed along a bank of windows facing the main industrial buildings of the campus, while the doors to at least thirty units punctured a plain white wall at his left.

Jalen found the room and quickly fitted the lock with a key. He flicked on the lights, which flashed and died. "Burnt out bulb," he muttered to himself. The second he finished the phrase and saw what the room contained, he shouted. "Oh shit!"

Without thinking, he had allowed the door to shut. Looking around, the contents of the room flashed across his imagination like satin cut from a nightmare. The grey light filtered in through the window, spilled onto a small bed, and illuminated a narrow door to the bathroom.

He withdrew his flashlight from its holster as the musty scent in the room wafted into his nostrils. A pervasive cold swept the room and bathed him in terror.

Each of the walls were lined with glass tanks vented to the room. Inside the tanks, cobwebs shifted in subtle breeze caused by Jalen's wake. Black and brown splotches hung in corners, scurried through the webs and speckled green leaves with oily stains. They moved. Jalen began to sweat, as if the heat in the room had suddenly been turned up. He slowly walked around the room. Horror crept up in his bloodstream. Dark. Angry shadows. The combination swelled with a gut-wrenching sensation of utter doom. At least thirty tanks contained many different species of nature's most horrifying insect. Spiders. And they all seemed vetted to destroy him.

As Jalen peered through the glass in a tank holding eight to ten monstrous arachnids, a hollow beep shredded the quiet. On instinct, Jalen sprinted toward the door and attempted to violently fling it open. It was locked mechanically. Trapped. A sensation of horror clawed at the insides of Jalen's brain. He gripped his radio, pressed the button and shouted for help. "Kalee get me backup now!"

"What's the problem, Ja..."

"Shit!"

The clatter of shattering glass and tumbling shelves engulfed the room in a rage of sights and sounds. Jalen sprinted across the room and jumped on to the bed. The shelves had collapsed, sending shards of glass across the floor. The shards glittered in the gray light from outside. It seemed that the rain had found its way inside. Spiders scurried across the floor, climbed on the walls, skittered across the window. Some left entrails of silk. Jalen's heart exploded in catastrophe.

They closed in on him. Thousands of them. Big ones, small ones. Tens of thousands of eyes, and tens of thousands of hairy, spiny legs. A particularly huge spider sprinted across the floor in a dazzling burst of speed, leaving what appeared to be the streak of a lightning bolt on the floor. Its white spot seemed to absorb the light.

The spiders on the walls seemed to multiply. They were coming for him. He flinched as chills raced across his flesh. Several of the creatures had already climbed onto the bed. Jalen attempted to kick them off, but they ran toward him.

"Help!" His screams echoed through the room and deadened. Adrenaline forced him to leap from the bed. A spot devoid of spiders appeared somewhere near the door. Without letting his feet make contact with the floor more than twice, Jalen sprung for that spot. But more spiders appeared, filling the clearing with hundreds of black dots.

Many hundreds of these spiders likely each stored enough venom to kill him. His heart hammered against the inside of his chest as he slipped, sending his flashlight and the key sliding across the concrete floor.

"Oh, God."

The tiny hairs near his ankles tingled. Tiny legs danced on his arms. Jalen looked down in horror to witness at least four spiders crawling on him. He flung them off with violent twists of his body, but more of them came. The darkness in this corner of the room pulsed with a certain energy Jalen didn't understand.

His ankles tingled again. Some of the spiders crawled across the flesh inside his pants. One climbed up the back of his scalp. Jalen swatted it away with fury as the sting of his own slap sent a scorching wave of pain over him. He shouted obscenities over and over again, writhing in the blackness where the dots scurried across his body like tiny stains that he imagined could eat his flesh until it consisted of nothing.

"NO!"

The tantrum seemed to subside as a subtle knowing filtered through his subconscious mind. He was done for. He flung a couple of spiders off his arm, gripped his taser and wildly zapped the floor around him. The bursts of energy stunned several spiders, but there were too many. They wanted him. Dead. He was dinner.

"Get me the backup! Kalee!"

"Jesus, they're on their way. What's happening?"

"AAAAGH!

A larger spider scampered up his neck and skittered toward his mouth. He closed his eyes, spun his head and slapped at it. A streak of his own blood wetted his palm.

Eight minutes. It took that long for light from the sun to reach the earth. As brief as that sounds, to a person in peril or bathed in the murky shadows of darkness, eight minutes could stretch into an eternity. Jalen howled, hoping that it would take less than eight minutes for the light to enter through the door.

A flurry of voices sounded from the hall. The metal of the key glinted in the light from outside. He scooted toward it, flicked a spider away from it and with all of the force he could muster, slid it beneath the floor. "Get me out!"

The lock clicked and the door opened. Jalen used his taser to zap a host of invading spiders as he crawled out of the room.

Barry helped him to a standing position and he sprinted away. The door slammed behind him, but Jalen didn't look back. His screams scattered in the gray light and seemed to become nothing more than whispers in a field left barren with crushed ideas.

Tingles flicked across his back and his arms and his scalp. Though no spiders crawled on him, he swatted and slapped at himself until the sensation reemerged somewhere else.

Eight minutes, and light. Eight legs and dark. He flung himself against a wall at the end of the corridor and slid down to the floor as if in defeat. Barry and two other officers ran toward him, issuing a series of orders that somehow did not sound like words to Jalen...only clipped parts of speech that communicated neither emotion nor reason.

# 15

# A Cross in the Galaxy

Because the nearest fire station was less than a mile away, the paramedics arrived within minutes, once Kalee gave them detailed instructions on the easiest access to Hotel 40. They climbed the stairs quickly and attended to Jalen.

His pulse, moments ago erratic and uncontrolled, began to calm. His eyes darted in all directions without focusing on anything. The corridor around him began to twist and contort as a bleak gray light flooded them all. Barry stared while rocking his shoulders up and down in anticipation. The other two guys from the weekend crew seemed flustered, but powerless.

A tingling fluttered against his ankle. His heart leapt as he swatted at it but there was nothing there.

"Gonna need you to look at me," one of the paramedics said. His voice sounded dead, as though he uttered the sentence in a musty vault lined with pillows.

Training his eyes proved difficult. His breathing started to slow, but he wheezed under the strain of adrenaline anyway.

"Bloodshot. Erratic," one paramedic said to the other, who'd identified himself as Bob Laggert.

Simon Vallegas was the printed name on the other EMT's tag. Jalen's vision could not focus. It looked as though Vallegas drifted across tranquil ocean waters in a canoe.

"Pretty good scare," Laggert said.

"Jalen, Jesus," a familiar voice said.

Jalen refocused his gaze on Kalee's frantic expression. Lines of terror seemed to have gripped her face. She seemed older, like age had suddenly seized her face and stretched it almost beyond recognition. He darted his eyes in all directions before paying attention to Vallegas again. The med shone a tiny light into his eyeball and pain shot through his skull.

"Tell me about your pain level," Bob said. "On a scale of one to ten."

"One."

"No obvious bite marks, but your stress level is out of this world."

Jalen wanted to blast a scathing reply, but instead, he frowned and tried to look at Kalee. His heart slammed two heavy beats as the heat in his veins began to cool.

"You know what that makes you, buddy?"

"Lucky," Vallegas said.

Yes, Jalen thought, because luck made all the difference in the world with his decision to investigate the residence by himself with no backup, even though he knew better. He shook his head and allowed a bitter frown to shine through the agony.

"Your situation doesn't appear to be severe. Vital signs appear to be getting back to normal. But I'd recommend a visit to the emergency room just to be sure. Spider toxins can stay in the bloodstream for hours."

"What I don't understand is why this guy had spiders in a temporary residence," Barry Said. "Don't make sense."

"No," Jalen said. "Just a...hobby?"

"I bet he pursues snake hypnosis at home. Maybe dreams of running a T. Rex training seminar in his off time."

"There's no accounting for taste," One of the weekend officers said.

"How did it happen?" Kalee asked.

"No way...no way to be sure. Booby trapped. I think."

"What?"

"Only makes sense that way. He rigged it, but I don't know how. Investigate it," he said to Barry.

"I'm not going in there."

"I don't think you hear me," Jalen said. His arms twitched and he slapped his wrist while wincing toward Kalee.

"You'll get a ride to the ER?" Vallegas asked.

Jalen nodded.

"I'll take him," Kalee said.

"When we get the...uh...pests taken care of we'll run a sweep." Barry promised.

Jalen stared at him. He had to force his eyes not to dart off down the corridor, where he swore he saw hundreds of tiny black dots scurrying toward him. His legs flinched as he pushed himself backward against the wall. He noticed the blood on his uniform and allowed his muscles to slacken.

"And you've gone all PTSD on me."

"Look for hidden cameras. Some kind of triggering mechanism. It locked me in and collapsed all the shelves simultaneously."

"You need to take the rest of the day off," Bob said. "Go home."

"No," Jalen said. "Got work to do."

"Jalen, I think you should listen to him." Kalee looked concerned. She raised her eyebrows and knelt on the floor next to him. "We'll get to the bottom of this sooner or later and the cops are working on it."

"Gets stranger and stranger," Jalen muttered. His knees tensed and his biceps flexed. He flung his gaze around the corridor and watched the paramedics stand up and walk away before anyone said another word.

Life always constructed reason even in the direst of circumstances. Without reason, only chaos could exist. He looked down and considered the situation.

"I'll be back."

"Hopefully everything will be back to normal by then," Kalee said.

"Never will," Jalen conceded.

She shrugged and stood up while allowing precious seconds to pass. She glanced at Barry and the weekend officers and said nothing.

"You're in charge now," Jalen said, looking at Barry. "Don't do anything I wouldn't."

Barry uttered half a chuckle, narrowed his eyes, and glanced down the hallway. "That opens up a whole other world of possibility."

"Ready to go, boss?" Kalee flashed a look of stark sincerity across her face and then extended her hand to help Jalen up.

When he returned to his feet, he looked down the tiled corridor. Several black dots scattered as they streamed from the room.

She offered only small talk as they made their way across the campus back to Building 27, where Kalee parked. Jalen managed to keep up with her, though she walked at a brisk pace for reasons Jalen did not understand.

Long streaks of gray folded across the sky with gloomy lines of yellow stealing moments of sadness and somehow transforming them into something resembling light heartedness. The mood remained dire, but for some unexplained reason, a sense of curiosity enriched the gray and added a warming sensation. The rain had to cease sometime, he thought.

Kalee drove a small, silver Toyota. It seemed to match her personality. The cup holders and compartments were neatly stuffed with an array of items only a woman would keep in her car. Marie lived the same way, but didn't maintain such organization.

A few drops of rain flicked against the windshield as she drove toward the gate. An expression Jalen did not fully understand engulfed her face. Age crinkled her nose and her eyebrows were raised. Still, her eyes communicated neither contempt nor interest.

Instead of speaking, she let seconds turn into minutes as she made her way to the hospital.

*"It's a hard life,"* Jalen heard her saying. Her voice floated in the air like distant echoes from a memory that was plunging into the vast abyss of oblivion. *"You never know sometimes which way is home, but you still return."*

It took a moment to realize Kalee hadn't said anything. Instead, memory spoke those words.

"It was a rainy day, wasn't it?" Kalee asked.

Jalen feigned confusion for a moment, but then nodded slowly while he looked out the window.

"I shouldn't have..."

"It's done," she said. "Living in regret doesn't help us accept the future. And it certainly hinders the ability to appreciate the present."

"How can you appreciate a time like this?" Jalen said. He frowned and rested a fist on his cheek. A tickle teased his leg. He bounced both knees up and down until the sensation dissipated.

She shrugged. "You learn to, I guess."

The conversation thinned. The mist in the air pushed against the mountains and obscured the peaks in fluffy gray billows. On one of the nearby hills stood a giant illuminated cross. On a clear day, its light travelled for miles. Though he'd never been up there, someone once explained that the cross was at least thirty feet tall and some church who owned the land around it had erected it as a beacon to weary travelers.

Jalen had never been certain about the existence of a God who controlled everything, but in times of need, he thought, what was the risk, other than damage to his ego? Then again, more than two thirds of the metro area seemed highly religious. In truth, that quality had attracted him after relocation. The people were friendly and warm and the city's endless recreational possibilities drew him like a magnet.

Oddly, that recreation transformed into a viable scapegoat when life went sour. The spring runoff from heavy mountain snows over the winter had raised the water levels. Normally, they said low water offered the best thrills, but nature could often deliver unexpected results from the simplest set of constants.

Jalen closed his eyes. Stars too numerous to count sprung to life, rotating around a giant mysterious entity that imagination illuminated more than fact. Life always had a reason. Somehow, a way home always appeared. Yet this blackness defeated everything. As life careened toward the veil of infinity, the one constant remained the disorder of darkness. It expanded through time like a canvas that somehow erased every media that adorned it.

Order meant disorder. The realization that nothing could be re-assembled in quite the same manner it existed before smashed the frag-ments of his consciousness until only powder remained. From creation on, everything fell apart. Even reason. But what would happen when it all vanished from existence?

When he opened his eyes, he could no longer see the illuminated cross on the mountainside. Instead, he witnessed the blue glow of the cross atop the twelve-story hospital tower.

"This guy, whoever it is orchestrating this…He's got to be pretty smart," Kalee said. "How did he know you'd be looking there?"

"We don't even know who set that trap," Jalen said. "Part of me wants to say Cambridge set it up, but anyone could have."

"You think it was designed to kill?"

"Maybe, but not very efficient, it seems."

She offered a flat smile, but it vanished as she pulled into a parking spot in the underground garage.

"You're good, too," she said. "I've got a hundred bucks that says we'll find him."

"Sure about that?" Jalen said. "Thought you would have learned your lesson by now." He tried to imagine the final score of the game, but found that his thoughts failed him.

A curious smile parted her lips. "Some things," she said, "are more certain than a soccer game."

# 16

# Orion's Shield

An ache that was not unexpected prodded at Jalen's brain. He attempted to massage it away, but it returned with enough force to push him back in his seat. If Friday had been a nightmare, then Saturday's events trespassed into full-on hell. His dreams were blackened windows into a dreary landscape Jalen didn't dare enter. Burned out tree stumps protruded from a black mass where no man roamed. Occasionally, a giant spider would skitter across the window making hollow knocking noises and then pause to stare through the glass into Jalen's shattered eyes.

The cursor on his keyboard beckoned him. He considered his words carefully before beginning to craft.

*This is a world we have made for ourselves, but no one is in it for themselves. Causes unite us and separate us against whatever evil we perceive to rule the day. The battle comes quickly and scars rage across our land. We fight not for our way of life or our home, but for our heroes. And the war will never go quiet.*

"It's shit," Jalen said to himself, or at least he thought so.

Marie stood behind him quietly observing and reading his words as they inched across the screen.

"Then why do you write it?"

*Because it lets me see the world from afar,* he wrote.

"And that's so much better than exploring life and building something with someone else. You want seclusion, maybe you can have it."

Jalen spun his chair around, looked up to her face, and glared. The sun dove through the window. For the moment, the rain had ceased, and the skies had cleared. In a sudden surge, spring lurched forward, and life began anew.

"What did I do?"

Marie glanced away and pretended not to hear him.

"Now who's on the wrong side of the bed?"

"You going in to the office again. It's great. Never get to see you anymore and it's always like this."

Jalen studied her body language while slowly folding his arms across his stomach. She shifted her stance, spun her hips, made a motion toward the door, and then shot a quivering frown at him.

"I can't live with a man who's afraid to live."

"You don't know what it's like."

"And you won't tell me. I'm done with this. Hell with it. Maybe I'll catch up with you online."

"The hell are you saying?"

She bit her lip and her eyes glassed over. "Don't look surprised. It's been over for weeks."

"Go," Jalen said. He could no longer pretend he cared. Rather than watch her leave, he spun and faced his screen. He backspaced all of his writing, slapped the keyboard and heavily pounded out another sentence.

*What lies beyond the end?*

No answer came to him. He leaned back in his chair, balled his fists, and glared at the screen as if it were his sworn enemy. How could he let her leave so quickly? Especially when it didn't begin so quickly?

He felt his frown twitch and then stood up, folded his arms again, and paced. And now this falls apart. That son of bitch yesterday even had the nerve to call him lucky. Oh, if he'd lived in Jalen's mind or taken a five minute walk wearing his shoes, he'd see that occasional, small miracles punctured the madness that perpetually surrounded him. He'd know. And he'd hate every minute of it.

The front door slammed. He waited to hear her car start, which took a good minute longer that he'd expected. Only once she pulled out of the driveway did he emerge from the room. He peered out the window at a cloudless sky. A pocket of fog lingered over the mountain and beads of water shimmered on all the cars in the neighborhood. Forecasts expected another round of showers later, but for now Jalen was glad to have the sun.

When he arrived at the office, he saw Kalee enter the front door of Building 27. For some reason, he didn't really want to talk to her. Instead of turning off his car, he remembered how she'd left him. She had driven him back to the office discussing something to do with her sister and a barbecue she hoped wouldn't get rained out. Jalen had tried to imagine what her sister looked like but had realized that the only image he could conjure was a slightly more disjointed version of Kalee herself.

She had dropped him off at his car with the motor still running. They had discussed whether Jalen would be in on Sunday with a clear undertone of not wanting to. Jalal rarely worked weekends, but he hadn't worked a single Sunday in almost three years.

Kalee had smiled at him when he'd gotten out of her car. "Take some aspirin, or something to help you sleep. You've had a tough day."

Instead of dropping into more discussion, he'd offered a simple nod and started on his way home. He had followed her out of the parking lot and then for a little more than a mile down the main boulevard. Kalee had turned to get onto the freeway while Jalen had kept straight.

Jalen stopped reflecting and exited his car. The sun crept over his face like a warm blanket, but he didn't stop to appreciate it. The office sat quiet. Both of the weekend guards patrolled the hallways, while a man named Barrett watched video footage at Laurie's seat. Kalee had already taken her seat. He frowned and glanced at her before logging into his computer.

"How was the evening?" she asked.

"Same old," Jalen lied.

"Did you get enough sleep?"

He nodded and thought about it. He had. Marie had disposed of every bottle of wine or bourbon or brandy in the house and the garage. She hadn't said as much, but she'd intended to help him. Her tactics hadn't helped. It was a good thing Jalen kept a secret stash of vodka stored in his desk. He'd left it in the bottom drawer with all of the papers, old bills, and magazines he never read. That was possibly the only place in the house she'd never look, but Jalen didn't have to be so secretive anymore.

"I see," Kalee said. They didn't speak for more than two hours. Jalen busied himself by examining known computer code within programs he had access to, which were not many. The Lynx Technologies website didn't stretch far and wide like some would suspect. The product identifications were brief and limited. The website didn't share much about the history of the company, either. Jalen knew how to examine code embedded into websites, which could be used to hack in.

The examinations lasted longer than he'd anticipated. He shrugged and decided to take a break. When he got up, he told Kalee he was going to go patrol, but she knew he never patrolled. She perhaps thought about joining him, but didn't move.

On his way to the cafeteria, Jalen decided to take a look in the chem lab and the cleanroom. He stood in the chem lab staring at the washing sink for what seemed like ten minutes. A chemist entered and bustled around for a few minutes as if she didn't even notice him. She grabbed a notepad that sat next to a white board and departed moments later.

The police had cleaned up well and it appeared that everything was back to normal. He shrugged, turned around, and left without seeing anything worthwhile. The cleanroom had always been, well, clean. Cambridge had left no trace other than the tablet, the phone, and the badge. As Jalen thought about it, Cambridge seemed to transform from a villain with a violent streak to a man in trouble looking for escape. That scenario fit well enough to explain his death, but after that the pieces were hard to assemble. The cops believed the killer was murdered and Jalen couldn't disagree. But using a steam valve as a murder weapon? That didn't even happen in those crime shows on TV.

He peered through the windows without dressing down. Few people worked the room today. Capacity often lessened during weekends due to temporary lapses in demand and shipping delays, but shutting down the fabs entirely would result in mass losses. The business end of the complex often didn't make sense, but Jalen never desired to enter that world.

After determining that there was nothing left to see, he went to the cafeteria for a hot cup of coffee, decided on two, and then headed back.

Inspecting line after line of code required certain distractions to break up the monotony, lest Jalen go crazy under the pressure of his own thoughts. He often found that those little pieces of imagination, when not used constructively, could build up enough to collapse his psyche. When that happened, rebuilding and repairing seemed almost impossible.

Kalee was not at her desk when he returned. He scanned the office and didn't see her. Either she'd stepped out for some errand or entered the storage room to look for something.

He didn't wait for her. He gently sat the second coffee next to her keyboard and walked back to his own station.

The code seemed to stack up, line by line, into a black wall that shielded a uniform veil of white from whatever perils Jalen's mind could unleash. Seemingly misplaced asterisks and hash marks created an odd connect the dots pattern. Jalen stopped a time or two to attempt to withdraw meaning from them, but failed. Whoever had written this code seemed to embrace a creative side. Some actions required relatively simple code to produce a desired effect, but the beauty of writing code lied in the fact that there were multiple ways to achieve some ends. Jalen didn't know how to write code and didn't know what all of the brackets and symbols meant, either. But patterns existed everywhere.

After more than two hours, his eyes began to droop. Kalee had returned to her desk and finished off the coffee but hadn't said anything. Jalen hardly noticed her presence.

"Son of a bitch," he whispered.

Five lines of code sat neatly spaced in the center of the screen. Two characters in the center line seemed hyperlinked to something. A hole he could not climb from burned in the center of his mind. For now, nothing but the link mattered. Instead of clicking on it, he highlighted the text and looked at the link address. The text didn't link to a webpage or even similarly designed code documents for similar systems. It directly led to an email document. This had 'virus' written all over it. He didn't open the link and continued scanning. Again, this peculiarity smacked of something. He'd seen ideas like that before, but didn't understand the extent.

Except for one thing. He did. The revelation troubled him. He shifted in his chair and looked up to Kalee, who had busied herself entering items into a spreadsheet. She was gifted enough with the spreadsheet program to make her own games out of it. In fact, she'd built a sort of trivia quiz where each step depended on the outcome of the previous step. He hoped she wasn't making a game.

He looked up at her.

"Can you do something for me?" Jalen asked her.

Her eyes wandered for a moment before looking at him. She nodded slowly after leaning back slightly.

"Can you dig into Kale Stanger's profiles?"

"Are you serious?"

"We can do it if we have probable cause. I say we do."

"Jalen," she started, looking away. "Is this even related? It's bad news if he finds out, company policy allowance or not."

"If we fall, I'll take the fall for you."

She hesitated. "It will still be linked to my station."

He nodded and continued by wrapping his head around more segments of code which all seemed to collude against him. His head began to pound and a dull ache pulsed away somewhere in his stomach or his heart or his lungs. Trying to remain focused grew more and more difficult.

*Time for another drink.*

Jalen pulled away from the screen, swore, and then stood up. "I'm going down to the cafeteria, you want some coffee?"

"You know, there are rules about how much of that stuff you can drink before giving in to hallucination."

"Take that as a 'no,'" Jalen said.

This time the walk proved more difficult. He couldn't get his mind around the simple fact that he was missing some vital piece of information. What did Stanger have to do with anything? Could he even trust the computers on this one? *How can we trust the machines we built to help us without fearing that they will control us? Trust might be an abstract that computers can never understand, but it is a key element of the human experience. Trust is earned, and without understanding it, a person cannot strive for it.*

"You're going crazy," Jalen said to himself.

*Crazy is only an interpretation of something you don't fully understand.*

"Shit."

He returned with a pair of health bars instead of coffee. The wrappers promised lasting energy that would not die out as fast as caffeine. The wrappers also claimed the best taste, as if taste were a quantifiable entity rather than a subjective one. If nothing else, Kalee would be amused.

She stared at her computer screen when he entered again. She shrugged and glanced up at Jalen, as if to silently ask him to join her.

He dropped one of the health bars next to her hand and attempted to smile. "What do we got?"

"You're not going to believe this," she said.

"Stanger had emailed Kazinsky four times, and one other email from an unknown source mentions the tour guide by name."

*Crazy?*

"The emails are mostly about some zip line tour Kazinsky's company offers. 'Great views and even better amenities.' Do you think he's involved with Cambridge too?"

He stared, wide-eyed at her screen. "I...I'd stake my house on it. Find out where that link goes to." Jalen pointed at a linked portion of text in the email.

"It's linked to another email," she said. "Can't he just insert it as an attachment like any normal person would do?"

"That's the same damn message embedded in the code I was reading. That son of a bitch."

She rolled her chair away from her desk and folded her arms across her stomach while staring down to her feet.

"Let's get him."

"I'm not going to be a part of it," she said.

"Then I'll do it myself," Jalen growled.

"Hey thanks for the coffee and the...death-by-sugar bar. But your priorities need a little bit of work today. If you want to investigate Stanger, I'd suggest you call Lawrence and get the police to do it. Because this can only end badly for both of us."

He didn't need her common sense. Not today. She used it for a variety of reasons and it almost always served her well. Sometimes, though, it could work to her detriment.

Grunting and returning to his computer, he bit into the mound of sugar Kalee had accused the health bar of being and then dropped the rest of it in the trash. *Great taste, my ass,* he thought.

As good as he was at writing computer code, Stanger wasn't adept at hiding. He didn't even attempt it, which seemed strange. But Stanger had murdered two people in cold blood right in the middle of campus. He had to be confronted.

Slowly, he began to build a plan as he kept a close eye on all of Stanger's movements. Every thought his mind constructed strengthened his case against Stanger. And with him behind bars, Jalen could find his way back to what he'd long since accepted as normal. The paranoia and mistrust. The heartache without a bitter end.

Hours passed. Kalee stood up to leave for home after a while. Jalen didn't move. When the night crew showed up, he simply stared out the window at where spring was beginning to offer some kind of temporary hope. The flowering trees blurred together in his vision like showers of confetti out of focus.

Darkness spread across the city early. A flash indicated the arrival of a storm, but thunderstorms in this city were both rare and mild. Wind had kicked up and then stopped entirely.

Stanger's personal life revolved mostly around his professional life. Lynx Technologies had given him a cell phone in his name for private use. This gave Jalen an idea. If Stanger hadn't been interested in covering his tracks on his PC, then why would he go to greater length on a cell phone, especially when a cell phone's data is more secure?

Jalen found his inspiration to be accurate. It hadn't taken him long to find out where the phone's signal was coming from him, and that allowed him to track it.

It seemed surprising that Stanger had elected to work on a Sunday. People like him often opted to go golfing or hang out with the family or schmooze politicians, or at least in Jalen's perception.

After finding the signal, Jalen tracked it. The signal originated from Stanger's office in Building 11 and then travelled the corridors of Buildings 7 and 9. After that, he went outdoors, but not to the parking lots. Instead, he made his way to the north side of campus where the sports facilities resided. His signal paused at the soccer pitch and seemed to remain there for more than five minutes.

Now or never, he thought. He grabbed his jacket and left without saying a word to any of the night crew. If needed, he could always radio for help. Then again, the sports areas seemed the least secure portions of campus. From the office to the soccer pitch would be a healthy ten minute walk, but at a run it would take around five minutes.

Rather than run, Jalen decided to walk at a brisk pace. Given the weather conditions and the limits of his own stamina, this pace would have him wheezing by the time he reached the facility.

The pitch stood mostly abandoned. A single overhead lamp illuminated the track, which lent a ghostly aura to the area. Jalen scanned the darkness beyond the limits of the light and saw Stanger, dressed in black, running along a short stretch of bleachers. Without thinking, he ducked behind an equipment shed and waited, watching.

Stanger rounded the bend in the dirt track at a healthy pace. The light seemed to dance on parts of his face while his features bathed the other regions of his face in shadow. Sinister would have been a great word to describe Stanger, but Jalen didn't care about labels.

After rounding the bend, Stanger came to an abrupt stop. Jalen ducked his head away in the dark. A muffled *humph* emanated from his area and died as the rain began to fall more heavily. "Damnit." The voice sounded more frustrated at the weather or his pace than anything, but Jalen didn't poke his head out until he once again heard Stanger's footsteps brushing in the dirt.

After checking that Stanger's back was turned, Jalen moved stealthily across the grass and into the pitch. He trailed behind Stanger and had to adjust his pace to catch up with him. After a hundred yards, Stanger paused again and looked around. For some reason his gaze didn't cover the area directly behind him. Jalen became conscious that his breath was beginning to strain in the humid air. He attempted to quiet himself, which only seemed to make it more painful. He couldn't keep the pace any longer.

When Stanger picked up his pace again, Jalen sprinted the last sixty feet or so. At the last second, Stanger stopped. He'd heard the intruder. Without thinking or adjusting his run, Jalen pounced. He landed on Stanger's back with a dull thump. The man was strong enough to buck him off with surprisingly little effort. In response he ran again, faster. Jalen sprung to his feet and used his soccer speed to attack once again. Stanger saw it coming. The light overhead illuminated a surprised expression, but one littered with strands of anger. Jalen took a swipe at the back of his head, recoiled, and aimed to strike again.

Rather than attempt to run again, Stanger spun and landed a heavy blow around Jalen's shoulder. The pain seemed to gouge a hole in his muscles, but he didn't relent. A heavy breath and a grunt. The man's right fist spun out of the darkness and swooshed across Jalen's ear while he attempted to parry. His forearm clashed with Stanger's elbow. On instinct, Jalen grabbed the arm, twisted upward in a violent swish, and then swung. Rather than stumble, Stanger gasped and lunged over, widening his stance. He stared at Jalen. His eyes were like chunks of coal embedded in a pale field of cheat grass.

"What do you want?"

Jalen twisted harder. He tangled his legs with one of Stanger's feet and shoved him forward. Stanger tumbled face first in to the mud. A stray bolt of lightning briefly illuminated the scene beyond what light the lamp provided. Jalen breathed in heavily and shoved the back of Stanger's head into the ground.

"Where do you get off? Goddamnit!"

His shoulders gave a mighty lurch, which was enough to fling Jalen to the ground. The hell if he was going to let him get away. He clutched for his taser and grasped one of Stanger's hands.

"You killed him! Cambridge."

Instead of retorting, Stanger issued a grunt and shifted his shoulders. Jalen crawled to his side and kneed him in the ribs.

"You son of a bitch, get off."

"You're under arrest."

Stanger swore and jutted his elbow hard against Jalen's abdomen. Jalen didn't flinch. He grasped the taser, shoved it against Stanger's back, and pulled the trigger.

He fell motionless without fighting back. Jalen limped to his feet, grasped the man's shoulder and pulled him up. The shot from the taser stunned him well enough that he couldn't move his arms or legs. Jalen dragged him across the grass and then decided to radio for help. He kept the weapon at ready and waited just over five minutes for his backup to arrive.

No one emerged from the gap between the buildings, but a set of headlights rounded a corner in the parking lot, turned left, and crossed the drainage ditch. Jalen recognized the vehicle as a site security truck. A man in his thirties assisted Jalen with hauling Stanger into the bed of the truck. They didn't say anything until they were both inside the truck.

The other security guard, Mike, sighed and shook his head. "Jesus, do you have any idea who you just gunned down?"

Jalen nodded slowly and shivered as the warm air touched his wet skin.

"It's not good news." Mike seemed to ponder the idea more than he should have, but Jalen got the idea that Mike was simply attempting to diffuse whatever tension existed between them before explaining further the consequences of Jalen's actions. "Kale Stanger, Administrator of Public Finances. Second in line to CFO David Cunningham. Guy ranks higher than me, higher than you. Higher than your boss."

Jalen shifted his shoulders, looked out the window at the flicker of light dancing off of the wet pavement, and bit his lip. "He's a murderer."

# 17

# Scorpio

Wielding only suspicion proved a frustrating endeavor. Jalen's knees bounced up and down and his palms began to sweat. Certainly his eyes would be bloodshot by now. For the moment, he only frowned and ignored his captor, who sat quietly in handcuffs waiting for the police to come.

The rain outside had stopped twenty or thirty minutes ago and a steady mist remained as a reminder that spring weather could be fickle. Kale Stanger sighed, leaned back in the guest chair, and rested his head against the wall.

"You gotta let me go," he said. "My wife…" Another sigh.

"Love to hear about your fetish for murder?" Jalen looked up at the clock and turned a page in a magazine he pretended to be reading. Now that he had the perpetrator in his grasp, he had little reason to continue the investigation.

Regardless of the obvious holes, Jalen pulsed with victory. A celebratory drink wouldn't be too much to ask for, but first he had to get rid of Stanger. Lynx Technologies would likely promote from within to fill Stanger's void, but they'd almost certainly respond by placing another incompetent fool in the position.

"I don't know anything about it," Stanger said. "Other than what I read in the paper. And I wouldn't even know how to get to that dungeon."

"Don't got any dragons here, or pretty princesses to run off with. Only two counts of murder."

"Didn't this Cambridge guy kill the tour guide?" Stanger placed his hands on his knees, glanced at Jalen without making eye contact, and then allowed his facial muscles to relax.

"Name was Kazinsky," Jalen said. "You know that. Found his name in your email. Did you and Cambridge team up to take him down and then you double crossed him? How much money was in the offing?"

"I'm not saying anymore without a lawyer."

Jalen faked a chuckle. "You don't have Miranda rights in here, this isn't TV." Jalen opted to press harder. "Besides, only guilty people demand a lawyer. I've seen the cop shows, too."

Stanger put his knees together, drew his head away from the wall, and flinched his eyebrow. Wrinkles of weariness spanned his face for a moment, but he quickly extinguished them and bowed his head so he could stare at his feet.

With a subtle grunt, Jalen slapped the magazine on his desk, spun, and glared at Stanger. Without being smug, he'd somehow managed to derail Jalen's plan. He didn't speak. The moments passed before someone else in the office spoke.

Lynette, the lady watching cameras at night, looked up from the monitors and said, "Cops are here."

"Thanks," Jalen said.

Stanger looked up but remained hunched over. He eyed Jalen with curiosity and offered yet another sigh.

"How does thirty to life sound?"

"You're never going to make it out of this," Stanger said. His voice remained flat and sterile as if he'd trained his reaction into sounding ordinary.

"Brilliant."

He looked down and then glanced at the window when the flashing lights outside appeared. "You're going to get fired. You don't just apprehend a high-ranking corporate official and accuse him of killing without the consequences. You should know that."

"Doc's gonna understand," Jalen said. Instead of fighting back, he waited. The front doors of Building 27 would be opening any second. Jalen stared at the office door. Then he stood up, walked to the door, and unlocked it.

"Officers Lawrence and Carson appeared in the lobby and strode to towards the door. Jalen watched them for a few moments and then turned around. Lawrence didn't look pleased.

The cops entered the room without much fanfare. Lawrence eyed Jalen with a steely expression. He lowered his eyebrows and tightened his jaw.

"Meet Kale Stanger, Administrator of Public Finances, and your prime suspect," Jalen said.

"This guy did it?"

Jalen nodded.

Lawrence stared at Stanger for longer than Jalen would have deemed necessary. A certain uneasy feeling swept his face and his eyes seemed to gather in the mist from outside and churn it into another storm. More than fierce, he looked perplexed. Composed, but sparking with energy.

"Put him in the car," Lawrence said to Carson. "And give the hand-cuffs back to Murray."

Carson nodded, released the cuffs, and allowed Stanger to stand under his own free will. Stanger wavered for a split second before finding his balance. Carson led him outside to the car, leaving Lawrence and Jalen alone in the office.

Officer Lawrence pulled a chair toward him and then sat down with his elbows on his knees.

"You don't have the authority to make an arrest," Lawrence said.

"I've got the authority to detain people for any security or safety means," Jalen said. While his sentence was true, such detainments almost always resulted in escorting the dangerous party off campus until such a time that their badge status is reviewed and either reapproved or declined. Having a badge revoked usually resulted in the firing of the employee. In the case of a contractor, the individual would not be allowed in any Lynx Technologies building for up to three years.

"It's not the same thing," Lawrence said. "Did you tell him he was under arrest?"

Jalen made a move to nod his head but didn't finish the gesture before Lawrence started speaking again.

"Then you overstepped your bounds. Maybe I should have you pack your bags."

"But?"

Lawrence sighed but didn't peel his eyes from Jalen's face. "You're too valuable to our case."

Jalen nodded but didn't say anything.

"It isn't my decision what to do with you over this misconduct, so I'll leave that up to your boss. The problem is, we're still going to need you running computer diagnostics and other techno stuff our guys can't do."

"It's done," Jalen said. "I caught him, now we can all go home."

"Not exactly," Lawrence said. He glanced at the window and then retrained his gaze on Jalen. He leaned back and placed a fist under his chin.

Jalen swore under his breath.

"See for all of your good investigation skills, we can't drop our case just because we have a guy in custody who a security guard claims did it. Not with all the evidence in the world. We build our own cases. Are we going to investigate Mr. Stanger? Absolutely we will. But we can't keep him in custody for very long. If he's guilty, so be it and good job. If he isn't, we both know where that's going to lead."

"So I'll keep digging on him," Jalen said.

"We'll take it from here."

An ugly idea formed in Jalen's head, spreading its disease like a plague intended to wipe out all thought. From Stanger's body language, Jalen guessed that he'd perfected his act. Look innocent by showing all the right signs, and when they least expect it, attack.

For all he cared, Stanger had set the trap in Kazinsky's room. It wouldn't have been hard for him to get the key. Rigging the shelves to fall seemed genius, but it made Jalen's blood boil.

Without a courtesy goodbye or a handshake, Lawrence departed the room. Jalen leaned back in his chair. The day's weight settled on top of him. Over the course of the weekend, so much had happened that Jalen was already having difficulty discerning one event from another.

A stain crept up from the bottom of his heart like acid eating away at the fabric of the life Jalen had clung to. It was a cancer Jalen didn't know how to treat. How could one heart, so detached in spirit and so distant, inflict such destruction? No matter how hard he tried, it didn't matter. He could not erase the bleakness behind the memory.

***

Cold. The morning felt like winter. The bite of the wind, the chill of humidity, and the settling of the air conspired to push Jalen closer to the edge. Sleep hadn't been plentiful and dreams had plagued him. Dreams of cold.

"She's in a better place now," Kalee had said.

Jalen hadn't responded. Ice water poured down his cheeks like freezing rain. The lamp beside the table emanated with an orange light that suggested warmth but couldn't raise the temperature in the room.

"You can't expect her to stick around forever, not the way things work."

"I'm...You can't do this to me. Gonna die."

Her voice had sputtered and broken apart as her facial expression drifted further away, as if tethered to an ancient memory not entirely her own. "Besides, we both know what's best for you. Get some sleep."

"Can't."

"Be careful."

*Be careful. Careful!*

"Shit! Shit, no."

Jalen sat up straight in bed, his spine aching from a cold sweat and his eyes darting around the room without resting on any of the odd shapes that composed his universe. His heart shattered in the cavity of his chest, leaving a swamp of blood. The voice was mirthful, yet as serene as a spring dew. It wasn't real. How could it be?

He showered, but decided to skip writing and breakfast. The prospect of sharing the dream scarred him. He frowned as he left the house, leaving her void behind.

Who had she been talking about? The heart of the conversation had leaked with the scent of death, but hints of another life sparkled. What better place?

"Wasn't her," Jalen said. "Maybe."

The path to work didn't seem so easy. Jalen approached a light that had just turned green seconds ago. Before he got there, without having allowed a single car to go, the light changed to red, skipping yellow entirely. He made a mental note to contact the city and let them know their signals were malfunctioning.

Then again, Jalen's mind could have been the culprit. The drug of choice last night had been a glass of vodka. He'd relaxed on the couch, numbing his senses to everything before finally giving up the ghost and retiring. Life seemed simpler with a beverage. He yearned for simplicity. Against all odds, when everything else failed, the one true ally—that awful betrayer—answered each question with cold, sterile facts.

The light stayed red for fifteen seconds or so before switching to green again. Ahead, all of the lights turned green. And all of them managed to change back to red before he got there.

"Goddamnit."

Monday morning traffic merged from the freeway in long lines of headlights burning bright against an orange sky. The sun began to lift upward behind the mountains, scattering its light through haze and cirrus clouds. Jalen greeted it with a sigh.

Lynx Technologies came to life at 7:00 am, with or without him. He parked in his usual spot and took his time walking through the doors. The first thing he saw caused his heart to sink.

Kalee sat forward on a sofa in the lobby, her expression sharp. She turned at her waist and fixed her gaze on the white-haired man Jalen called boss.

He approached and paused when he got there. Kalee looked up and smiled.

"Good morning, Jalen."

"Good morning," Jalen answered.

"Just who I needed to talk to," Doc said.

"You don't say."

"Heard about your little altercation last night. The board is ready to put you on indefinite administrative leave. Chinese for 'you're fired.' Can't tell you how pissed they are."

"Stanger?"

"He's here."

"Supposed to be in jail," Jalen said through gritted teeth.

Doc lost his swagger. He leaned forward and wrinkled his chin. "You're lucky this time, but don't let it happen again."

Jalen nodded and walked toward the office door, but a blue jacket caught his gaze and he stopped.

Officer Lawrence assumed a dominant stance and put away his phone. He approached Jalen swiftly.

Jalen issued a grunt and faced him.

"Stanger's innocent," he said. "You had the wrong man."

"So quick?"

"We worked through the night, sort of a hot button item down at the station. Good frame-up, maybe, but we detected a flaw pretty quickly. You know the guy calls a mechanic to change his license plate?"

"What are you saying?"

"He doesn't know the first thing about how to operate a steam valve. He's vaguely aware such a thing exists."

"An act," Jalen growled. "He's playing you."

Lawrence nodded and inched closer to him. "Don't think we don't know when someone is playing with us. Want to guess what Stanger was doing that morning up until we found Cambridge?"

"Having coffee?"

"Taking a cab from the airport. His plane landed about two hours after you found the tour guide's body. He took off on a business trip to Jakarta Tuesday night. There's no way he could have been back on campus to commit murder so quickly.

Jalen fought back the urge to battle. He swore under his breath and pretended the news didn't bother him. Still, something seemed amiss about Stanger. Shade. It was as if he bathed in its fury, contemplating a range of actions so severe that it made Jalen gulp.

What Lawrence told him might have been true, but Jalen didn't make mistakes. The emails and the code suggested only Stanger's involvement, but there had to be more to it than that. He determined to find a way. Some incriminating evidence existed somewhere, lurking in the shadows, ready to lash out at the slightest moment of aggression.

He only had to wait for it.

His face reddened. He trembled and cracked his knuckles while Officer Lawrence lathered him with inquisitive glances. Before Jalen could take a step, a hand brushed his shoulder. He spun, almost as if expecting an attack from some vicious monster, but only Kalee stood there.

"You're in too deep," she whispered.

Great. They got to her too.

"Want to tell me about it over coffee? I'm all ears if you want to talk. I'll just listen, it'll be just like you're typing in your diary."

"You..."

"I've always known about it."

Shots of anger poured through him like venom from a cobra that coiled up somewhere inside. Flames emerged in his eyes, but became doused by the beginnings of a tear. The enemy existed all around him. The world had become strange overnight, as if a dream had spilled over from the night and scarred the day beyond recognition. All Jalen wanted to do was fight, but no worthy opponent stepped up. The danger of memory stung deeply and all else stood quiet.

# 18

# Magnetic Declination

A slice of cold air drifted between them. Neither spoke until they'd traversed the corridor out of Building 27 into another realm all too similar. Building 24 had been constructed as a multi-phase project consisting of five different parts. Each specific phase denoted different areas of the building. Closest to Building 27, an E adorned all of the room numbers. Room number 24E165 would prove easy to find because a user would know first that it was in Building 24, Area E, and second, that it was on the fab level, as opposed to mezzanine levels, sub-fabs or interstitial zones, where the area E room number would start with 0 or 2.

Jalen paid attention to a cart loaded with fresh silicone in plastic cases. A woman with short hair and a dark complexion pushed the cart to rest outside of a cleanroom, pulled out a chart to mark it, and then began to open the pass-through. She noticed Jalen looking and smiled.

"I don't read your journal," Kalee said. "I never have. But ever since you started here, I noticed you would occasionally be typing something. And then one day, I was running a maintenance scan and noticed the document."

"Should have labeled it differently."

"You don't need to be secretive about it. Lots of people write in journals."

"Lots of psychopaths."

Kalee wrinkled her nose and quickened her pace. Her feet squeaked on the floor but drowned away, leaving only the hum of the fab equipment behind the pass-through.

"I didn't mean...It doesn't bother me so much, but when you are expecting all of your personal thoughts to remain safely tucked away. You sort of try to protect those things. You guard them like your life and maybe even more."

"I know," she said slowing down. They passed through a set of double doors that were always open and the room numbers changed to 24D prefixes. "You've had a lot of time to think. But what happened over the weekend?"

"Guy got killed, took a bath in acid, now his killer's got his face smashed in. About the extent of it."

"That's not what I meant," she said lowering her voice and speaking slower. Her arms swung wide, the squeak of her shoes returned, and her expression morphed from concern to dismay.

The light reflected off of her glasses, which somehow magnified her eyes into enormous spectacles that shimmered like celestial bodies spinning billions of miles away. Jalen noted her posture, which seemed to be a little too crisp, given that it was a pre-coffee Monday morning. The mood she portrayed somehow made Jalen feel worse. Right about now another sip of vodka might do the trick.

"You're deflecting," she said after a wide pause carved a gulf between them.

She tightened her facial muscles at once, making her look cynical. Not helping.

He looked to his shoes and pretended to be interested in the layout of the tiles and the way the reflections danced off them like tiny, luminescent ballerinas. She might as well have been asking him about what his latest journal entry said, what it meant behind the surface of what it sounded like it meant. He wasn't in the mood for the carnage, but then again, choice evaded him.

"She left me," he said. His words cut through his flesh like poisoned barb wire glowing white-hot.

"Marie?"

He nodded slowly.

"Not good timing. I thought there was a lot of potential there. I mean, how long had you been seeing her?"

"Too damn long," Jalen said.

She tried to look confused, but Jalen didn't buy it.

"She could have saved us the trouble and got out months ago and it wouldn't have made any difference to me. But she just keeps staying until we can't stand each other. And just the sight of her makes me want to—"

"Lash out in your journal?"

Jalen bit his lip and silently issued a scathing comment about her interrupting him. He swallowed and continued. "I don't know how it got like that. Just little things every day. Build up and then suddenly World War III."

"Why didn't you ask her to leave? When things got bad."

"I'd settled into the idea of her staying forever. You might think things like that, but you don't take action because deep down, she's the best thing that ever happened to you."

She nodded slowly and shortened her strides. An idea played out on her face and then it faded and died. Her eyes narrowed, but still sparkled in the light.

"I don't think that's true."

"You were rooting for me." He furrowed his brow and looked away.

"What I'm saying is, how can the best thing that ever happened to you make you so miserable?"

"Wasn't her," Jalen said, his voice rising more slowly than it should have. In one of the cleanrooms, a large red light started to blink. Someone would need to have a look at that, but it wasn't Jalen's job or expertise to track down why some machines decided to malfunction. Monday mornings.

"But it was something deep enough to call it quits over."

"Like I say, lot of little things."

She nodded as if unwilling to continue the strands of the conversation. Jalen looked away and paid attention to the room numbers, which had dwindled down to 24A107. The corridor shifted about 30 degrees up ahead, and then took a hard right. The corridor passed a bank of windows on both sides that stretched twenty feet, and then the corridor ran into another set of double doors. If a road sign were placed at the intersection it would have said "Entering Building 22."

"What were you talking to Doc about?" Jalen said.

She looked less than pleased with the new direction, but visibly decided to go with it. She shifted her shoulders and brought her arms closer to her sides.

"It was about that breach of protocol," she said. "The backup. And he knew I'd been snooping, but he understood the intent, I think."

"Do I need to talk to him for you?"

"You'd probably better steer clear about now. I think you're on a short leash, which means you have to be really careful."

"But we have to catch him," Jalen said.

A sour look spread across her face. Her nose wrinkled when her eyes sunk.

"He didn't do it, Jalen." She bit her lip, but allowed herself to pursue one step too far. "God, you're so stubborn."

"Stanger did it. I don't care what the police say. I've seen it with my own eyes and you have too."

"I don't know what I saw."

"Think about it."

"He's too high up the food chain, it isn't going to work. You'll be hitting the sidewalk and me, I'll either be promoted or forced to work with someone with a longer fuse than you. Two things I don't want right now."

Jalen sneered. "And I'm not interested in peace, or even war."

"Maybe you're not. Just watch your step."

"Would you look out for me?"

She shook her head and her eyes seemed to shrivel to pits. The cold streak between them returned and expanded. Life had not always been fair. No stroke of justice could assuage the guilt or the sorrow over what had happened three years ago. Her insistence on helping and Marie's own hard-headedness conspired to disallow peace. The gears of warfare churned in his brain, but its battlefields remained bathed in a murky fog where neither gunfire nor bloodshed had transpired.

"I gotta watch him," Jalen said to himself.

Kalee heard him, but didn't respond for more than a minute. Silence reigned. The squeak of shoes, the hum of equipment, the clash of boxes and carts running into walls, doors slamming, all rolled into an explosion of sound meant to pry Jalen from the here and now.

"Your compass is a little off."

Her voice seemed to echo, yet languished hollow in his ears. She had her way of introducing thought so severe that it made his head throb. That simple sentence spoke volumes. Jalen considered its many facets before settling with the obvious explanation. What we choose to see—what we have conditioned ourselves to see, doesn't indicate the true nature of things. The best guide would always be a roadmap, or something else that charts our course from afar. What we see from the ground often takes on an entirely different meaning. In the case of following a compass, Jalen could only follow where the compass said north resided. But the earth's own magnetic field interfered with the magnetism of the compass, which in certain regions caused the needle to spin up to twenty degrees off. Over the course of miles—over the course of life, one could end up nowhere near where they intended to go.

Damn her for making too much sense. Instead of chastising her or changing the subject, Jalen allowed the conversation to wither away and die. They each ordered a coffee from the cafeteria, but Jalen elected to go with a side of omelet.

Passing comments aside, they didn't converse for the remainder of the trip until they entered the office. Jalen almost didn't want to know what his associates were up to. Probably more rubber band wars or some other frivolous activity meant to saw time off the clock.

Jalen settled back into his chair, watched Kalee flip through a stack of papers, and then brought up the program he'd used to track Kale Stanger's cell phone. Jalen shook his head when he saw it. The phone was turned on, active, and was not blocking access. The idiot either had no idea or nothing to hide, which had its way of making Jalen feel uneasy.

He watched anyway. Stanger sat in his office most of the day. If Jalen wanted to, tracking his online movements and his file access within Lynx's servers would have been easy and maybe even the correct avenue. But the physical world was a different place than the internet world. As long as Stanger stayed in his office, Jalen had no reason to be suspicious. When he left was when he drew suspicion. Stanger headed to the cafeteria for lunch, stayed there a half hour, and then wandered the corridors of Building 11.

He entered the board room on the fourth floor of Building 11 and stayed there for over an hour. His movements did not seem to indicate wandering. If he didn't do something foolish within another hour, Jalen felt he would go crazy. *Come on, you bastard.*

A single punch on a keyboard drew Jalen's attention. He started to look around the room, but Laurie spoke.

"Hold on, now I know I've seen this truck before."

Jalen rolled his eyes and refocused his attention on the screen. Two other people ran to her aid, looking both impressed and yearning to hear more.

"Last week, I think, maybe around Tuesday."

"I'll check out the creds," Marcus said.

Marcus rushed to his computer and brought them up as quickly as possible.

"Jalen," Laurie started. "South gate, delivery truck. They're letting him in."

"Where?" Jalen said.

She put up her index finger and stared for thirty seconds while she watched the escort truck pull out in front of the delivery vehicle. "Looks like Building 25, bay door. Same place that guy went on Friday."

"That was odd enough to make you question it?"

"Once, no, but twice in less than a week's time, that's something."

"Credentials check out," Marcus said. "The truck is registered to Selway Transportation. They run a small leasing service on their trucks just in case the party making the delivery can't handle the load."

"Any link to Burton Cambridge?"

"Negative."

Jalen sat up and leaned forward to bring up Selway's webpage. It seemed that the company specialized in light mechanical transport for industrial purposes. They lacked the equipment necessary to take heavier loads. Cambridge hadn't used one of Selway's trucks.

"Get Barry and check it out," Jalen said. "Report back to me. Tell me what's on the truck."

Marcus abandoned his computer, grabbed his gear and rushed out of the office. Kalee seemed silent during this. He glanced over to her. She looked somewhat interested, but acted as if her work had her so engrossed that she couldn't spare a single second to take part in the conversation. He thought about asking her for comment, but Kalee had constructed a solid reputation. She mostly did what she was asked to do. This probably had something to do with Doc, but he decided not to ask.

"He's arrived," Laurie said. "The angle of the camera doesn't cover that bay door. It's impossible, unless we were to install a new camera."

"Not a bad idea," Jalen said. "I'm going to request some funding do to a total overhaul of our operations here. New software, new cameras, new protocols. Mabye corporate will finally listen."

"And maybe they'll bury their heads even deeper in the sand," Laurie said. "They don't understand that we're ten years behind the times."

Jalen slapped his palm on the desk, closed the webpage, glanced at the little dot that located Stanger's phone, and then stared at the tablet.

He picked it up and flipped through about two dozen apps, looking for emails, note pads, sketch pads, anything that could offer another clue. Other than the three apps that Jalen had long since aborted, nothing came to the fore.

*There's no one,* Jalen told himself. *Cambridge was an accident.*

The police hadn't updated Jalen on their progress, but he understood that some things took time, especially on the forensics side. Some murder investigations could take months or years to see through. Some were done in a week or less. Considering the complexity this case dripped with, he wagered up to a year or two before they could finally put it to bed.

Whoever and whatever was going on would take less time than that, and no matter how hard Jalen worked, no matter the vigilance he exerted, Lynx Technologies remained vulnerable. Maybe it would take another murder or two for the corporate execs recognize the need to better fund security. Jalen understood the game. Its vitality could not be understated. Yet, the company pushed more and more resources to research and development in hopes of gunning straight for the top. World dominance amongst the memory tyrants.

Watching Stanger could have drained his time. He wondered if was a waste, but continued to watch him anyway. After the board meeting, Stanger made a few calls, which Jalen could probably listen to, and then headed back to his office. He wondered whether this had something to do with the company's possible expansion into the Indonesian market. So much potential there remained untapped, the company promised. Build a new plant, raise wages to five bucks a day, watch the assets mushroom by the hundreds of millions, and then attempt to buy out the last remaining competitor. It would be enough to make them number one.

This could have been the work of corporate greed, Jalen guessed. But greed itself didn't seem a strong enough motive to physically hunt down and murder two guys who had little to do with executive decisions.

With Stanger beginning to look innocent, Jalen scrambled to find something new to latch onto, something to occupy his brain and force the demons out.

A simple radio call seemed to do the trick.

"Jalen, this is Marcus. We got a truckload of metal storage drums, some hoses, and a mechanical coupling device, but the driver is gone."

Jalen threw the radio across the room and shouted. "Damnit!"

"Jalen," Kalee said. "Stop. Take a break."

"Our security isn't built for this." He stood, walked across the room, and picked up the radio. After an exhale during which he closed his eyes and attempted to calm his nerves, he pressed the button and addressed Marcus and Barry. "Find him. He couldn't have gotten far. Search the tunnels."

"He's going to get away," Kalee said. "If you don't watch that bay door."

"We can't" Jalen said. "No cameras and no manpower."

"There might be a way," she said. "I'll look into it and get back to you by the end of the day."

"If we don't catch him by then, he'll be gone. Want to see another disappearing act?"

"Forget I said it," she said. "I won't try to help anymore."

"Kalee."

She shook her head, blinked, and then looked back to her computer. Jalen watched her eyes reading endless words on a screen for long enough to make his head hurt. He was willing to admit he needed her help, but his approach didn't seem to work. Yet it was not something he could magically change and make it all better. He could only think to immerse himself in work yet again and maybe the ache and the desperation and whatever other emotion decided to rampage through his skull would depart.

"I'm sorry."

She didn't respond. The light from the screen flashed and reflected off of her glasses. The silent treatment was a method at which Marie excelled and he didn't need that. She told him over and over again that she wanted to help and then declined when it got rough. Just like Marie.

The day wore on and Marcus and Barry didn't return. Jalen waited until darkness approached outside. Kalee packed her bag, grabbed her jacket and went home. Laurie waited until the night crew arrived to give up her post. Still Jalen waited with no word from them. He attempted to radio them three times but got no reply.

At about ten minutes to eight, they both walked through the door, disarmed, and declared that finding the delivery man was a lost cause. Still, the truck remained. He thought about it and an idea came to him. He grinned and didn't wait to put his plan into action. The night crew would help him if he needed it, but a taser would be enough. The imagined taste of victory exploded somewhere in his brain. Adrenaline surged through his veins.

# 19

# Gravitational Lensing

"That's a bad idea," Barry said before exiting the front door. "Get some guys patrolling, but don't go underground yourself. You won't catch him yourself. It's not all about you."

Jalen shook his head and pulled his radio out. The night crew had already started to arrive, but since night patrols of corridors never presented themselves as major areas of need, patrols were light and spotty. Jalen almost didn't want to know what took place in the office when he was off, but as always, he'd convinced himself that worrying didn't suddenly dump more weight into it. The less he knew, the better. Sleep, while rare, remained an important concept.

"Gonna be fine," Jalen said. "I'd invite you to stay but it looks like you have plans already."

Marcus walked out the front door, leaving Jalen and Barry as the lobby's sole occupants. Barry raised his eyebrows. "You can *order* me to stay."

"You want me to do that?"

"Up to you."

"Stay," Jalen said, remembering the ferocity with which he'd told Marie to go. He wished he wouldn't have done that, but some of the fault had to fall on her. "Keep up with HQ, lock down all known access points to the tunnels."

"There could be hundreds we don't know about," Barry said. "I doubt my buddy over in engineering even knows how many ways a person can get down there. But I'll have some guys watch the ones I know about."

"Check and see if we have cameras pointed at some of them. We'll keep in touch. See if my plan works."

"You have a plan? That's gotta be a first."

"I didn't say it was highly evolved," Jalen said, lowering his gaze. "Fact, it comes with a fair amount of risk."

"You're telling me," Barry said.

"Move," Jalen said. He turned around and said nothing more to Barry. A certain feeling that Barry only stared until Jalen evaded eyesight embattled his mind.

Jalen had one more stop before heading for the tunnel. Stopping there didn't start out as part of his plan, but he found that following goal layouts exactly as written often involved greater risk of failure. New information, new ideas, and changing conditions played a vital role in all plans. Flexibility was key.

The Building 5 interstitial mechanical room likely stood vacant while the machinery tirelessly hummed the night away. Jalen half-ran to the door that led to the stairs, hoping this little side trip would pay off.

"Steam valve controls...why so isolated?"

When he reached the door, he quickly swiped his badge across the reader. Nothing happened. Another attempt seemed futile, but he swiped again. A red light appeared next to the reader, alerting him that access was denied. This info raised a red flag, but Jalen paid no attention. If the room didn't allow him access, then it wouldn't let anyone in.

Instead of backtracking to the end of Building 27, where he knew he could access the tunnel, he continued on his trip away from the office. Jalen took a side corridor that jutted off from the doglegging main corridor in Building 5. This corridor narrowed, led around a series of bends, through a couple of lounge-like areas, and then down a darker hallway where blank doors punctured the white walls. The corridor looked like it led to a mechanical area.

After trekking through that confusion, Jalen turned around and glanced at a small sign on the door. Building 1B labs lined a wider corridor that branched off to the right. Jalen hadn't realized that he had exited Building5. Building 1B was one of the first buildings to be constructed on the campus of Lynx Technologies, back before the company knew they wanted to dominate the international market and guide memory pricing.

Back then, the company was known as Lynx, LLC, before the sweeping name change to Lynx, Inc. Jalen didn't understand the difference, but the way legend painted it, the move strategically placed Lynx amongst a handful of companies positioned for growth as the information age exploded.

The growth had expanded the campus exponentially in the following years. Less than five years after Building 1B opened, Lynx had assembled a sizable portfolio and quadrupled in size. Not long after that, Buildings 4 and 5 were constructed simultaneously and adjacent to one another.

The sign indicated that Fab X stood ahead. Each fab included up to dozens of separate cleanrooms. For some reason, the company chose not to number each fab based on the number of the building or buildings the fab was located in (some of the eight fabs encompassed parts of two or three buildings). He suspected that Fab 1 sounded too elementary and made the company look like a second-rate manufacturer and Fab X sounded more impressive.

Jalen surpassed a long cleanroom with five access bays and five work bays. The rooms lasted until it appeared that the corridor ended. However a narrow pass jutted off the main corridor at a blank wall. He took a left and came face-to-face with an unidentified door. This door allowed him access when he scanned his badge.

Instead of a stairway, an oddly shaped mechanical room stood behind the door. Pumps and other equipment hummed and churned to a deafening roar. He paced the room, looking for a way out, and then saw what appeared to be a hole in the floor. Stainless steel railing barricaded the hole. Up to a hundred pipes turned vertical along the far wall of the oblong trench until they disappeared from view. He searched for a steam line but didn't find one. Instead of calling it off, he walked to an opening in the railing and looked down. The pit extended deeper than Jalen anticipated. At least twenty feet separated him from the bottom of the pit. Piping extended out of shaft walls, routed horizontally to group up with other pipes, and then extended into darkness below.

Jalen turned backwards and carefully descended the ladder, while keeping an eye on the floor below. He glanced back and forth until the floor above seemed to disappear.

The mechanical space in the pit was narrower than Jalen expected. In fact, a claustrophobic person would feel quite uncomfortable. The hole wasn't so much a pit as it was a trench. Several dozen pipes lined the wall adjacent to the ladder and joined with even more piping that came in through a horizontal notch in the concrete wall. The piping extended fifty feet or so before bending hard left. Jalen flicked on his light to illuminate more clearly what the sparse florescent lights could not. He tried to pay attention to the yellow labels on some of the larger pipes. Two large, insulated lines labeled TCHWS and TCHWR seemed to dominate the bank of piping.

At the end of this trench, the pass turned left and seemed to widen enough that Jalen could easily walk straight ahead instead of shuffling sideways through the maze of piping.

After the bend, the piping rack extended down a tunnel so long and so narrow that Jalen could not see where it ended. He quickly came to realize that he'd been in this tunnel recently. Sure enough, about thirty feet from the bend, the piping spread wide where a ladder extended maybe ten feet to another trench, where he'd discovered the body of Burton Cambridge.

Jalen shone his light down the corridor and strained his eyes. A mysterious figure crept slowly along the bank of piping to the right, as silent as possible. Trying to equal the man's silence seemed a strange endeavor. Plenty of noise from random pumps and valves filled the trench and at that distance, hearing noise at either end would have been impossible.

Advancing more quickly, Jalen followed. The man stopped. On instinct, Jalen turned off the light and ducked into a shadow. When the figure turned to move once again, Jalen emerged and kept the light at his feet. A nearby light flickered. When the figure seemed to adjust his pace, Jalen understood that the person was aware of his presence. He responded by pressing forward at almost a run.

The man disappeared from view moments later. Jalen slowed when he approached the gap. The figure reemerged less than a hundred feet away. It appeared that the man followed a certain pipe as it traversed along the wall. Jalen peered to the piping at his right and studied the rack. The TCHW lines had reduced in size, making them seem less dominant than before. Somewhere along the line a large white plastic pipe at least two feet in diameter extended along the floor. Jalen shuffled sideways to avoid it while keeping his eyes on the intruder.

Beads of sweat bathed his forehead in heat. He wiped the sweat away with his sleeve and kept going. His pace quickened as he headed into a wider portion of the tunnel, where dozens of pipes jumped into the fray. A network of tangles spread piping in all directions overhead. Up to a hundred new pipes somehow merged onto the rack. The rack split into multiple tiers to accommodate the space needed. At this junction, twenty foot-wide corridors split off in a tee while the main corridor widened beyond fifty feet. A maze of pumps, blowers, and other equipment lined the left wall on large, concrete platforms. From each pump and each blower, large pipes shot up vertically and joined together to pass through the deck above.

Hundreds of feet later where the corridor shifted its angle and descended a shallow slope, the tunnel got even wider. The man continued to follow the pipe, which had shifted to overhead. Jalen switched off the light and continued to follow in the shadow.

With a sudden swoop the man turned hard right. Jalen flung himself against the bank of piping where shadow dominated. He crept along the piping without being able to see where the man was headed. Could this have been the delivery man? At this time, no one else seemed to be down here.

When Jalen reached the point where the man had inexplicably disappeared, he paused and peered around the corner. Another long, narrow corridor split off there. The corridor descended another shallow incline that lasted about sixty feet to a double door. The door was open, revealing the darkness that expanded behind it.

Jalen waited there for what seemed like ten minutes and then almost gave up when something moved in the shadow. Jalen darted to hide behind a valve with a huge wheel attached to it. Now less than twenty feet away, the man stopped to observe the tangle of piping overhead. Many of the pipes split off to run down the side corridor to the door, but many more pipes jumped onto the network of racks.

The man seemed to grunt, lowered his shoulders, and crept across the corridor to where a heavy welding curtain denoted a small construction site. The man didn't bother with the curtain. Another corridor, somewhat hidden, split off behind a concrete wall and paralleled the main tunnel for a little less than twenty feet. This corridor was narrower and darker. To its left, the tunnels opened to a tee that extended wide enough to drive three cars abreast. The short leg of the tee extended one hundred feet to the overhead door where the delivery man had parked the vehicle. It would seem that the man returned to his truck, but decided to snoop in areas he had no business visiting.

The dark of the tunnel perplexed him. Why hadn't the lights come on? Had the motion sensors been deactivated? In truth Jalen wasn't certain the lights in the tunnels were attached to motion sensors. In fact, as the thought settled upon him, he came to realize that all of the lighting was manual, which meant there had to be a switch nearby. Jalen thought about trying to find it, but decided not to in case the mysterious person was not aware he was being followed.

The corridor descended a long ramp that pushed the depth of the floor at least fifteen feet lower than the main tunnel. Jalen crept along the wall, where several pipes seemed to dead end or cut through the wall out of sight. At the end, a heavy double door etched a dark gray rectangle in the dark. A flash of memory in his mind alerted him to where he was. Not a good sign.

While the darkness seemed to billow and fold, it allowed a moment of clarity. Four diamonds in a greater diamond of white adorned the right door. During training seminars, the videos made it a point to stress how dangerous these areas were. A red triangle with a yellow flame indicated flammable materials, while a green one noted that noxious gases could be present. But the third diamond, the one front and center blazed with three wide arcs of yellow against a sea of black, could not be mistaken for anything other than possible radiation.

Jalen shifted his weight against the wall and watched the man read the door. He slithered into shadow to the right as Jalen watched. A hollow clanking sound interrupted the muted hum of equipment. Behind the door lied danger greater than anywhere else on camps, yet the visitor seemed to seek it out. The door was equipped with an exquisite locking system that forbade anyone without proper clearance from entering, which included Jalen.

The chemicals in the room behind the door were well confined. The vault was constructed of heavy stress concrete more than two feet thick. In the center of the concrete, where single strands of rebar ran, a heavy sheet of lead further protected the vault from the outside world. Should anything happen, the setup would ensure no one on campus would be hurt.

Jalen turned. The clanking sound returned and Jalen froze when a conical light flashed across his face. His veins turned to ice. He swung his fist at the shadow but felt only the rush of humid air against his fist. Before Jalen knew what was happening, the dark enclosed him. The sound of the equipment was harrowing, distant, and cold. The heavy sound of metal scraping against concrete filled his eardrums. He rolled to his side and kicked out his leg. Nothing. Pain. Sharp, jolting pain smashed against his scalp like the force of thousands of headaches, while dark stretched out its arms to embrace him. The scent of blood filled his nostrils, followed by the bliss of nothing. Nothing but decay.

# 20

# Supernova

The world around him spun like a cyclone circling toward extinction. The blur of rain and tears soaked his face as panic set in. The central boulevard inside the campus of Lynx Technologies glistened with the sparkle of wet pavement. Disc-like waves spread across the tiny puddles and criss-crossed. Shivers pummeled his spine.

The water dripped from his scalp. With Building 11 behind him, Jalen strode with purpose, pressing forward though the wind cut through him like a butter knife. Kalee struck his mind, her face glowering with the coals of anger over Jalen's latest tirade. She shook and her image vibrated and dispersed.

To stop it from taking place, he had to walk faster. Ducking headfirst into the wind and using his forearm to shield the rain, he picked up his pace. After passing the campus's central nitrogen plant, the ramp at the back of Building 25 appeared.

Despair collided with purpose in his mind before melding in a murky concoction of emotion too crude for his heart to process. Exactly what was about to happen he didn't know. He didn't want to know and he didn't want to find out. Somehow the consequences would be too ghastly to imagine.

The image of 25 bounced as he broke into a sprint. The rain further blurred his vision. In nightmare after nightmare, unexplained tears carved rivers in his face, his eyelids drooped, and the corners of his mouth sagged into wretched reflections of his former face.

Some scars—a bright flash like orange lightning illuminated the bottom of the ramp. A burst of flame bright enough to blind him shot up into the sky. The embers expanded. A concussive blast of sound shook the ground beneath his feet. Jalen's toe met a protruding metal ring in the concrete. His knees buckled and his heart raced. The blossom of fire dissipated, leaving behind a towering column of smoke. The rain streaked through it. When Jalen's mind caught up with him and motion returned to his limbs, he stared at the scarred remnant of Building 25. How many people were in that building? How many lives were lost?

He blinked. A hallucinogenic light hovered somewhere in a hidden chamber before coming to rest on an array of wide yellow arcs across a canvas of black. A skull appeared before his face clamoring as though rotten flesh had just peeled itself away from the bones.

A scream punctured the night as the din of the explosion trailed away. Jalen leapt to his feet. Survivors. He had to call someone now. Anyone.

Jalen's eyes flitted open as a cold sweat dampened his forehead. He shook from head to toe, trying to make sense of it all. The nightmare. Panic and ache dulled his nerves as the images from the dream faded and ebbed. He wrung his fists together, sat up, and buried his face in his palms.

Could Kalee have been in the building in search of him? His heart sunk with the thought as the feeling of ice battered his muscles. "No." Jalen said. "It wasn't..."

But was it? Had any of it been real? The tunnels had been dark. He remembered following him toward the chemical vault. The darkness had expanded, leaving only a crater carved against the black. His fist had missed. So had his foot. And then, the void. Shouting interrupted the blackness for one surreal moment.

"Jesus, Jalen, you've had too much to drink...No? Shit. Relax, you have a concussion."

The voice had wavered in the dead air, but had it been real? And if any of it had been, how did he end up in his own bed bathing in cold sweat?

His body trembled. Whether or not the events of the previous night carried the sting of real memories, the explosion could not have been accidental. While true that his dreams had never proven prophetic or even resembled future events, the case of murder could turn into a terrorist attack.

An explosion that size could...Jalen's heart rate somehow quickened. How exactly did he get home?

He sprung out of bed, ran to the shower, and then got ready. He elected to skip breakfast. Perhaps his thoughts weren't an emergency, but he had to tell someone what he saw.

Just as he tightened the knot on his tie, a car horn sounded. He peered through the window. The car's headlights shrouded his vision in sheets of halogen. He gulped when he realized that his own car was not parked in the driveway. The car horn blared again. He grabbed his jacket and ran out the door to greet whoever had showed up to give him a ride.

He paid attention only to the cold and the grass still wet with dew. His intuition had scarred him, yet the demons had not been flushed away.

"How are you feeling this morning?"

An ache pierced his skull. He frowned and looked into Barry's eyes, but his body twitched and squirmed in the seat.

"Still edgy."

"Wha...what happened?"

Barry raised one eyebrow. "I could ask you the same question. What was it? Alcohol induced coma?...Don't bother fighting, I know you. No. Someone in the office thought they heard someone attempt to radio. It wasn't me, so I got suspicious. I thought I knew where you were going. And then I see you laying on the floor with blood on your scalp and a pipe laying next to you, I got a little nervous. You sort of woke up for a minute, but you were hardly aware of your own existence.

"I got you home after I turned on the lights and determined that your head must have hurt, but maybe not enough to visit the ER again. I wedged an aspirin in your mouth, after laying you down on the bed and then poured just a little water down your throat. Knew you'd have a rough night, so I left and told you I'd come pick you up."

"He attacked me," Jalen said quickly without letting the bluntness of Barry's story sink in. His heart trembled in rhythm with the drone of the motor.

"Who?"

"I don't know who, damnit." Jalen abbreviated his story, leaving only the key details. He didn't expound on the fact that he hadn't seen the attacker's face.

"It had to be the delivery guy," Barry said. "People don't like being followed. Given the choice I'm not so sure I wouldn't do exactly what he did, if I didn't know it was you."

"Gotta get him," Jalen said.

"The office has been on it all night. They monitored the gates, but the truck never moved. It's still there. Who knows if he's still on campus?"

"Why wouldn't he just drive away?" he said.

"I don't know. He plans to finish his delivery, maybe?"

"He was interested in the chemical vault. Shit's flammable as hell and maybe even nuclear."

"No one can get in there," Barry said. "There's two or three people in the entire world who can access that, and none of them are corporate officials."

"It could have been him," Jalen argued, remembering the altercation with Stanger. "You know it too."

"He didn't do it, end of story," Barry said. "Maybe your head isn't right for you to come into the office today. I'll call Doc and tell him Kalee will be in charge."

"The hell you will," Jalen said, his lips trembling. "You don't know what could happen. If he could blow that vault, it might kill hundreds. Or more. You don't just ignore that."

"You want me to call Homeland Security?"

"The fallout and the radiation could affect thousands more people, whoever lives downwind." Breathless, Jalen finished.

"What makes you think that?"

"I had a dream."

"Oh, God. I'm turning around."

Jalen swallowed hard and pressed. His hands quivered and his face seemed to melt into an eerie frown. "Listen to me, you son of a bitch."

Barry raised his hands, keeping his palms face down.

Hurrying through the important points of the dream proved an excursion through the scarred landscape where images of his dream faded into dust. He was sure his eyes were bloodshot.

"You're serious?"

Jalen nodded.

"You know whose job that is," Barry said. "Yours. Ours. He won't blow up the vault because we won't allow it."

Jalen rode in silence for more than a minute before he dug his phone out of his pocket. He dialed her number and waited.

"Oh, it's you," she said. "I thought you'd be on Jupiter by now, clawing your own eyes out."

"Shut up," he said.

"What do you want?" Marie's voice pierced his eardrums. He'd never heard her so concise, or the rhythm of her voice so sharp.

"When are you gonna come get your stuff? That teddy bear is about to meet its maker."

"I'll be by today and I'll leave my key," she said. "After that, I don't want you to call me again."

"We can work it out," Jalen said.

"Bullshit. Always comes back around and I'm not taking any more emotional abuse. You don't need me or want me anyway."

"Been talking with Cassie, I see," Jalen quipped.

"Leave her out of it."

"Maybe I will. You working today?"

"What do you care?"

"I'm just...It's been a rough night, that's all."

She waited for more. Her breath sounded venomous at first, but seemed to cool into the tender remains of something resembling concern. After a moment, the breathing stopped. Twenty seconds passed and neither hung up the phone.

"Rough life," she said. "Don't think I don't understand. And your answer is always the same. Get drunk off your ass."

"I didn't...That's not even accurate," Jalen fought back. "I got attacked last night and my memory's a little fuzzy still."

"Knew this was gonna happen," she said. The timbre of her voice dropped an octave and Jalen shivered. "Maybe you deserve it."

Jalen grunted, pulled the phone away from his ear, and then pounded his fist on the screen with enough force for it to crack. "Don't know what you're talking about..." he mumbled. "Bitch."

"Shouldn't have made that call, my friend," Barry said.

Jalen shot him an icy glare.

"Maybe you should bring it up with Kalee."

His heart sank lower, and his hands trembled again. "I don't know. I don't think she wants to talk to me anymore either."

"You done repelling everyone? Don't take my word for it, but you need help. I can set you up with the on-site shrink if you want."

Jalen gulped and leaned his head backward. The fire of his emotion often got the better of him, true enough. He understood why people seemed to recommend psychiatric help every time an episode like this took place.

The remainder of the trip produced silence. Jalen's lips quivered and the scar on the back of his head ached with fury. He clenched his fist, closed his eyes, and pretended to sleep. Maybe the tumult in his heart would calm and he'd feel what he considered to be normal again.

When Barry parked his car next to Jalen's he exerted a fake sigh and looked at Jalen. "Take it easy today. For your sake, and for Kalee. I heard something about her the other day."

"God, I gotta be the most bipolar person on the planet."

"That's not funny."

Jalen frowned and massaged his scalp with one hand, trying to work the knot away. He wondered if any blood had soaked his pillow or if it had scabbed over already.

"Least the lights were working properly today," Jalen said.

"City needs to get that fixed before someone goes on a vehicular rampage," Barry said. "People react severely to that kind of stuff."

"As long as they don't think it's a public safety issue, they'll leave it alone," Jalen said. "Ain't broke, don't fix it, they always say."

"Yeah, sometimes you need preventative maintenance. Which comes back to you and the psychiatrist."

"I'm not going on a rampage."

"You could decide to tase everyone who moves wrong, though." Barry attempted to smile and swung the car door open.

"Not funny," Jalen said.

"Not at all."

They strode toward the office door and an eerie sensation spread across him. Why had Kalee been in a dream where she didn't belong? He cracked his knuckles and looked up to Barry. "You said you heard something about Kalee?"

"Lord, I'm not telling you that," he said, lowering his voice.

"Why bother with gossip then?"

"You can't control what people tell you, but you can choose not to spread it around," Barry said.

"So damn honorable," Jalen said.

"No, but I know when to do the right thing."

Jalen issued a sigh and allowed Barry to enter the office alone. Rather than force himself into the action, he leaned against the wall and attempted to gather the strands of his emotion the best he could. Believing what Barry said was one thing, but allowing the sensation of defeat to crumble in his bones didn't seem like a pleasant way to spend his time.

He closed his eyes. The fire of the explosion reached higher and higher, coalescing into a giant orange mushroom. The figurative smoke singed his eyes like dry heat pressing against his pupils. His heart sunk and a lone tear cascaded down his face. He wiped it away, squared his jaw, opened his eyes, and marched through the door.

# 21

# The Event Horizon

*H*umanity's last hope lies barren at the edge of the dark from which nothing can escape.

Jalen typed into his journal, feeling strangely invigorated as if the stress had risen off of his shoulders. Kalee watched him for a moment, but he pretended not to notice.

*You and I, we are nothing and everything. Even part of the dark. The dark does not simply take us in, whether against our will or as an invited guest. It destroys us. The matter in our flesh and bones, even what we may consider to be the soul, stretches and thins as it falls. Each molecule eaten but never spit out or regurgitated. The edge of this black hole is where we as a species cease to exist.*

Jalen rubbed his eyes, feeling the sting of whatever nightmare he'd lived through last night. The nightmare seemed to carry over. He had no call to speak to Marie that way. It was her right to do what she thought she needed to. Her opinion had always mattered to him, up until several weeks ago. When pushed to the brink, he fought back by attacking the weakest area, or at least what he saw as the weakest. No, Marie wasn't weak. But she wasn't part of the great opposition, which was too strong to take down.

"Shouldn't have made that call," Barry had told him.

Barry didn't normally dispense life advice, but Jalen took notice when he did. What was that he had mentioned about Kalee? He didn't even remember it now.

When he stopped typing, Kalee peered at him over the top of her glasses. A stern expression squared her jaw while her eyes suggested some sort of concern. "How's your head?"

"You know," Jalen said. "Got my skull smashed in with a galvanized pipe. How do you imagine it feels?"

"I see," she said. "Not that I was interested in the patronizing, but what the hell?"

"That's not what I meant," Jalen said.

"Maybe not, but your tone didn't have to be so rough."

"It's not exactly that simple, or that I can really control it. Imagine if your sister decided to burn the entire family fortune to run off to Vegas with a guy she hardly knew and then blew it all in Monte Carlo or something. You spend half the night crying, wondering how she could be so stupid. Then come into the office and try to make your voice sound pleasant."

"Not *my* sister."

Barry piped in. "If you get married in Vegas, what would you want with Monte Carlo?"

"Ever been there?" someone asked.

"This got away from me," Jalen said quietly.

Kalee suppressed a grin while Jalen attempted to formulate a plan to deal with the bad guy, whoever he was. He thought about calling the police, but by now he suspected that Lawrence would try to explain what cops thought of speculation. The thought caused Jalen to frown.

"I've been there," she said.

"Mote Carlo?"

"And Barcelona, Venice, Naples, Greece."

Jalen understood all at once what she was talking about. Eight years ago, the love of her life swooped in and rushed her off to some sort of fantasy world where no murder for hire ruined the sanctity. It was good and the Honeymoon was to die for. Two years later, the man knocked off a bank, got caught, shipped off to prison. The divorce followed. Maybe that was what Barry had alluded to.

"Did you know Naples is where Neapolitan ice cream was invented?"

Jalen looked at her. "Did you know Greece is where the Olympics were invented?"

She wrinkled her nose. "Tell me more."

"Zeus told me not to."

She laughed. "Did he now?"

After a shrug, Jalen plunged back into his work, attempting to find out more about where the truck came from and possibly who the driver was. The funny thing about privately investigating personnel at a different company was that the management suddenly acted all 'cloak and dagger.' As if Jalen hadn't honed the skill of finding out who the employees were. He could do it. A certain amount of illegal hacking could go a long way.

"You know after a bump on the head people start to do some strange things," Kalee said. "I've heard stories about concussions. Never had one, but I don't imagine they are pleasant."

"Which takes us right back where we started," Jalen said without looking up from his screen.

"So I guess did you get some sense knocked into you or are you 'whacked out?'" She stared at him, perhaps hoping that his expression alone would communicate what he thought, but Jalen didn't want to play along.

He shrugged. "I had a nightmare," he started, wondering if he should tell her that her face meaninglessly appeared. A swallow allowed him to continue. The third time he told the story, he felt like he could dredge up more of the emotion that had come with the scene, but the more he conjured, the more fiction slipped in.

"Did you want me to tuck you in?"

"It's serious. Don't know if we should call it a premonition or not, but we gotta be on high alert. That's why everyone is out looking for this guy."

"Found him," Laurie said. Everyone stopped what they were doing and stared at her. Instead of gaping, Jalen stood and half-sprinted to her desk to get a peek at the security camera at the north gate. "Same truck, same driver," she said. "I'll have them lock it down."

She picked up the phone and started pressing buttons while Jalen thought about it. He glanced at Cambridge's tablet when an idea flashed over him. "No. Let him go."

"What?'

"They're not going to react too kindly at police HQ or corporate if I go detain the wrong man again. We'll need some more. But I think I know how to bait the trap."

"Come again?"

Jalen strode over to the tablet, breathed in deep and grabbed it. He brought its screen to life and started pressing buttons. Kalee followed him and watched.

"Hope this works. I'm thinking this guy is in with Cambridge, maybe even there to finish his job. That means that whoever he is probably has a contact saved into the email. After I figure out the password, hopefully the emails aren't encrypted. He'll get nice and suspicious when dead Burton Cambridge contacts him. I do it right, maybe I scare him right into coming out."

"You do know the risk of that, don't you?" she said. "If this man killed Cambridge, you can bet he'll know various ways of attacking."

"I know. High risk, high reward. The second he makes his move, the police will be there to bring him down. This guy set a trap for me, so maybe I should return the favor."

"I don't know," Kalee said. "What if he expects it? What if he's the wrong man?"

"Well then I guess it's been nice knowing you. Maybe we can still hang out."

"Be careful."

*Be careful.* Her voice seemed to carry on a cold breeze, fluttering, diving, and scattering like emotions of the past.

"Can you do me a favor?" Jalen said. "Never tell me to be careful again."

She didn't know. "Pardon me for caring."

"This had better work," Jalen said. He punched a few buttons on the tablet before downloading an application that promised to cover his tracks should anyone be snooping. When the download completed, he opened the user's email, changed the password, and dug through a small sample of messages. The user had wanted to meet someone for coffee. Dinner and a date, followed by murder. The email that mentioned the elimination of the tour guide stood out. Jalen read it again, hoping that a different device would divulge more detail. It didn't. Several emails had volleyed back and forth between a MZ1961 and Cambridge. The mystery man couldn't have picked a more obvious email name.

The conversation had been about video games. "Have you played the new Call of Duty yet?" "It's a real killer."

*So are you, Cambridge,* Jalen thought.

"Not as good as the new Halo," Cambridge said. "I got all the way to where that Elite punctures your gut with his energy sword, but maybe I have the difficulty too high. I can handle the Grunts easy enough, but those Elites are badass."

"They are Supers, and they always move in a pattern. It only takes a couple of tries to figure out what they're going to do, which makes it easy to counter them. You wait behind the corner for them to throw their grenades, bury one in fire, and the other three will charge you. Unload a plasma grenade, which should weaken their shields, then start picking them off. I had to punch one of them in the face three times when I was almost dead. After that, it's all Brutes."

*The hell are you guys talking about?*

Jalen decided to do a little Google research and find out what some of the characters were. They could have been speaking in code, Jalen thought, but if so, the code was advanced enough to prevent any snoopers or hackers from figuring out what it really was they were up to. He had no interest in playing Halo. Computer games were not his forte. He didn't have time for them.

Elites, it seemed, were tall, heavily armored, and highly skilled aliens. Their common weaponry included plasma pistols, plasma launchers, and some sort of machine gun, while some carried long, shiny energy swords. Brutes used their bulk and strength to best opponents. Their weapons included a more 'primitive' array of machine guns and grenade launchers, but they also carried huge hammers that would defeat most enemies with a single blow. Grunts were stupid, relying on numbers and an armory of plasma grenades to bring down what the Wiki page called Spartans.

So, in code, the grunts would be people like most Lynx employees. And Brutes...Security officers? Jalen already knew who the Elite was.

After reading the remainder of their conversation, Jalen found another email from someone in Indonesia. He read it quickly. "We're looking good here. Send your guy and we'll put this one on ice."

Jalen's jaw dropped. He read it again, whispering, "Stanger, you son of a bitch."

"Did you say Stanger?" Kalee asked.

"Shit."

"He just bought a plane ticket to Salt Lake."

"We gotta stop him."

"No we don't," Kalee said, emphasizing the 'we.' "Maybe you can get airport security to nab him."

"He just got back from Jakarta on a business trip. Bet you'll never guess who this Cambridge character emailed two weeks ago. Strorgensen-Under-score-John, whose email signature is in Indonesia. Can't be a coincidence."

"You think Stanger is going to try blowing up the vault? I don't know about that."

"Might be," Jalen said. "But he might also be a potential victim. I'm not so sure I want to wait around to find out."

"International?" Kalee said in disbelief. "And it all happens to come at a time when Lynx is trying to become the world's number one memory provider. Which means we're all pawns."

"Not it doesn't," Jalen said. "It means we're Grunts."

She shot a sideways glance at him, then rolled her chair backwards toward the wall. A slow gesture with her hands indicated apprehension, but Jalen knew the right time to attack.

He pushed the button to compose a new email and fired it off to Driver 8127 and the guy in Jakarta. They'd respond to this and he knew it. What he didn't know was how. Jalen mentally tried to prepare for all possible outcomes. If Driver 8127 came back, Jalen knew just where to find him. The hook was baited. Now he just had to wait.

After allowing himself a few minutes to be proud of himself, sitting back with his fingers laced behind his head and a smirk stretched across his face, he turned back to the screen and opened up his journal again.

*We are not yet falling in, being obliterated one atom at a time, but we are fast approaching on the accretion disk. It is only a matter of time before humanity is not even a memory. The best case scenario is we all become radiation from the nuclear reaction that has merged us with the great singularity.*

# 22

# Cybernetic Crimson

Dusty yellow light poured into the office through the windows. For a moment, Jalen caught himself staring at the spectacle. Without a break, Jalen doomed himself to fail. His mind, his muscles, everything would shut down and the engine that powered him would become as lifeless as an obsolete and overworked computer.

He resettled himself, turned in his chair and faced his screens. Kalee typed away at something but paused when Jalen looked at her.

"Coffee?" he asked.

She picked up a small Styrofoam cup and swirled its contents with a bleak smile. What was that, an excuse?

"Health bar?"

A wider smile parted her lips. She sat the coffee down, leaned back and pushed her glasses up her nose. "I'd love to."

They quietly stood and exited the office. Not unlike the average Monday morning, the corridors were alive with hushed and clipped conversation, possibly having something to do with the ever-evolving murder case, or the rumors of a new Asian plant.

Jalen observed. A young woman stopped to chat with a man twice her age in a blue coat. He grinned, tilted his head sideways, said something, and then strolled away with a victorious stride.

"It's a busy day," Kalee said.

"Monday."

"My favorite."

Jalen studied her as she glanced at a bulletin board in passing. He gradually began to slide further away from her, and when she realized the space had grown, she altered her course. Anything to make it look like they were walking together rather than two complete strangers who, by sheer luck, happened to be walking in the same direction. He tried not to notice after the second time.

"How are you doing today?"

"You know." He tried to make it sound like everything was fine and that life hid some sort of meaning he had to hunt for.

She nodded and swung her arms. "Have you talked to Marie?"

"Don't remind me. Called her this morning, something to do with her stuff still being all over my house. Asked her when she'd come pick it up, told her I was sorry, and invited her to work it out. Then she got all defensive on me, we fought, and a couple of low blows later here I am still struggling to make sense of everything. It's all become so..." He raised his palms and allowed a strained frown to surface on his face. "Fragmented."

"You remind me of my divorce," she said.

He gulped. It was best not to bring that up in normal conversation, he'd learned. As painful as it must have been, she didn't elect to share anything. As a result, Jalen only knew the particulars of what happened, but not how and what it felt like. Then again, he almost didn't want to know.

"Everything just sort of got away from me. I know it's not the same thing, but maybe you can learn something, if you care to. I sometimes woke up with no idea what was real and tried to convince myself that the worst parts were sort of an ongoing nightmare. Maybe like, if you tell yourself something often enough, you'll eventually believe it."

"You don't strike me as the kind of person who believes that," Jalen said.

"No, but what's it hurt?"

"Good point."

She glanced at him before turning her focus to a young woman in a white jacket and goggles who'd stopped to stare at something as if a huge idea had just flashed in her brain. Something in the air today made the whole place seem more alive.

"It wasn't just about the bank robbery. He made some stupid choices and so did I. They drove us apart, and with that kind of space, you allow mistrust to fill in the gaps. Right before the trial, I accused him of something I shouldn't have, he told me about the problems at work, and how he might be out of a job soon. Didn't think I'd be there to support him. And how could I be while he was in prison? He made some new friends, some new enemies and turned into some stranger who only slightly resembled the man I married."

"You don't need to say anymore," Jalen said, attempting to offer some form of comfort.

She drifted closer to him. Jalen pretended to be distracted by some poster on the wall advertising a benefit concert at a downtown plaza.

Kalee tilted her head and meandered around a puddle on the floor. When she returned to his side, she continued. "It was then I decided to move on and do what was best for both of us. Sometimes, for whatever reason, things don't work. Maybe that's how it is between you and Marie."

"You're suggesting I quit on her?"

"Nothing wrong with a little persistence. I'm just saying you should probably analyze the situation pragmatically and then decide what you really want to happen. In the end, some things can't be fixed."

Jalen allowed her words to make an impact, but said nothing more for several minutes. The silence stretched and thinned as the Monday morning hoopla progressed. "Maybe it was the hit on the head. Still spinning."

"If that hadn't happened, then we might not have found out about this whole angle with Stanger and Indonesia," she said. "So thank you."

Without so much as cracking a smile, Jalen said. "Happy I could oblige. Maybe tonight I can get my leg broken so we can figure out who's pulling the strings."

"That's supposed to be good luck."

Simpler small talk filled the corridors as they walked. She said something about wafers, Jalen chimed in with his opinion, and then without much warning, they shifted to discuss the weather and the news. This lasted them the remainder of their trip. They both brought back a cup of coffee and occasionally sipped.

When they entered, Marcus stood up, nodded at Kalee and then stared at Jalen. "Airport Security has Stanger tied up, but they won't hold him for long. What do you think we should do?"

"Convince him to go underground?" Kalee said.

Jalen shook his head. "He won't do that. We need to make him question his trip enough to call it off. I'll go hack that email address and see if I can get a message to him, hoping to reschedule."

"You think you can do that?"

He'll have some sort of encryption to bypass," Jalen admitted. "Once I figure that out, I own the place."

"Still no movement on the noose operation," Laurie said.

"Noose operation?"

Marcus nodded. "My idea. We decided we should have a code name. Essentially, what we're trying to do is hang him, right?"

Jalen couldn't be sure who spoke, but someone interrupted with an invalid point. "That's why Germany decided to call their blitzkrieg 'Beat the Crap out of France.'"

"We give this enough rope, he might hang us," Jalen said, thinking fast. He set his coffee down on the desk, grabbed the tablet, and said nothing more. He could set an example in this situation, and often this action succeeded in getting everyone to work without wasting time on meaningless conversation.

He sat down, took a sip of coffee, and went to the options application on the device. He stared at the menu list for several minutes before trying to decide how to tackle this problem. With the security apps already shut down, the risk of being bitten from a different angle seemed low.

Instead, he focused on building a mental map to the applications and how they were interconnected. Sketching the diagram on a sheet of paper seemed useful. He drew three circles with lines connecting all three. Inside the circles he wrote the names of the three apps. Next, he drew another circle he labelled data. How could he connect the fourth circle to the other three? Something had to be communicating with these apps and these apps had to store their data somewhere, even if only the apps could access the data.

On the side of the page, he scribbled the possibilities: hard drive, cloud, server, and remote.

The first location proved easy to crack into. He managed to bring up a coded notepad that should have stored all of the data from the apps. Even if one or more of the other options was in use, the hard drive would likely contain at least an echo.

The echo proved easier to find than the actual data. He scanned through the code relating to the three apps by separating them from the rest of the computer. By bringing them to a central point in the hard drive, the links became more defined. With that accomplished, he searched for backup files, thinking that somehow, the apps would eventually need to store something on the hard drive. He scanned by his 'abort' commands looking for more.

If some data had been erased, backup files could often be used to reconstruct the original data, unless the backup files were also deleted. Luckily, the backup files saved themselves every so often in a folder completely unconnected to the apps themselves. Sixteen backup files resided in a temporary folder. After so often, some backup files were programmed to delete themselves after so many days. This seemed to be the case because, otherwise, he would have found many times more than sixteen. He quarantined all these files and copied them into a folder he would later attempt to load onto his computer.

After more than fifteen minutes, Jalen crossed out the 'hard drive' option and considered eliminating 'server' and 'remote.' True to his intuition, the 'server' option had never been used. In fact the device seemed independent of network ties. The wi-fi had been enabled the whole time, but it connected to nothing. After verifying that nothing pointed to a network, Jalen crossed that off the list.

The other two options would be much more difficult to track down. The temporary folder was cluttered with a litany of different web pages, some with questionable behavioral traits, and some whose motives seemed more honorable. He recognized one page as the football-related message board that Cambridge had connected to at home. That site seemed the only website he'd accessed on both devices.

He couldn't rule out the 'cloud' option, so he attempted to bring up remote connections. Some applications could be used to monitor use of another device and thereby even control that device with the right discipline in place. It didn't look likely from the start, but Jalen pursued it anyway.

Almost an hour later, he crossed 'remote' off the list, which left possibly the most difficult road still open. When connecting to a cloud, security could be slim. The device could download a debilitating virus or encounter malware designed to remotely take control of the device and even hold its hard drive for ransom. Taking this route presented numerous perils which Jalen didn't dare face unprotected.

He grabbed the phone Cambridge had left and verified that the two devices had never been connected. The ridiculous firewall that attempted to mark everything as a possible virus would help to eliminate any threats on either device. He started by connecting the phone to his computer manually. He planned to use the phone's wireless signal to piggy back from. Without something backed up onto the computer, the connection would be shaky and more dangerous. He doubted that any malware could find its way through the cable into the Lynx security server.

He then plugged the tablet in as if to charge it. This would not allow him to access any data from the phone or the computer, but it was good enough to get the tablet to recognize the phone's signal. After testing the connection to make sure it worked, Jalen dug into the tablet's questionable past.

Two adult websites raised eyebrows, but Jalen doubted whether Cambridge would be reckless enough to allow that kind of site access to his info. Instead, he intended to use a more innocuous website. The message board seemed as good a starting place as any. The message board recognized the username and password to log him in automatically. After that, scanning through Cambridge's profile information was easy. Nothing in his browsing history or post count raised any suspicion, but he found a link embedded into some of his profile text. Hoping that clicking the link wouldn't download software to cripple the device, he swallowed hard.

"Here goes nothing."

The connection seemed to be secure. In the event of disaster, the phone would serve as a backup to the tablet. Jalen scanned the webpage and considered tapping one or two links. Then, he saw the golden connector. In the upper right portion of the screen a PDF link appeared. While PDF documents some considered notoriously unsecure, they could be used to house other information. Jalen tapped the icon to download the file. The file had already been accessed once before, because the device asked Jalen if he wanted to save over the existing one. He clicked 'yes' and found himself looking at something that wasn't a PDF. He had never had anything to do with the dark web, but there was no mistaking this page as just that.

"Holy shit," Jalen breathed.

"What's going on?" Kalee asked after a moment of silence.

"Cambridge was on the dark web, linked there by some message board he visited to talk football, which I doubt happened all that often. And he's not selling or buying anything."

Instead, the page was used for communication purposes. Jalen found no evidence supporting the theory that Cambridge had been talking to the delivery man but discovered that the page was used as a cloud where data could be securely uploaded and downloaded. This connection seemed to allow another device connected to the cloud to control the tablet. He found that only two other devices had been connected to this cloud.

"Let's make it rain, then," Jalen muttered.

And it rained. The trap Jalen had expected to pop up wiped out the connection to the phone's signal. If Jalen got lucky, he could stop the bleeding by disconnecting from the computer, which would leave an 'orphaned' window open. The connection would only be totally lost if he navigated away from the webpage.

With a little work, he established the base of connection, which tracked the signals of the other devices. Jalen noted the behavior and tried to mentally record the IP address. Using that, he was able to track its signal.

Assuming that the signal came from a local source proved foolish. Rather than staying put, the signal bounced around all over the globe, originating from Sri Lanka, traveling to South Africa, Norway, Russia, Indonesia, and then North Korea. In Korea, the signal disappeared entirely.

"You've got to be kidding me," Jalen said.

He noticed his computer screen flash again.

"Wait, did you see that?" Kalee asked.

"Saw it," Jalen said. "This son of a bitch is starting to infect our system." He unplugged both devices from the server, allowed their screens to go dark, and then stacked them on top of each other.

Right on cue, the firewall did its job by quarantining the virus and asking Jalen whether he wished to eliminate the threat. He clicked yes, and the damage ceased. He gulped hard, expecting Doc to storm through the office door at any moment.

"What happened?" Kalee said.

Jalen hesitated and stared at the devices. "This delivery man is a smart sonofabitch. He used the cloud to reroute his signal all over the world until it ended up in North Korea, probably to be swallowed up by the government there. Then the webpage downloads a worm that somehow made it onto my computer."

"Weird," she said. "I thought that flash was the end of us."

Jalen stared at the devices and allowed fear to swell within his veins. Whatever this was has just become exponentially more complex.

If humanity had long ago entrusted its own existence to computers, the machines were beginning to take over every aspect of life itself. In the future, people would bleed zeroes and ones as computers began to adapt to human behavior. Internet-enabled pacemakers, auto-programming insulin pens, and even brain wave receptors would begin to be hard wired into those foolish enough to allow it. Computers were invented to make life easier, but life was becoming so easy that some people literally needed computers to live. The vicious cycle would never end, not until the reign could reduce mankind to nothing but wires and hardware.

Kalee's concern, while not as steep as Jalen made it out to be, rang true. He gulped hard, sipped his coffee, and answered her. "Maybe it was."

# 23

# Cobalt Sixty

Less than an hour later as the hum of the computers seemed to escalate, Barry entered the office hoping for a break from patrolling the corridors. He looked exhausted, yet still ready to exert the work necessary to catch the delivery man. Kalee worked to find out who he really was, but he'd proven much more elusive than Burton Cambridge. Jalen believed that to mean something, but Kalee remained cautious.

"How's it going out there?" Jalen asked.

"Hectic as a Monday morning," Barry said. "But this isn't doing us any good. I've got three guys hunting in the tunnels and they haven't found anything. Davis did find the pipe that clocked you last night."

"Lot of hiding places. You checked places outside of the main tunnels?"

He shook his head slowly with a curl of his lip. When Jalen made eye contact, he shifted his eyes. "I think you might be getting a bit obsessive over this."

"Keep searching then," Jalen snapped.

"The man's gone, damnit. He took his truck and left campus. How do you think he'd get back?"

Before Barry could finish, the tablet emitted a ding. Jalen spun around, wild with anticipation, before approaching the device.

"That's gonna be a virus," Kalee said. "It seems like our delivery man is good at setting up traps online. If he can do that, sending a Trojan through email would be easy."

"I don't care if it's a virus." He scowled and lit up the tablet's screen. A single email had arrived in Cambridge's inbox. Jalen rushed to open it and then read the message aloud.

"Spartan team one, move to auxiliary. Disassemble unit and report back."

"It's coded," Jalen said. "What does it mean?"

Barry rubbed his forehead above his eyebrow. He stepped back toward his desk and appeared to stagger. Jalen shifted his stare to Kalee, whose fingers furiously typed on her computer. She only offered a half-second glance at Jalen. A spark seemed to ignite her eyes behind her glasses. Her hair swayed forward and backward as she battered the keyboard with even more furious strokes.

The office phone pulsed, adding to the clamor. Marcus sprung for it before Jalen could move a muscle. He spoke with short, muted sentences as if he were a doctor discussing the last wishes of a dying patient. A single nod indicated that something good had happened. Jalen watched as the conversation seemed to stall and then glanced at Kalee.

"He's not available," Marcus said. "No. He says he's in danger, and considering the circumstances, I'd say you believe him." He paused. "Absolutely, a lot has happened down here in the last twenty-four....Ten four."

Jalen stared back at him as if to prod him for answers. "BPD has got Stanger in custody and he's irate. Detective Lawrence—that's what he called himself—promised to be here by the end of the day to chew us a new one."

"Fill him in. Write a report and fax it."

Marcus started blazing away at his keyboard before Jalen finished speaking. He then turned to Laurie, who stared at him as if waiting for orders. He thought about speaking, but instead, tilted his side sideways and raised his index finger. He walked away down the small corridor that led to the file storage area, the printing room, and the server room. He punched in his access code to the server room and entered. Six large servers stood end to end against a wall. Another door provided mechanical and electrical access to the servers, which stood above a shallow raised floor using the same kind of removable tiles the clean rooms used. Jalen examined each of the machines, and decided that temporarily disconnecting them from the master servers housed below Building 11 was prudent. Using the control monitor, he disconnected them, and then examined the wiring just in case a physical disconnect became necessary. He didn't know the first thing about the wiring, but knew there had to be a way to do it without shutting down the entire network.

After checking his work for errors, he exited the room and went straight for the file storage room. He burst through the door and vaulted straight toward a bank of filing cabinets that flanked the far wall. The keys resided on a large ring they stored in a desk drawer. He unlocked several file drawers before finding the right one. The cabinet contained a mass of wires, a simple mounting kit, and two unused cameras, which had been decommissioned in favor of upgraded products just over a year ago. He searched for an installation guide and found it wedged against the back of the drawer. Removing the wires and the cameras, Jalen also found the driver disk and hurried back to Laurie's desk.

"You know how these work?"

"I'm not sure these are approved for use," she said, lowering her voice.

Jalen shook his head. "I don't care. Tell the boss to talk to me if he questions you about it. We're going to need some around-the-clock surveillance of the chemical vault. Can we get these set up?"

"I'll install the software," she said, thinking quickly. "If you bring a laptop down there, you can check to make sure they are connected properly. "They're remote capable, so not totally safe with our system."

"I know. But this is going to work."

She nodded and labored away with a fury she hadn't displayed during the week. In fact, Jalen didn't remember witnessing such dedication among his staff as right now. Either he was doing something right or they each understood their responsibilities and upped their game.

"We have problems," Kalee shouted, staring at Jalen.

He spun and ran to her.

"Underscore-John just used his email address to sign up for a mailing list to some online magazine. He's not in Indonesia."

"USA?"

She nodded. "The delivery guy is Martez Williams, works for United Transport under an alias. They keep his true identity under lock and key for some reason, I can't imagine why. I'll flag this to gate security right now."

"Do it."

*Ding.*

Jalen's spine stiffened, sending his back upright in a split second. Kalee stared at the tablet while Jalen rounded the desk to grab it. His heart leapt when he read the simple reply message someone named MZ1961 wrote. "They're onto us."

The tablet began to buzz and vibrate. His fingers clenched the tablet as his muscles began to tremble. With a sudden lurch, he flung it across the room, where it collided against a wall and went black. "Shit!"

"What the hell happened?" Kalee said.

"They know we're onto them! MZ1961 is Martez Williams!"

She shuddered, lowered her gaze, and stared at her screens. "But then who is Underscore?"

"Jalen?" Laurie had finished her work installing the drivers for the cameras. "We got them linked up. You want to see?"

He strode over to her and kicked the remains of the tablet aside. Adrenaline pulsed through his veins and a vicious headache began to spin in his brain. He glanced at her screen and waved his hand in front of the lens. "Good work. I'll get them mounted, and I need you watching my back. I'll have a light. If anyone comes, alert me by radio."

"Will do," she said.

Jalen grabbed the cameras and brought them over to his desk.

He arranged them side-by-side and looked up at Kalee. She rose from her seat and made her way around the desks, stepping carefully. Barry rolled his chair over to them to join in the conference.

"I have some concerns about this whole thing, man," Barry said. "This is dangerous as hell. We need to get law-enforcement out here immediately. I don't think you should do it alone."

"He's right," Kalee said. "We don't want you getting killed trying to be the hero."

"I'm no hero."

"This guy is bad news," Barry said. "He's got us right where he wants us and we're walking into another trap. Remember the Trojan? The spiders? If this guy rigged all that, there's no telling what he could be cooking up."

"Williams plans to bomb us," Jalen said. "We have to stop it. He already knows we've got Stanger secured. How many lives is this going to cost us?"

"Only one, if we are lucky," Barry said. "You want to work alone, then you got it. I'll watch your back, but after this, I'm done. I'll get a new job."

"What are you talking about?

"Jalen," Kalee started.

He glared at Barry and brandished a harrowing frown. That scar might never go away. The entire time, Jalen believed that Barry was on his side and wanted him to help.

When he released his stare at Barry, he quickly shifted his focus to Kalee. Fire pulsed in his heart, boiling the tension between them into steam.

"I believe you're doing the right thing," she whispered. "We're not about to stop you."

"I have to do it," Jalen said.

She hesitated, glanced at the broken tablet, and then back to Jalen's face, which Jalen thought might have been melting with the fury of his own emotions. "I'm not going to tell you to be...you know what. Let Beth go. You need this."

His frown erased itself as a powerful pang of regret seemed to swallow his heart. "I can't."

*Yes you can.* Beth's voice echoed in his brain. *Just follow your heart.*

Jalen stood up and tapped his foot, glancing away from Kalee every other second. Her eyes flashed with concern, radiant with power. Whatever she knew about three years ago, it was more than Jalen had thought.

Instead of following her advice immediately, Jalen launched a cold stare at Barry. "I do need your help," he said.

"Yeah?"

"Get with your friends in engineering. Ask them if they can disconnect our servers from the main."

"Are you crazy?"

"It's a precaution," Jalen said. "If they decided to attack us where they know they can get us, we can limit the damage to only this room. I've disconnected already, we just need to unplug entirely. Think you can do that?"

He nodded. "This is going to set Doc off, you know that. You were skating on thin ice already, so it's been nice knowing you. Send me a postcard from wherever you land."

"Marcus," Jalen shouted. "How's that fax coming?"

"Just sent it," he said.

Jalen grabbed a poly tote bag with the Lynx logo plastered all over it and gently lowered the cameras and the wires into it. He walked back to the storage room and found a set of tools that would help him get the job done. He would be able to find an unused flood light and an idle ladder in the dungeon. He pushed the tools into the tote along with the mounting equipment, and then carefully wedged his laptop into the bag.

With ice pouring through his veins, he turned to Kalee, who had stood up and started walking back to her desk. "I'll be back. Have some good news waiting." Then he glanced over at Laurie.

"I won't let you down," she said.

When he turned back to the door, his gaze drifted across Kalee's expression. It seemed all wrong for the situation. Instead of what she normally displayed, emotion seemed to dance at the corners of her mouth. The damage had been done. When he closed the door to the office, he studied his memory of her expression. Interest and concern had been replaced by the swaying strands of horror and despair. She never let her guard down. But this time, something seemed different as if an untold concoction of energy had touched her and transformed her into someone he hardly knew.

Lunch had come and gone without Jalen even realizing that precious moments had passed. The office seemed locked in some sort of time capsule where life erased hours within what seemed like only a few minutes.

His heart became an unsteady isotope of some reactive substance that could only be synthetically produced. Its power lunged at him from unexpected caverns within his soul. Everything changed before his eyes. Everything he knew and had taken so long to assemble had begun to crumble into billions of tiny pieces, as if each atom of his heart was being ripped away from the whole.

Life always went on. Somehow. But not the way it had always been. The forces of change cascaded freely through him, bending the laws of everything he thought he knew. What had Kalee's expression meant? Would Barry really leave him?

Kalee had mentioned Beth by name. Three years had seemed to transform his memory into something where faces didn't always match up with names. He hadn't heard anyone speak her name and indeed hadn't thought her name in more than two years. Now that it came back around, it gouged a crater in his heart, the likes of which he could not climb out.

Facing the world and the horrors it unleashed once came with little effort. Today, it resulted in annihilation.

Dozens of workers filed through the corridors, pushing carts, sharing small talk, laughing, and squeaking their heels. They had no idea. To them, life resumed, unaffected by the torrent of events that shredded Jalen's mind. Maybe he would need the shrink, and maybe not, he thought.

He rounded the corner into the narrow hallway that led to the underworld—the industrial underbelly of Lynx Technologies. The noise from the main corridor drifted away and he relished the silence as he walked.

Behind that blank door, energy surged through the dark. He gulped hard and swung the door open.

# 24

# Cat's Eye

Warm air blasted him, causing him to close his eyes. An eerie glow pulsed from somewhere out of view as Jalen stared into the pit. Giant ducts and a bank of pipes rose up the wall close enough to the stair landing to touch. He slung the bag over his shoulder, peered into every corner, and then crept down the metal grate stairs. The maze of piping appeared, followed by the pumps and blowers that paralleled the opposite side of the wall. Jalen looked both directions when he approached what he would have defined as a corner.

The scant light stretched toward the end of the narrow tunnel, causing it to disappear on the horizon. The pipes and ducts at the far end seemed to meld together into a shimmering orange glow. He squinted and stared. Across the way, where the large intersection area stood, Jalen heard a beeping sound. A worker wearing a hard hat rode a motorized lift and stopped to stare up into the mass of piping.

Jalen attempted to wave at him, but the man didn't pay attention. The widest portion of the tunnel, where the bay door punched a hole in the wall, looked like a better-lit junction of two freeways. Every pipe led in that direction. Jalen lowered his head and slinked along the wall in the shadow of the large pipe bank he'd followed before.

This afternoon, no mysterious figures stalked these tunnels. Jalen took it all in, careful to look in every shadow should the delivery man emerge once again. This time, he wouldn't run the risk of leaving Jalen alive.

The small opening that led into the parallel corridor exuded only dark. Beyond that darkness, the floor sloped downward toward the doors to the chemical vault. Jalen shuffled across the expanse of floor space before approaching the welding area. He heard he clink of tools on concrete, stood back and tried to peer into the cracks in the lead curtain. Someone shuffled in there, oblivious to Jalen's presence. He swallowed, wiped a bead of sweat from his forehead and peaked behind the curtain.

The worker stopped what he was doing and, still clutching a tool, stared at Jalen.

"Security," Jalen said. "Show me your badge."

Jalen grasped the grip on his weapon as the man leaned over to place his heavy tool on a mobile work bench that also supported a set of blueprints. He reached behind the overalls he wore and displayed his badge. Jalen squinted and examined it.

Already knowing the answer, Jalen asked, "Seen anybody lurking around here or heading down this little walkway here?"

"Just me," the worker said. "Fabbing up a run of solvent vent line, needed to follow the line."

Jalen nodded. "Got a light?"

The man felt his overalls where his breast pocket should have been, then looked sideways, apparently wondering why Jalen asked for a smoke.

"Floodlight," Jalen said.

A look of relief crossed the man's face. He relaxed his shoulders and let the badge dangle around his shoulders. "Seen one across the hall about a football field down on the right." He pointed and narrowed his eyes.

"Ladder?"

"Beats me. There's usually one across the way right there. A couple guys been doing some painting over there lately. Make sure you got a flash-light."

Jalen understood and made his way toward the darker corridor he'd seen the delivery man enter before he explored the corridor to the vault. A set of double doors separated the main tunnel from the side tunnel. He shoved the door open with his shoulder and pulled his taser. He readied himself to fire in case he needed to.

The dark enveloped him. A fluorescent light hanging from a chain in the middle of this dusty tunnel scattered its dim light through the area. This tunnel housed multiple banks of pipe that seemed to scatter in all directions. Piles of tarps, rags, painting equipment, hard hats, and maybe even rodents littered the floor along the wall, where several pipes stubbed out of the concrete floor and dead-ended. A crowbar leaned against the wall next to a paint sprayer.

The painted portion of the corridor seemed small, but Jalen found a door that led into what might have been described as a small, makeshift office. The door stood ajar and Jalen kicked it open, ready to flood the room with his flashlight. More dead-ended pipes stubbed through the concrete at various locations around the empty room. In one corner sitting above a folded-up tarp, a paint-splotched metal ladder extended about ten feet to where only a few squares of drywall obscured the overhead piping. In the opposite corner stood a small, portable floodlight with a stand made of flimsy steel tubing. He shuffled across the tarped floor, grabbed the floodlight by the handle, and dragged it toward the ladder. He clenched the flashlight in his teeth as he folded the ladder and held it ready. He had stashed his bag along the wall near the door. Again peering in all directions, he propped the door open and hauled out the ladder and the floodlight.

A narrow tunnel jutted off just across from the room. It extended around fifty feet into a realm of blackness. Jalen thought he saw some plumbing equipment down there, but only shone the light in that direction for a split second. Gazing into this dark realm was like staring into an abyss where escape loomed as a remote possibility. He clutched the ladder under his arm and swung his head to illuminate the tunnel.

This tunnel took a hard right just ahead. A steel ladder ascended one wall into a den of black. The rectangle of dark seemed to push through the substructure to whatever building he lurked under. That trench probably extended hundreds of feet and carried an array of piping. It looked similar to the trench where Jalen had found Cambridge's body.

A faint clinking noise interrupted the distant drone of equipment. "Anybody down there?"

No answer came.

He turned around and strode through the dirty hallway with the ladder under his arm, his bag slung over his shoulder, and the floodlight in his hand. His teeth began to ache from the cold steel of the flashlight handle. When he pushed out into the main tunnel, the curtain opened and the worker named Tom emerged carrying what appeared to be a clipboard. He rushed past Jalen and nodded at him as he searched for the stairway. Jalen peeked behind the curtains once again and saw that the welder was turned off. A plastic caution sign stood next to the curtain warning passersby of danger and noting the requirement of hard hats and safety glasses.

Wasting no time, he plunged into the dark, rounded the bend, and then descended the incline toward the vault. Jalen elected to position one camera facing the entrance to this tunnel. He dropped his gear and let the ladder crash into the concrete. Searching the wall for an outlet, Jalen once again thought about what Kalee's expression might have meant. Did she know more than he did? Or was she just being careful while trying to contain Jalen's rage? Numerous possibilities existed, but Jalen valued Kalee's presence in the office. She excelled at what she did without Jalen having to ask her for anything.

The outlet was bolted to the wall ten feet away from where Jalen parked the ladder. He wedged the metal cover open and then plugged in the thick round cord.

The light sprung to life, illuminating a sufficient portion of the corridor, but leaving the area between the pipes and the ceiling in shadow. He erected the ladder quickly and then clutched the mounting bracket and the heavy screws. He climbed up about seven feet so that the camera was positioned above eye-level but no so high that Laurie couldn't see anything.

Pushing the bracket against the wall, he drilled four holes in the concrete. He checked to make sure the camera would swivel properly in case his installation angle deviated from the angle necessary to view the vault door. After verifying that adjustment would be possible, he grabbed four metal pins encased with plastic. Small barbs extended away from the pin shaft at an angle. Jalen had heard these pins called Hiltis, but couldn't remember where that came from. It seemed like a brand name, but Jalen couldn't be sure.

When the mounting plate was secure, he descended the ladder and grabbed the camera. The cord coiled around a painted metal bracket at the back end of the device. After unraveling it and determining that it was long enough to plug into the outlet, he carefully screwed the camera down to the plate. He then swiveled it and aimed it directly toward the entrance to the tunnel, so that it would record any intruder.

Jalen plugged the camera into the outlet and made his way toward the door, again searching for an outlet. The light from the floodlight reached this area, so he only needed to reposition the base and the angle of the bulb. After finding the outlet, he dragged the ladder toward the pipe the intruder used to club his skull in. Just above where he'd fallen, he positioned the ladder, climbed the steps and drilled the holes.

The light didn't seem to be bright enough or abundant enough to do the trick, but Jalen didn't care as much as he should have. He wrung his hands when the bracket was secure. Another faint clinking sound interspersed with pump motors. He looked up toward the entrance to the tunnel just as a shadow moved and fell still. His heart sunk.

He grasped the taser and pointed it toward where the shadow moved. "Hello?"

Of course, no one answered. Whoever had been watching him kept their distance and remained bathed in shadow for as long as Jalen stared. "Shit," he whispered.

He plugged in the camera and then placed his laptop on the floor. The intranet signal was just strong enough to connect the cameras. After making sure both cameras were turned on and accessing the network, he punched in the access code to make sure the closed loop system worked properly. These cameras could be tampered with, but the point in installing them was to protect the physical and personnel assets of Lynx Technologies. Camera one, which pointed at the entrance, produced a sharp image on Jalen's screen. He nodded and looked in that direction, then glanced at the screen. A shadow moved across the camera and disappeared.

Ice poured through his veins. "Show yourself!"

No one emerged from the dark.

He pushed the radio button and addressed Laurie. "Did you see that?"

"It's working," she said. "Camera two ready?"

Jalen stared at the screen and connected the second camera to the network. Again, something moved in front of the screen.

"Goddamnit, I'm armed!" Jalen screamed. "Come out or I'll shoot."

*That little taser? I got one shot.*

"Laurie," he said, pressing the button on the radio.

"I see it," she said. "Good work."

"Did you see what passed in front of the camera?"

"I think it was a dangling cord," Laurie said. "Clear it out of the way and you're good to go.

Jalen gazed up at the area in front of the camera. He checked to make sure the motion sensing abilities of the cameras were activated before moving. A small wire seemed to block part of the camera's lens. He dragged the ladder back up the slope and inspected it. As he pushed the wire out of the way, a drilling noise pierced the dark.

"This isn't going to work, you son of a bitch!"

A flash of light scattered in the dark above the pipes. Electrical energy crackled around a loose wire that rested in a gap between two disconnected ends of galvanized conduit. Jalen tried to follow where the conduit led but lost it in shadow. If that wire served the outlets and it carried more energy than intended, it could send a surge through the wiring and disable the cameras.

The clinking sound of metal on concrete continued, followed by the howl of some other distant piece of equipment.

"Tom, is that you?"

The conduit sparked again. He stood up, crept along the wall, and unplugged the floodlight with his foot. Darkness encroached from all sides. He shuddered. The howl returned and intensified. Holding his weapon at the ready, he made his way up the ramp. When he reached the jog in the wall, he gulped hard to gather his nerves. With a swoosh, he flung himself into the darkness, ready for a fight that somehow didn't start.

The howl grew louder until it could shatter his eardrums. The glow of molten metal and sparks flickered behind the curtain. "Tom?" He yelled as loud as he could.

Briskly, he gripped the curtain and thrust it open. The arc welder blazed with energy as it shot sparks at Jalen. He made his way around the perimeter, keeping his eyes focused on the obscured walls behind banks of piping. The arc welder fell off the table just as Jalen lunged to turn it off. With a huge crash, it sounded like something had broken. Jalen waited until the nerves settled, attempting to extract human-caused sound from the mechanical groan of electric and pneumatic motors.

Jalen searched the portions of the tunnels within his view for the welder. "Son of bitch," Jalen said only loudly enough for himself to hear above the pitch of the motors.

He looked around. Someone moved across the way, lurking in the dark where the double door led to the office where Jalen had found the ladder. He darted around the back side of the curtain and waited. Jalen stared into the dark, trying to make out the figure.

"Campus security," he yelled. "Come out with your hands up!"

The figure seemed to dissipate in darkness. "I know you're here, you crazy shit! You can't hide." The man slinked away into the dark. Jalen sprinted across the way with his taser and flashlight held high. Plunging into the humid dark produced a row of sweat on his forehead. He breathed heavier as he became aware of a lingering pain in his knee that had resulted from crashing into Lieutenant Marlon in the halls outside the chem lab. He limped but kept running until the corridor ended.

Smaller branches fed off this tunnel in narrow, shallow trenches that ran perpendicular to the main corridor. No light emerged from any of them.

"You're trapped now!"

A ghostly echo sounded behind him. He spun on his feet to come face to face with what he could only describe as a bat. The nocturnal kind. He shooed it away and spun around. "Goddmnit, I'll kill you!"

Silence. The bat swooped overhead and then dove into one of the dark trenches.

"Barry get somebody down here! We've got an intruder!"

The radio crackled. "Ten four, backup on the way."

Jalen relayed where he was, exited the hallway and slung the door shut. In the absence of a device, he could use to block the door from swinging open, he sprinted back toward where the cameras observed the vault.

"See anything yet?" he asked Laurie.

"Negative, just a flash of light or two every now and then," Laurie said. "You okay down there?"

Jalen gulped. Sweat poured down his face and his body trembled. He peered out of the dark waiting for anyone to emerge from the doors. Less than a minute passed as he attempted to calm his nerves. "I'm not alone," he said, gasping for breath.

Seconds later, a roar erupted from a room adjacent to the main tunnel. He clutched his weapon and sprinted in that direction.

# 25

# Shadow of Io

Jalen's vision of the scene undulated like dim light blurred with rain. He flung himself into the shadow of the pumps, slinking along the wall as the noise made his head spin. Shuffling sideways to avoid colliding with a set of pipes vertically arranged on the wall, he peeled his eyes. On instinct, he looked back at the welding station and the double doors across the way. Due to the angle and the mechanical equipment, he could no longer see the doors. So far, no one had emerged from the dark.

More than one person had to be playing him right now. He spun around a loose assortment of pipe fittings, scooted along the concrete wall, and then climbed a three-foot-high concrete platform that moored six blowers. Ducts large enough for a fully-grown man to walk inside stacked through square holes in the concrete ceiling. No light filtered through the remaining portion of the hole, but Jalen guessed that some kind of flashing had been installed to separate the air masses of the two spaces.

In the top of the platform, a small sink lay flush with the concrete. The drain routed through the concrete to presumably underground. To avoid tripping on the sink, he sidestepped without accounting for a metal duct that descended through the ceiling and swooped left into a sort of header that fed the blowers. His head collided with the metal and he staggered. The pain rocked his skull until he could regain his balance. The hum of motors grew louder with each step.

Jalen leapt from the platform, keeping his knees bent to avoid destroying his legs. The landing opened up to a large expanse of floor that housed several different types of equipment in addition to mechanical pumps. He sprinted into the room, feeling a batch of hot air blast him from above. He stretched out of the way and looked up into a grille at the bottom of a duct. The room seemed to be vacant.

"Anybody here?"

"Of course they're not going to show themselves," Jalen said to himself.

Once again believing that he had the room sealed, he lurked in the shadows against the wall and made his way to a long piece of equipment fed by several smaller pipes. Along the wall, a series of electrical panels stood as if united for a common goal. One or two of the panels sprung conduits of various sizes out the tops. The conduits spread out and then regrouped into a common rack that trailed a group of pipes and headed out toward the main tunnel.

Jalen observed the glory of years of mechanical construction, the product of which he'd worked in for more than three years without realizing how industrial the campus was.

A dripping pipe overhead produced a puddle on the floor, which Jalen found himself standing in. The water formed a tiny creek that flowed straight toward a drain in the floor. He couldn't tell what kind of liquid had been dripping, but it seemed to be a construction error. The seal between a coupling joining two ends of pipes dripped. The metal was corroded badly enough to warrant reconstruction.

He scanned the floor around him and saw that some of the concrete floor around the panels had been ground smooth. Jalen's disturbance in the water caused just enough of the liquid to flow across the smother portion of the floor toward one of the panels.

A small gutter flanked the perimeter of the panel, extending about an inch thick. The gutter housed a piece of steel to which the frame of the panel was bolted. But for a tiny gap in the metal, the wiring penetrating the floor into the bottom of the panel had been isolated. Jalen dove toward the gear to stop the water, but too late. Inside of the metal, the wires sparked. The odor of decay seemed to burn around him. A single spark floated through the crack and fell into the liquid.

Fearing electrocution, Jalen attempted to roll out of the water. Before he could move, flames engulfed him.

"Oh, shit!" he screamed to no one.

He rose to his feet and ran headfirst at a blank portion of the wall between the panels. The electrical charge had ignited the liquid into a sheet of fire. The flames licked at his ankles, singeing hairs and charring the fabric of his clothes. Slamming his shoulder against the wall produced a cascade of pain that seemed to numb his entire arm. The fire on the floor had spread. If it reached the pumps, they could explode.

He rolled himself across the wall until the fire in his clothes was extinguished. What remained of his clothing smoldered. Jalen sprinted toward the pumps to stop the advance of the flames, somehow. Somewhere in this cavern a fire extinguisher decorated a wall, but he could not see it. The flames spread near the pumps and began to die without leaping onto the pads and starting a massive electrical fire. Without thinking he sprinted toward the entrance to the room at what appeared to be a narrow notch between banks of piping. This little corridor led back to the main tunnel.

Trying to think hard, he dashed back toward the double doors across the way from the vault, crouching low into the shadows where he could. The scene had erupted in chaos. Flashlights swirled around in the dark, Illuminating barren patches of concrete walls that were stained with leaking liquid. The pain in his scalp seemed to spread. His ears had grown numb from the growl of equipment in the pump room and the deafening roar of the blowers.

Both of the men carrying flashlights had emerged from the tunnel where Jalen had installed the cameras. They shrugged when they saw Jalen sprinting toward them.

"No one's here," Marcus shouted.

"Bullshit! He ran in there." Jalen pointed at the double door. Sweat seemed to boil on his skin.

"The hell happened to you?"

"It was another trap,' Jalen said, knowing that further explanation would delay their attempt to catch the intruder.

They burst into the dark corridor, kicking painting equipment away and then invaded the office. A quick search revealed no one, and they dispersed into the various tunnel arms. Jalen turned left just across the corridor from the office. This particular tunnel looked like a dead end, but Jalen managed to squeeze through a gap separating a water heater from a nearby wall. After pushing past the equipment, he found himself in a chamber that smelled like gas and the carcasses of several decaying rodents. The narrow tunnel took a hard right and then jogged left again. A bank of piping penetrated the slab above and scurried down the wall. Two of the pipes continued underground while several others branched off and reduced themselves into nothing but clear plastic tubes.

Considering that this tunnel had been constructed for such a simple purpose, Jalen swallowed hard. He spun around and twirled the flashlight in circles. Above him something dripped onto his face.

"God, not again," he groaned.

The droplet of water cooled his skin, but Jalen didn't feel it again. He looked up into the nothingness. Yes, bats could live in here, he decided. Give them some way into the tunnel and they'd thrive in the environment.

Jalen made his way back and squeezed between the water heater and the wall. As he shuffled, something touched his foot. Angling his flashlight down with a sudden twitch, he pushed against the water heater. Something lurked and then he saw it. Several hairy legs brandished themselves in his direction. Hundreds of eyes. "Oh, hell no!"

The spider crawled across his shoe. He flung his foot, hoping the insect would fly through the air away from him, but those sticky legs held on. And then it climbed. Jalen struggled to squeeze through the gap, pushing with all his might on his other leg as though the spider immobilized him.

"I'm gonna need backup," he said to himself.

When he'd wedged himself free, the spider asserted its power and began to climb up his pant leg. He kicked it away with his free foot and slammed it against the wall. "Get off me!"

He emerged from the side tunnel breathing heavy and darting his eyes in all directions, expecting more of them to pour out of hidden catacombs and press him into a corner as he screamed for help. The void seemed to answer his plea. The walls seemed to close in around him. Suddenly, the chamber became tight and constricted. The main tunnel did not offer much more light. The light that did leak through the open double doors grew faint as the rays bent. Flashlights could only reveal pieces of the puzzle.

He stepped past the tarps and painting equipment and sunk himself deeper into the void. Bats, spiders, rodents. Everything you'd expect underground below an industrial facility. Not only did they slink though the dark, it seemed as if the dark had instigated a certain gigantism effect that made the creatures grow to more than twice their normal size.

The hairs on the back of his neck tingled. He swatted at himself, danced, and then darted into the darkness when a flashlight showed the way.

Barry stared at him. "A little paranoid?"

"Wha...? Shut up, it's not funny."

"I didn't think so. There's no one here. You imagined the whole thing."

"The hell I did."

Marcus emerged from a trench and climbed down the ladder. His eyes seemed bloodshot as if he'd seen a ghost.

"Something's not right down here," he said.

Barry scoffed. "You guys are out of your minds. I'm going back to the office."

Jalen growled and stepped toward him. As his muscles tensed, the glow of the flashlight spun in erratic circles. He could pierce Barry's mind with his gaze he was sure. "Goddamnit, I saw him down here, Jalen said. Williams was here. He's who attacked me, and he's found a real good hiding place, I'd say."

Glancing back and forth between them with a scathing air of defiance cutting across his frown, he allowed his heart to sink. Could it be possible that Barry was onto something?

Then it dawned on him. "Holy shit, what building are we in.?"

"Under, Marcus corrected him. Guessing from some of the valves in that trench, I'd say maybe 18?"

"He got into a clean room somehow. Some of these older buildings don't have subfab spaces, some do."

"Sure about that?" Barry said.

"Didn't just disappear into thin air," Jalen grated. "I know it."

Barry sighed and stepped backward as Jalen grasped his radio and turned around.

"Kalee, you there?"

"I'm here."

"Lock down all cleanrooms in Buildings 15, 17, and 18. Please."

"What about 20? Marcus chimed in.

Without turning to face him, Jalen spit out an answer before the answer revealed itself to him. "Twenty doesn't have a cleanroom."

"Got it," she said. "Working on it now."

"Thanks, Kalee."

"Gotten all soft now?" Marcus said. "It doesn't seem like you. Tell me, what have you done with my boss? He's bald, black, sort of looks like you, but kind of a hardass."

Jalen pushed the radio back onto its clip on his belt and glared at Marcus. Marcus had been scanning the chamber and only raised his light when it became apparent that Jalen wasn't going to answer him.

"Just kidding around," Marcus said. "'Sides, you wouldn't want her and she sure as hell wouldn't want you. Word has it she's..."

Barry shushed them, pointed his light at the floor and pointed toward the double doors. Jalen could see just enough to make out the shadow of his finger. The doors began to slowly pull closed.

Without exhaling a word, Barry crept toward the door as the square of light reduced to a sliver. Water dripped on them from overhead. Sweat beaded on Jalen's brow. The pipes overhead seemed to groan with a sullen lurch like the gasp wedged between two painful sobs. A twitch at the back of Jalen's leg caused him to jump, but he didn't whisper anything. One by one, they drew their weapons.

Barry grasped the door handle and flung it open wildly. It crashed against a makeshift rail that protected a pair of metal conduits on the wall. The three of them vaulted from the dark, ready for the attack.

"Shit! Damn!"

Jalen lowered his weapon. The welder had returned from his break and seemed to be looking for some supplies. Why was he closing the door? "Seen anything?"

"Just got back from engineering. This door don't normally stay open, didn't see anyone inside, so thought I should close it. You guys scared the Jesus out of me."

Marcus reached into his pocket and pulled out a folded sheet of paper. He quickly unfolded it and showed it to the welder, who looked confused. Jalen stared at the face of Williams. Kalee must have printed out the picture and gave it to Marcus before they rushed to join Jalen in the tunnels.

"Seen this guy around anywhere?"

"Nope. Been working down here off and on Friday and today, but I never seen him before."

Jalen nodded at him and trudged back toward the stairs that led up to Building 27. His shadow seemed to stretch and morph with other versions of itself as he walked. The dreary lights battered him from all sides. The dark within him glowed red hot, searching for a crevice through which it could escape. His muscles trembled.

As he closed his eyes, the lights pressed against him, warming his flesh. For the moment, all was golden. Foam rose to the top of a glass. The liquid sparkled in the dim light. She was there, sitting across the bar. Her face and hair glowed as golden as the liquid, reflecting the dim light. If humans could carry halos, she must have carried hers in her purse. Her smile flashed in his mind and then disappeared.

Was it Beth or the beverage? His facial muscles drooped. A concoction of both wormed its way through his heart, scavenging for bits of darkness on which it could prey. *God*, he thought. *Make it stop.* He clenched his fist muscles, shoved the memory away, and then pictured himself sitting at the bar alone. Instead of beer, clear vodka filled his glass. His sorrows seemed to reflect on the surface of the drink. The effect would be instant and gratifying. It was the only thing that could dull the pain and keep it at bay.

Jalen shuddered at the thought and climbed the stairs, wiping a band of sweat from his forehead. *You need it. Take a sip.*

# 26

# Particle Collider

When Jalen pushed the door to the tunnel open, the light seemed to drill into his corneas. He couldn't see for several moments as his eyes adjusted to the light. His head began to throb again. After walking crooked for a half-minute, Jalen's eyesight gradually sharpened. Rather than saunter back to the office in defeat, Jalen shortened his stride and worked his legs briskly. He imagined he must have looked ridiculous, but he soon came to realize he wasn't the only one hustling through the corridors.

The office buzzed with life. He violently swung the door open and stomped toward his desk, unaware of his frown. Kalee looked up at him, but diverted her gaze out the window. Instead of addressing the few who labored away at their desks, he walked straight to his chair and sat down. He covered his face with his hand and noticed Kalee looking at him again.

"Are you okay? What happened?"

"Another trap," Jalen replied. "Walked right into it too. How the hell does this keep happening? One minute I'm chasing the guy who killed Cambridge, next I'm on fire."

"You've been on fire from the start," Laurie sneered.

Jalen shot her a wry glance.

"One more booby trap and I think I'll go postal."

Kalee leaned forward, resting her chin on her open palm with her elbow on the table. The light from her screen danced on her glasses. She stared for a half-second too long before an uncomfortable twitch emerged in his wrist.

"Log onto your IM, I want to show you something."

He raised one eyebrow and, leaning back, he punched in his password. The messenger immediately notified him that Kalee was typing as her fingers began to tap on the keys.

> You told me you wanted good news. I think I have it :).

"Smiley face? Really?"
She didn't look up. Her fingers pounded the keys and paused.

> Just listen. I was working out some things with Underscore, and I think I found him. Let me show you.

Jalen sighed and waited while Kalee tapped another message. Instead of offering more words, she sent him an image that looked like a snapshot of her screen, which had a small map tucked away in the corner.

> That's where he is?

Kalee caught Jalen's attention by putting an index finger to her lips.

> They might be listening. I saw that flash again.

Crossing his ankles and letting his wrist twitch again, Jalen typed another message.

> I see. And they have no idea how to read our IMs. Good idea.

> Sarcasm? Really?

"Well," Jalen fumbled.

> I think Martez Williams has been hacking us.He's on site.Hence the charred clothes.

> It's probably easier to hack from on campus, anyway. There are lots of

"Shut up," Kalee warned.

Jalen crossed his wrists and stared at her. His expression probably looked wary and a little flighty, but it didn't matter. "Give me a break, talking by IM while we're sitting right across from each other is weird."

She stretched her fingers and began typing.





Her fingers blazed across the keyboard. Her face seemed frozen in a furious state and for a moment Jalen wouldn't have been surprised if he saw steam shoot from her nose. For the next several seconds he glanced back and forth from her to his screen.

His cursor started to move.

"Just watch," Kalee said blankly.

The mouse moved over an icon in his task tray. When it sprung open, Jalen found himself watching a video. The video showed the screen changing from a webpage to the same signal tracking software Jalen had used to try to track down the communication between Williams, Cambridge, and Underscore.

Jalen typed another message.



She didn't respond.

The video showed Underscore's web activity. His signal was only mildly encrypted and only rerouted through several North American servers, none in Asia. Jalen continued to watch and his heart began to pump faster. When the signal stopped bouncing around, it seemed to land somewhere in the metro area. The recording then showed the IP address linked to a GPS, which showed the location of the signal. Jalen eyed it and compared it to the small map on Kalee's screen shot.

> They always trip up somewhere.

> I think I'll have Doc get you a raise.

"You don't have to…"

"Thank you," Jalen said, trying a little too hard to indicate sincerity. He closed the IM chat and the video and pushed away from his desk. He spun around when the office door opened.

Barry entered, looking somewhat dazed. "Son of a bitch is like a ninja."

"Cleanrooms are locked down," Kalee said.

"Yeah, Marcus and another guy are checking them out. I think we'll have this Williams guy sitting in our chairs in fifteen."

"Unless he manages to escape, just like Cambridge," Jalen argued.

"I paid that welder guy five bucks to watch the tunnels. There's no other way out."

"You idiot!"

"I trust him," Barry argued. "I don't think he's in on it and he's got a pretty good weapon at his disposal. You can do a lot of damage with one of those welders."

"Tell me you got engineering to help with that issue," Jalen said, staring at him.

"Yeah, Hank, one of the electrical guys came and unplugged it. This office is now independent. Five bucks says Doc walks through that door within ten and fires your ass."

"Tell him to call me," Jalen said.

"You quitting?"

"Jalen," Kalee said. "I really don't think this is a good idea. I already called the cops. Don't go alone."

"The cops?"

"They'll let you help them question Underscore; I told them to."

"What if you were wrong?"

"Don't make me tell you to be—"

Jalen sighed and stared at her. "I will. Nothing's going to happen to me. I've got my weapon, too. You can ping my phone, whatever you want to do. Then I'll get with the cops, and we'll grill the guy about Williams and this whole thing will be over. At the end, maybe some of us still have our jobs."

"Sounds like a decent plan," Barry said. "Let me come with you."

"No. Need you back here helping to bring in Williams and detain him."

A subdued exhale told Jalen all he needed to know. He grabbed his jacket, badge, and keys and departed.

A stinging sensation crept up his leg and a dry ache pounded at his skull. He attempted to pass Kalee a smile, but all he could communicate was lathered in pain.

The cool spring air bit at him. He programmed the address into his car's GPS and waited for it to bring up directions. This operation would require precision and an awareness to potential trap situations. Instead of listening to the sounds of the road, he turned on the radio and decided to take in some sad pop song about a girl regretting her choices. The next song talked about the sun and the moon.

His mind began to wander as he kept straight on the main boulevard leading away from Lynx toward the city center. In Switzerland they had some kind of facility where they tested atomic properties by launching parts of atoms at each other. The leaders of the physics field congregated there, testing theories and attempting to explain the grand scheme of things. The work had been fascinating, but rang hollow to Jalen. If they did determine the meaning of life, and even the makeup of every subatomic particle in existence, would it really change how Jalen chose to live? In there, cold emotion ruled. Those physicists were paid handsomely for their efforts. Their job description didn't entail wondering about consequences or emotional tolls, or even the state of humanity as it spiraled toward its own doom.

Jalen swallowed. Mankind's spirit, his compassion, and his energy were stored in a hard drive somewhere building the pieces into a complex imitation of life. It mapped its way toward a hole by inventing more and more procedures that removed the ability to make decisions. There was no need to act, if an application did it *for* man.

His phone began to ring. He picked it up, expecting to hear from Kalee but instead heard Lawrence blasting commands at random.

"We're *en route*," Lawrence said. "After that, we've got some talking to do, you and me. Stay there and don't do anything stupid. We'll find Martez Williams and charge him."

"I'm on my way," Jalen said.

"Goddamnit, no!"

"I don't care about your orders, *Detective*. Arrest me if you want, but it's my job to protect the workers and assets of Lynx Technologies."

"Turn around," Lawrence said.

"No."

Lawrence yelled something back, but Jalen didn't hear it. His motor revved as he pulled towards a stop light. The tires squealed on the pavement. Jalen slammed his foot into the brakes, but nothing happened. He tried the door handles with a furious twitch and then slammed his fist into the horn to warn other drivers that he was running a red light.

"This can't be…Oh God!"

Jalen fought the brakes and the accelerator but could not control the vehicle. He laid on the horn as the force of acceleration pushed him back in his seat. He forced the automatic transmission into Neutral, but the speedometer needle had already passed ninety. Only one thing could stop it.

He swallowed hard and slammed the shifter into reverse. The car lurched, spun, and launched Jalen forward. But the speed was insurmountable. Instead of skidding to a halt, the car spun sideways. The tires regained their grip on the pavement just as the transmission gave out.

Jalen swore and punched the vehicle back in gear, but there was nothing he could do. The tires squealed as the vehicle rolled backwards toward a fence. Jalen looked into the mirror, horrified. Between the fence and the boulevard, a canal cut a groove in the landscape. Its waters had risen to the brink just in time for the planting season.

He punched the brakes. Nothing. Trying to think fast, he whipped the steering wheel hard to his left. The car spun and Jalen screamed. The tires slammed into something hard, but the vehicle had built enough momentum to overcome the obstacle. Jalen sprung himself forward, reaching for the emergency brake.

The spin became a violent tumble. Shattering glass showered his face. A deep ache throttled his legs. The concrete gave way to a strip of desert cheat grass, still green from the rains. Terror gripped him. The roll folded the top of the car in in on itself. Acting on instinct, Jalen shielded his face.

The car bounced over the strip of grass and then a sharp downward motion took hold. The smashed windshield vaulted toward him. The roll had ceased, but Jalen heard a heavy splash as the car lost all momentum. Water flooded the interior of the car. Jalen gargled water, released his seatbelt and thrashed in the water. The car bagan to sink. Jalen's eyes slammed against his eyelids. Cold battered him. Writhing, he managed to slide through the window, which had been reduced to a narrow slot. He clutched the car as it flowed downstream with the water. When the bumper slammed into the concrete edge of the waterway, he released the car and grabbed at the branch of an overhanging shrub. Its roots strained but held him.

Panic set in. The world spun in slow motion. The scent of blood poured into his nostrils. Consciousness waxed thin in peril, but Jalen could not move. Rest. The world righted itself and pain slammed his entire body. How did this happen again? His phone was in the car, sunken and destroyed by water.

Sirens pierced the harrowing ebb of sound as it tumbled toward oblivion. Jalen found himself suspended in space, floating amidst the cosmos like a lone piece of refuse, yet he had no body. Nothing. Only atoms, protons, and electrons. Terror exerted the only emotion. Something, somehow had to give. Beth's voice echoed into the expanse of nothing as if programmed into his own nonexistent skull. *Be careful.*

# 27

# Quantum Revolution

Hope scattered like shards of glass fleeing the force of an explosive storm. Sirens flooded his eardrums in unison with the hammering of the headache. Vibrating, bouncing sensations burst through him every now and then, pushing him floating through an uncertain state of matter like a lifeless body ejected from gravity. His broken thoughts battered hard inside his skull, fighting a war they could not win.

Jalen contorted his facial muscles into an expression of shock lifted from a bad dream, but he could not open his eyes. Whatever he could perceive around him moved in slow motion. Sounds altered their frequencies so that beeps and bips sounded like wavering groans.

"Conscious buddy? Jalen?"

"Ugh."

"We're getting you to a hospital, just stay calm."

Instead of waking, his body gave into sleep. He lay his head back, feeling the pressure of the straps folding across his midsection. The pain in his skull seemed to slink away into dormant realms where silence remained a mystery. The squeaks of wheels and the clatter of medical instruments colliding with stainless steel rolled into one congealing mass of sound which Jalen almost believed he could cut through with a sword.

"Good work getting out of that car. What happened?"

Jalen could only mutter nonsense. He flexed his muscles, and felt the overhead lights batter his eyes from overhead. He turned his head and kicked his feet.

His eyes pried themselves open. Two doctors assisted him, while the machines monitored his vital signs. The machines that helped protect life were all wired together into a common network.

"Can you hear me Jalen? Can you see me?"

Jalen shook his head and flexed his neck muscles before shifting his feet and his arms. His clothing had been removed down to his waist and he donned a blue polka dotted smock. The Doctors watched the monitors while prodding him with instruments.

"The good news is you don't have any life-threatening injuries. Blood pressure's normal. Heart rate started a little off the charts but returning to normal."

If that was the good news, Jalen thought, the bad news would be something along the lines of his insurance failing to pick up the bill and forcing thousands of dollars of debt down his throat. *Pay it back or we'll take your care back. Fair is fair.*

"What's the bad news?"

"Ah. How do you like hospital food?"

Jalen attempted to push himself away from the bed. His mind wavered and his muscles weakened. "I got a case."

"What's that?"

Leaning back and frowning, Jalen partially sang his response. "The blues."

Neither of them laughed. "It's a good thing you were able to get out of that car intact. Otherwise, you'd be feeding fish in the Snake River right about now. But you get to live one more day, maybe two."

"Huh?"

"I'm good at telling jokes, too."

Jalen smiled but forced it away into an unfamiliar territory as the day's events caught up with him. He looked around, almost expecting to see pipes, angry co-workers, and computers. There were computers, each tied to him and connected to a network so people could watch him from other areas.

Ten minutes passed. Jalen tried to count the number of beeps the machine that monitored his heart made, just to check if mortality still floated through his body. He shifted when the door opened and two people rushed in.

Kalee hurried to his side, her hair bouncing near her shoulders. She deposited her purse next to a chair and sat next to him without speaking. Barry followed her. A look of defeat etched itself on his face. He stood a few feet away from Kalee and folded his arms.

"What happened?" Kalee asked.

"My car..." Pain flooded through his body and then ebbed. "The sonofabitch hacked my car."

"Bad bump on the head, doc?" Barry asked.

"I'm not lying, and it is possible. These days some crazy could hijack your coffeemaker and use it for his own gain."

"Yeah," Barry said. "That will do a lot of good. Who needs caffeine anyway?"

Kalee glared at him. "Cut him some slack, it's happened before. Most of the time you can assume people have good intentions or at least aim not to kill you."

"So a hacker crashed your car into a canal for you? Maybe possible, but how and why would they do that?" Barry gazed from Kalee back to Jalen and then stepped away all at once looking pensive.

"The cops are coming in the front door," Kalee said. "Led by your favorite."

"Deflect him for me," Jalen said.

"There won't be any need for that," Detective Lawrence said. Lawrence glanced at the doctors and squared his shoulders. His tie looked brand new and pristine. "I need a word."

"Nice outfit," Barry scoffed.

Kalee stared.

"Looks like you managed to track down this elusive...what's his name? Martez? That was nice work, but Williams wasn't there. We raided the house, kicked a few doors in, seized a computer and a passport, but didn't find anyone hiding in the bushes. It's clever."

"That was supposed to be Underscore," Kalee said. "I tracked him to that address. Now you're telling me Williams was supposed to be there?"

"His house," Lawrence droned. "No weapons, no killer, no evidence of his involvement, other than what your people are feeding us. Not to mention Mr. Stanger is going berserk."

"For his own good," Jalen said.

"We looked into that," Lawrence said, motioning for his partner in the hall to join him. "He had a few contacts over in Jakarta, but it doesn't look like anyone would be out to kill him. What do you think Jakarta has to do with it?"

Jalen sighed and relaxed his neck muscles. "Makes sense. The guy I found on the dark web seemed to be from Indonesia. Ironically, the same place Lynx has been trying to open up a production facility."

"What's his name?"

"He goes by Underscore John," Kalee said, flicking a strand of hair into position. She pushed her glasses up her nose and stared at Jalen instead of glancing at the detective. A flash illuminated her eyes. A certain peace seemed to reside there, and his subconscious mind reached out for it.

"No good," Lawrence said. "We can't just run off to Jakarta and arrest a guy."

"Not like you'd find him anyway," Jalen said.

Lawrence grinned. "You did."

A growl formed in his throat, but he chose not to release it. Instead, he let his eyes communicate his grief. "He's real good at hiding. Besides, I think he's here in the city somewhere."

"How would Williams be orchestrating all of this while running around campus?" Barry asked.

"There are ways," Jalen said. "That's the most likely, but you got him right?"

Barry looked down. "Well, uh..."

"Shit. Are you kidding me?"

Barry shifted his shoulders and stared at him. "He's good at hiding. Online and in buildings, especially big buildings."

"He's planning on bombing the chemical vault," Jalen said. "How do you just let—"

"Your cameras are still on and we got people watching them. He goes anywhere near there and we'll catch him in the noose you designed."

"How do you know that?"

Jalen looked puzzled. "Why's he hiding down there? I can think of maybe two people on the planet authorized to go into that vault. Williams isn't one of them."

Lawrence stepped closer to Jalen and leaned forward. Jalen groaned and stared at him but rolled his head a half inch away.

"I know about you," he whispered. "I know about your girlfriend, Marie. I know what happened three years ago, and that's what you're hiding from. You can tell a lot about a person by their past."

"You don't know shit," Jalen said.

"That's not something easy to live with. I made some phone calls. We can get you to release your demons, just tell me go."

"Go to hell."

Lawrence relaxed his shoulders and shook his head. "You got a good bump on the head. The doctor says you'll be good as new."

*Good as new?* Jalen pushed his head backward into the pillow. If only Lawrence knew what he was talking about. Then again, no one could understand the nature of life. A person can't just glue a broken teapot together and call it as good as new. When things fall apart, no repair can quite bring them back to their pre-disaster state. The laws of physics dictated that. Why was Jalen the only one who could see it that way?

"Detective," Kalee warned, seeing the trauma on Jalen's face.

Lawrence raised his palms, walked away, and then motioned his partner to join him. Together, they would exact a new plan hinging on Jalen's mental state to bring down the entire company.

"You did good," he said, staring at the ceiling.

Kalee scooted closer to him. Her warmth flushed through his hand and then vanished before he could begin to enjoy it. Conflict played out on her face. Jalen could see it without even glancing at her.

Madness had always bound the human species. Life had always been fragile and worth protecting even as mass bloodshed ruled the land and bodies piled up along riverbanks, in concentration camps, and in shallow graves. Yet madness could never fully take its toll. Madness caused destruction on all fronts. Nothing could stop its march as it moved to mow down every living soul in its path. Still, civilization had been known for its strong points. Enemies could be defeated, and they were.

Yet, a new evil always rose up, more prominent and powerful than the last. Just like everything else, humanity could never grow back to where it was before evil took hold. Life could only move one way. Had humanity really devolved into something so opaque and sick as what lied ahead? Technology had spawned a new enemy, one just as powerful, but more efficient and precise.

Motive had always lurked behind every node of madness, but with the new realm—the new reality mankind had constructed for himself, a killer needed only opportunity.

What was evil anymore anyway? A thin line had always separated good from bad, but time had managed to widen the line and to insert an expansive gray area. Discerning where some people stood lacked reason. Crossing the line had become too easy. Jalen didn't even know where he stood. Bring down the killer, save hundreds of lives, but at what cost? Did his actions root to a so-called moral ground, or did he simply act in his own interest, and seek to destroy his own past?

Kalee scooted away and glanced at Barry before resettling his gaze on the injured man. "We'll get him," she said. "I'm going to find Underscore for you."

"There are traps," Jalen said. "You just have to be...be..."

"I know."

"You get some rest, man," Barry said. "I really should have seen this coming, but maybe you should have too."

"Barry."

He turned to him and filed a helpless frown on his face.

"Thanks for coming."

"Thank Kalee. She drove."

Kalee stood without removing her eyes from his scarred face. An expression bordering on warm sincerity brushed against her face. Even in an environment devoid of color, she could flood a room with textures and warm tones.

"I'll see you tomorrow," she said. "Don't come back until you're ready. I'll hold down the fort and assume all responsibility. We'll get Williams."

Jalen watched her stride toward the door as she glanced down at her feet. She dragged her heels while keeping her arms motionless. Instead of speaking, he let his thoughts dwell on the point where life balanced between good and an ever-expanding ocean of evil. His eyes closed and he fell asleep.

What seemed like hours later, Detective Lawrence prodded his shoulder. Jalen scowled when he saw him, but Lawrence's demeanor had changed.

He looked livelier and more personable, like a real man instead of a cold, hard cop. Still Jalen trod carefully.

"I can understand if you don't trust me. But why don't you tell me the truth for once in your life? Maybe you'll tell yourself the truth."

"Been doing that for three years," Jalen said.

"Scars heal. You know I got shot four years ago? Never caught the guy who did it. But sometimes I hardly know the wound is even there."

"I understand why they did it," Jalen said as an ache pushed through his leg.

"I do too. Wasn't ready, didn't see it coming. I treated the thing wrong the whole time because I believed I was doing the right thing. Sometimes you have to change your approach."

Jalen reserved the urge to choke him for coming here and offering his two worthless cents on life and the meaning behind it all, at least as he saw it. His knuckles cracked as he clenched his fist.

"You don't trust me. If I didn't know any better, you'd put some lead in me as well if you could. We may not get along, but we aren't that different either."

"Why should I talk to you?"

"It's contempt," Lawrence said. "You serve it up like it's the meal of the day, and after a while you tell yourself it isn't bitter. Then you sort of learn to live with it."

"A cop and a wise man," Jalen mocked. "Never thought I'd see that."

"No? Well then maybe I'm not that wise after all." He shuffled his feet and dangled his hand beside the bed. "Why don't you tell me everything you know about this Underscore guy?"

Jalen blinked and told him the story of how he'd found ideas on message boards which led him to the dark web and how he'd managed to lose his signal in North Korea. Lawrence didn't take notes.

"Let's build a profile," Lawrence said. "What does he like to do in his spare time?"

"Football. Broncos—the team. Video games."

"That's a good start." He leaned back and let the overhead lights brighten his face. "So he's passionate about who he roots for. He's got an eye for detail and strategy, lives and dies by the keyboard, so it would seem.

Where would he spend his average Thursday evening? Drinking in shady bars or holed up in a lounge chair eating popcorn and guzzling energy drinks?"

"The latter."

"Yeah, but what's his love life like? Think he's seeing anyone special?"

"I wouldn't know."

Lawrence nodded and flashed a smile. "You just don't want to say it."

"This guy doesn't adhere to stereotypes," Jalen said. "He's clever, and even though he didn't do it, he knows something about it, otherwise he wouldn't be strategizing on the dark web in coded language. Maybe we need to understand him a little bit more before we start to paint an inaccurate picture."

"A lot of people live by stereotypes. Some of them are even quite famous and almost universally despised. Know why they do it?"

Jalen shrugged and stared at the ceiling.

"Acceptance. To fit in. Once you got a crowd you don't care what others might think and how they deride you. It's your lifestyle, you chose it yourself, and you knew what you were getting into."

"I still don't know why you're here. You can do all this with your friends at the station. And have a lot more fun with it. You're just staring at an invalid security officer who's had a nasty run."

"And a penchant for getting into traps," Lawrence said. "I lost count, how many was that?"

"Just shut up and leave," Jalen said. "I know what you're doing and it's not going to work."

"You've got me all figured out, Jalen." Lawrence had the nerve to look surprised and even a little bit perplexed. He clenched his muscles and stared at Jalen's face for a long time.

Jalen swallowed hard. What had changed with Lawrence between an hour ago and this moment? He attempted to spin the notion into something positive, but failed. What drove Lawrence didn't seem to fit his style. When things moved wrong, they often destroyed themselves. Patterns dictated everything, even down to the smallest pieces. Patterns don't change without consequences. Even the tiniest shift in the rotation of a particle could destroy the entire structure of the atom, which would eventually tear apart the entire piece of matter.

Then again, Jalen's own structure weakened three years ago and his own destruction seemed unrelenting. He teetered on the brink of being wiped away entirely. Martez Williams had outsmarted him on more than one occasion. He thought about the patterns behind Williams' actions and came to a quiet resolution long after Lawrence left.

Time had come to turn the tables. And he knew just where to strike.

# 28

# The Third Law

Fog lingered in the valley after an overnight storm brought a torrent of rain and damaging wind. No thunder had awakened Jalen and he'd slept straight through the storm. Leaves and twigs were strewn everywhere in the neighborhood and entire limbs had been ripped from some trees. After heavy rains, the air became dense with water vapor. The day was set to begin a warming trend for the city, with highs breaking into the 80s late in the week.

The drive in the rental car lasted no longer than the average commute, about twenty minutes, but at least he didn't have to take the freeway, which at this hour would likely resemble a parking lot.

Kalee greeted him with a curious smile, while Barry looked helpless or lost. His eyes darted back and forth from Jalen to a visitor, who sat in a chair against the wall. Jalen turned his head to see Doc sitting with his graying hair against the wall and an aura of anger touching the corners of his eyes. His face seemed to droop when he witnessed Jalen's scars.

"Shit, you look terrible."

Jalen had taken a cab to the airport early in the morning, where he rented a car. He drove home and took an hour nap before heading to the office. "You should see my car."

"Let's talk in private," Doc said.

Jalen exerted a sigh and then stared. He had a lot of work to do. Doc stood up and led Jalen into the lobby. The sitting area looked cozy. A lamp adorned one of the end tables, while a neat stack of magazines and a couple of fake potted plants graced the coffee table, around which two soft chairs and two couches were gathered. Jalen took a seat on the couch but didn't lean back. The boss sat next to him, looking as leathery as ever.

"I can't pretend I didn't see what I did yesterday. And the shareholders and the CEO are going to have some questions."

"The network connection?"

Doc nodded and frowned. "You know how important that is. If we don't have that, we don't have anything. And you shut it down?"

"I did it for a reason," Jalen explained.

The boss sighed and looked away. "Yeah."

"Since I've been investigating this case, stuff has been happening. When I realized that my work came with a danger, I had the servers disconnected to isolate us from the rest of the campus should we get infected. Kalee says that this Williams guy has been hacking security. Which gives me an idea."

"No. No more ideas."

"I have to do it," Jalen said.

"For what? Your ego? Jesus, we have to let the cops handle this one from now on."

Jalen growled. "Goddamnit, the guy's inside already. Got some moves and he could ruin this entire company. I know what's at stake. I know I'm right."

"Don't snap at me. You're smart, I'll give you that. But there's just too much baggage." He paused and stared at Jalen as if begging him to provide a final statement. "But I believe in you. I didn't want it to come to this."

"Firing me?"

Doc nodded slowly. "I'm sorry."

Jalen clenched his teeth. "Don't say you're sorry, I've protected this company for years, and you know I've...shit."

"But, as it goes," the boss said raising his eyebrows, "I'm forced to let this thing play out. I'll have a talk with the big wigs, maybe settle this whole thing. If it goes well, we both win."

"What are you saying?"

"I'm giving you one goddamn chance to make this right. What's your plan?"

"Since Williams has been hacking us, he's opened up a two-way street. Signal is pretty elusive, but I know how to triangulate now. I'm gonna hack him and shove a killer virus down his throat."

"That means—"

"Yeah," Jalen said. "It'll probably damage our servers irreparably. But since I've isolated security from the rest of the mainframes, the damage should be minimal. When the triangulation comes in, we'll send in the cops and arrest Williams or shoot him."

"That happens and you'll definitely lose your job."

"I might either way. This company goes down and I—"

"Lynx is the second biggest memory provider in the world," Doc interrupted. "We're not going down. During the recession, losses were in the billions, yet we've stayed on top. And if we get a foothold in Indonesia, Samsung will be crying in their beer."

"Tell them to steer clear," Jalen said. "For some reason, the connection in Jakarta has been popping up every now and again. Tell them what I know, for the good of this company."

"They're not going to believe you."

"They have to. Can't let their money go to their heads. Blows up in their faces like I think it will and it might be the end of the tech sector in this valley."

"I'll caution them, but I won't risk my job."

"Kalee takes over when I'm gone," Jalen said. "Promise me that. She's been doing this longer than I have and is probably better at it, too. Tell me you'll give her the promotion."

"Assuming that she isn't taking part in these horrible decisions, you've got my word."

Jalen stood up to sprint back in the office, but Doc, still sitting there, began to rock his knee up and down. The frown never left his face.

"Jalen. This conversation never took place. Do what you have to do. Bring that sonofabitch down and we'll talk about getting you or Kalee some more funding."

"Will do."

The boss watched Jalen until the office door closed. Jalen strutted to his desk and got his system up and running. Barry wheeled his chair toward

Jalen and studied at him while Kalee rested her elbows on the desk and gazed across. Her expression seemed plain, but eager.

"What's on the ticket today?" Barry asked.

"Get ready to see some fireworks," Jalen said.

"Finally."

Jalen glanced at Kalee. "Can you please build me a virus?"

"What?"

"Williams got us, now we can get him back. This whole time, we've been the victims of his attacks and his traps. He won't be expecting a counter attack of this scale. We infect his system, get his signal, and send the cops to bring him down. I think it will work."

"That's going to bring this whole office down," Kalee guessed.

"Yep."

"Then I won't do it. Leave me out of it."

"Kalee."

She narrowed her eyes, pushed her chair against the table, and fidgeted. "Damnit, Jalen, this is too dangerous. I have my limits."

"Just made a deal with Doc," Jalen said. "You're going to be immune."

"I don't want to be immune. All this time, I thought you've understood me. I can only do what I think is right."

Jalen stared and frowned. "That's all I'm doing. Please."

She glared for more than two minutes, during which her expression morphed from anger to confusion, to torment, to sadness, and then to something resembling understanding. A tear formed at the corner of her eye, and she looked away. "What kind of virus?" she asked.

"Trojan. Make it as destructive as you know how."

"I've never done anything like this before. It's illegal."

"For some reason I believe the cops will give us a pass this time."

Barry leaned away from Jalen but continued to stare. "What do you want me to do?"

"Stand by. Things can get real interesting real quick. I'm going to blindside this guy. I lost the signal in North Korea through the dark web the other day and I can track that signal again. Sending out two signals now. One through the hacking and one trough the dark web. Those two intersect and we've got degrees, minutes, and seconds on his location."

"Holy shit."

Jalen logged into his IM and typed Kalee a message.



"What's that supposed to mean?" Kalee said. Her fingers danced across the keyboard with more grace than a ballet performer moving to the last few lines of *Swan Lake.* Her frown never ceased, but the passion with which her fingers moved invigorated Jalen's heart. He imagined her doing his job better than he did and allowed a subtle smile to break across his face.

"It's bait," Jalen said.

"It's working." The screens flashed.

Jalen slammed his fist into the table and pounded away at the keyboard, punching the enter key so hard that the keyboard's supports snapped. His cursor moved without him moving the mouse. An icon flashed and a web browser popped up. "Oh shit! He's controlling my system."

The webpage seemed to be some kind of windows support page, but didn't look like one he'd seen before. The hacker moved fast through a series of links. Jalen countered by narrowing the bandwidth. He opened Kalee's video, and then used a separate internet window to stream a heavy metal song.

"This is going to rock you like a hurricane," Jalen shouted over the noise.

Traffic on the dark web seemed to be light, but one user remained online. "Underscore John, Is that you? I'm starting to think you and Williams are the same guy."

Jalen started tracking on the signal, leaned back, and watched it bounce around the world. Underscore scrambled through the web by eliminating programs that reduced bandwidth. He shut down the rock song and the video, allowing him to log into a large-platform website Jalen had never seen before. He glanced at it long enough to see the word Jakarta flash on the screen, but the image disappeared, and a page loaded with links took its place.

"How's that Trojan coming?" Jalen asked.

"It's taking a little extra coding to get it just the way I want it," she said. "Give me five more minutes."

"I'll try."

The battle raged on. Jalen again slowed down the bandwidth, but this tame had a different idea. "Everyone start streaming something now. Cat videos, rock songs, I don't care what."

A few eyebrows raised and Laurie even shook her head and rolled her eyes. The office filled with chatter, and the browsing on the webpage slowed down. Jalen attempted to close out of it but failed.

Underscore performed a series of stunts that scanned Jalen's hard drive, but somehow didn't touch the network connections. The idea Jalen understood to be too simple. The antivirus software would stop that in its tracks. "Gotta do better than that," he said.

Jalen hammered his keyboard multiple times, opening pages, shutting pages, while watching the bandwidth use skyrocket. The dark web signal bounced to Hong Kong and then to India, followed by South Africa and Norway. He believed it was going to take a rest stop in North Korea, but interestingly, it didn't. The signal bypassed that hub repeatedly. When the signal landed in the United States briefly, Jalen minimized the screen and brought up a new one. The hacker's signal had to be strong to be using Jaleln's computer against him. That signal hit several worldwide hubs and then darted across the Western United States. Jalen narrowed the screen and watched them simultaneously while pounding on his keyboard to open up more and more webpages.

"Come on, aren't you going to try anything clever? My grandma can do better than that."

He typed into the instant messenger:

Nice try, asshole.

Kalee received the message and scowled but continued to batter her keyboard with efficient grace and a narrow fury burning in her eyes.

The virus alert system further lowered the bandwidth, which stalled the signal trackers. Jalen swallowed hard as the hacker began to puncture holes in the server with smaller jabs. Jalen believed the servers could withstand the storm for a few more minutes while Kalee built the virus. He glanced up at her, opened a new webpage designed to alert him when someone was hacking, which would set off alarm bells.

The hacker worked away furiously attacking firewalls in the servers. Jalen countered each hit by concentrating his efforts on overloading the webpage he was using. It only mildly went to plan.

He glanced at the signal trackers and smiled when they intersected near Omaha, Nebraska. He used that point and coaxed the trackers into revealing the home address of the attacker. "Don't tell me it's Williams's house," Jalen said.

"Shit!" The trackers shut down. Screens began to flicker all over the office.

"Kalee, that virus. Get it done, now!"

"I'm trying."

Jalen's monitors went dark. He slammed both fists down on the keyboard, slapped himself across the forehead, stood up, and approached Kalee's desk while she still had use of her system.

"It's as good as it's going to be," he said quietly. "Let it go."

The hacker's attempts to thwart Jalen had been a success, but Jalen remembered the address and wrote it down. Martez Williams had sent the signal to the same address Kalee used when she tracked the signal.

Another idea sprung to Jalen's mind like lightning. "That's where the server is located," he said. But what about the terminal? Let's see if that sucker can handle this."

Jalen blazed through the same steps he'd used to track the user's browsing through the hacking. Now that he had that location pinned down, the system would likely reveal the locations of all connected users. Two were in use, both wirelessly. Jalen managed to isolate the one seeing the most activity.

"Hack this you son of a bitch!"

Jalen pressed the 'launch' button a little harder than he should have. The destruction didn't appear to start immediately. Instead, it simmered as the user continued to slash away at the servers.

"Work it," he coaxed the virus. "Come on, do something."

"Jalen," Kalee said, sounding pensive. "I've got an idea. Instead of letting him do all of the hacking, why don't we hack him for a change? We'll get his home address that way."

Jalen nodded, swallowed, and started pressing buttons. His fingers worked furiously, and for a moment, Kalee's fingers began to dance with his.

He held back a smile when their fingers attempted to press the same key at the same time. Instead of letting the moment hit him, he trialed away and let her do the attacking for once.

"This is insane," Barry said, staring at a cat video on his screen. "Using this guy's own tricks against him. That's like meeting force with force. Like what Newton said way back when."

"For every action, there is an equal and opposite reaction," Jalen recited.

He clicked a few buttons while Kalee burned a hole into the user's security system. Jalen bared his teeth, raised his eyebrows, and dug in.

# 29

# Supercluster

The virus protection software on Kalee's desktop lit up like crazy, flashing warnings, attempting to delete harmful files, but they kept coming. Jalen swept the warnings away one by one as he worked. Kalee operated the mouse, clicking and moving in perfect harmony with the rhythm of Jalen's fingers.

The hacker seemed to be stationed in a higher-end house more typical of west foothills residences or more private suburbs. Jalen managed to activate the compcuter's webcam, which was aimed at the user's chest. Jalen attempted to swivel the camera but could not use the controls.

The desktop seemed as though it should have been cluttered with half-empty bags of chips and beer cans, but what little of the room Jalen could see appeared to be clean. The user's hairy arms remained in view the entire time as he typed away at the keyboard attempting to bring down whoever he dueled with.

Jalen burned through the user's hard drive as the Trojan tore it apart. "Steal that file," Jalen said to Kalee. "Let's let him know we're here."

"It could be a trap."

"Not gonna hurt," Jalen said. "When this is over, I think our whole system will be fried. I see that software going crazy. That tells me your virus is doing its job."

"I decided to go with a wrecking ball rather than a missile," Kalee said.

"Good choice."

Kalee downloaded the file and dumped it into a temporary folder that remained untouched. She stared at other files, downloaded more of them, and then began to dig into a Home Security folder. She examined the company as Jalen typed.

Jalen glanced up at the security company's profile page. He almost had to laugh. It couldn't have been that easy the whole time, could it? "Maybe we should go hack them, too."

"No need for that," she said almost as if she'd read his mind. "It looks like I found his street address. It's in the country. Southwest, in a higher-end subdivision. She released the mouse and scribbled the address down on a sheet of paper.

The Trojan ate away at Kalee's security files as Jalen worked.

"That's a nice security system," he said. "Wow. Clever. It's a fortress. Sprinklers, automatic door locks, lighting and heating controls, and we can probably make dinner from here. I can break it, but I don't have to."

"Are you sure?"

"Watch this." Jalen tapped a few buttons and turned out the lights.

Kalee didn't laugh, but a cool smile touched her lips. She bounced around through the hacker's hard drive stealing data both corrupted and clean. The user sprung out of the chair, looking irritated, and disappeared from view. The lights flashed back on, and the user returned to his chair.

"I think your lawn needs watered." Jalen found the controls to the sprinkler system and turned on the water. The man didn't move. He seemed to rock back and forth, as if enjoying the exchange.

Jalen typed to himself in the IM screen.

> Looks like the water is on, you'd better got take care of that.

The user pounded the enter key four times and leaned back. Kalee began to steal everything she could get her hands on.

The hacker didn't bother get up. Instead, he attempted to install a feeble defense system that started to kick in just a little too late. Jalen's heart rate rose as the monitors began to flicker. The music and the videos that surrounded him went quiet. Jalen looked up at a roomful of flashing screens. That would be the servers biting the dust.

"Got anymore tricks before this whole thing collapses?" she said.

Jalen operated the door locks in the house and quickly programmed them to sound an alarm each time the doors were locked or unlocked. That would get annoying. Unrelenting, Jalen battered Kalee's keyboard with more and more commands as she downloaded the contents of entire folders.

The sirens went off. The user stood up and sprinted away from the computer, then returned after silence resumed. Jalen locked the doors again, turned on the water, and flashed the lights. The user fought back by blasting chunks of damaged data at them. Jalen didn't even try to deflect it.

Within a few moments, he was able to program the locks to stay closed no matter what the user tried. For fun, he turned on the sprinklers and turned out the lights.

The sky outside had gone dark. Jalen became aware of that when he glanced around the room and saw all of the workers sitting there with nothing to do.

Barry stood up from his desk, motioned Marcus to follow him, and then pounded his fist into his palm. He nodded his head at Jalen as they both departed the office with weapons drawn and flashlights ready.

With the locks to the doors securely in place, Jalen offered a chuckle and then pounded the keyboard one more time.

"That ought to do it."

As he finished saying it, all of the screens in the office went dark. The user leaned down and stared into the camera for what seemed like thirty seconds before Kalee's system shut down. The Trojan had reduced both hard drives to rubble.

For a moment, Kalee looked as though she didn't know what to do. Jalen stood up and stared into her eyes for a second. A familiar glint flashed behind her glasses. She knew what was coming without Jalen having to explain it.

"Go," she whispered. "Take him down. I'll wait five minutes to call the cops."

Jalen rushed out the door and took one last second to glance at her. This could be his last seconds as an employee of Lynx Technologies. The time ran bittersweet through his senses. Coldness drifted through him, followed by an inexplicable warmth.

Through it all, Kalee remained the best friend Jalen could have asked for. Her advice never ventured into self-serving territories. Her kindness and the simplicity with which she worked around Jalen's worst demons touched him.

He nodded, faked a smile, and then closed the door.

Thick waves of traffic met him during the drive to the user's house. Adrenaline surged through his veins like waves crashing on a rocky shore. He shuddered, tried to listen to some music, but decided against it. More than two lights changed to red before he got there, but he blew through them anyway, carefully checking for cross traffic just in case someone thought it wise to tee-bone him into a canal.

Flashing lights appeared on the horizon as Jalen turned on to the boulevard that led to the user's subdivision. The subdivision, surrounded by both newer and older housing projects, was shaded by large, old-growth cottonwoods. Jalen punched the accelerator to the floor when the two police cars approached the street from the opposite direction.

They both turned and Jalen followed. He needed to see this, he told himself. If the man had managed to escape, fury would strike Jalen. His heart folded with heavy chugs as his breathing intensified. The hacker lived two streets over from the main drive in. The police cars almost collided as they approached, but Jalen followed close behind them.

As the cars parked, Jalen gazed at the exterior of the house he'd just attacked. The lights had been turned off. No blue glow from televisions flickered in the windows. All seemed quiet.

He flung the door open just as a half dozen cops assaulted the front door in a military-like formation.

"Come out with your hands up," one of them ordered into a bullhorn.

Jalen pulled out his weapon and walked up behind the cops. Detective Lawrence saw him but didn't have time to verbally abuse him for his stupidity.

"Come out, or we'll be forced to come in after you!"

Jalen stared at the door for a moment and then to the sprinklers. An idea came to him. The outside lights were turned off, but the sprinklers continued. The user's hard drive had been destroyed, which should have shut down the sprinklers. He paced back and forth in the driveway as his idea came to him.

He ran into the spray of water and kicked a sprinkler head clean off. A cascade of water shot up through the open pipe, and began to flood the lawn. Jalen didn't wait before sprinting toward the garage. He opened the small security console, which required a password to operate the garage door. He pounded the keypad repeatedly with his fist until the display went dark and the backlit numbers flickered.

"I got you, Underscore John," He yelled. "You're as dumb as you are...SHIT!"

A boom rattled his eardrums. He staggered away from the garage toward the cops, who began to back away from the house. The boom resonated again. Splinters of wood rained down from the second floor. A shotgun had just punched a hole in the siding. Jalen spun around to scan the neighborhood.

Quiet resumed as one by one, neighbors began pulling open doors to gawk at the commotion.

Instead of opening fire again, the residents seemed keen to wait it out. Lawrence sent a pair of cops to cover the rear door.

"You almost killed me four times," Jalen yelled. "But I survived, you son of a bitch!"

"Come out!"

Lawrence darted to the door, opened up his stance and kicked it four times before the frame splintered. The four cops stationed near the front door assumed their formation and invaded the house. Jalen thought fast and followed them, drawing his taser and readying to fire upon anyone that moved.

The flashlights illuminated the dark rooms well. Jalen lurked behind the cops, helping to check every room. Gunfire erupted. Glass shattered.

On instinct, Jalen ducked. The other officers returned fire into the dark. The hacker fired four rounds and paused. A volley of shots resumed a split second later. Four police guns shot two rounds apiece. Jalen's ears began to ring.

Hoping he wasn't about to get shot, Jalen huddled against a wall and pressed the barrel of his weapon against his face. Sweat poured out of his forehead. His feet and hands trembled. He worked back a lump in his throat and powered forward into the crowd of firing cops. More gunshots echoed from the room cops concentrated on. Silence, and then the sound of shattering glass. The officer kicked the door open and fired a round just as the hacker pulled the trigger. The slug plunged through the officer's forehead. A dazed look shot across his face, and he fell face first.

Instead of pausing, Underscore pulled the trigger repeatedly, spraying the cops with an impressive amount of firepower. The gunfire stopped after another cop had fallen. Rather than watch the carnage continue, Jalen sprinted to the end of a corridor and charged the adjacent wall. The shock of pain bolted through his shoulder. Drywall crumbled as Jalen broke through, but not without colliding with a stud.

Another volley of gunshots sounded. Someone screamed. The villain had been injured, Jalen guessed. He looked up and saw something dangling from a tree branch outside the window. Jalen laid still, pointed his weapon, and fired. The charged taser shot jolted the man's stomach. He twitched, stumbled backwards and fell through the window.

A crunching sound emanated from below. Jalen abandoned his weapon and crawled to the window. Two guns adorned a table near the window. The hacker had enough firepower to bring them all down.

Looking out the window, Jalen scanned the area, expecting to see a man fleeing. Neighbors lined the sidewalks, gaping at the house across the way. Jalen studied them for a second as the cops began to tear the room apart.

One glance down told him all he needed to know. The man lay motionless on top of a pair of crumpled metal garbage cans. Blood oozed from open wounds. The man's eyes seemed to stare up into the sky as if he witnessed the fiery glow of billions and billions of galaxies all bunched together.

A flood of victory poured through him, but instead of relishing it, Jalen slumped to his knees and buried his face in his hands. It had all worked out for the best, he told himself, but destruction reigned. For a moment, he could only stare at the wall.

The cops scoured the room and then invaded the rest of the house, shouting commands at each other. The two cops that had gone to the backside of the house had climbed the steps and attended to the two fallen officers.

Jalen's chest heaved as he stared.

One cop was dead. Jalen recognized him as Lawrence's partner. He uttered a scream, but his chest only seemed to pulse with a soundless lurch. The other officer was alive. The cops had already called for ambulances to assist them in caring for their comrade.

With one gasp, Jalen fell sideways, motionless. Minutes stacked up. He could only stare. This job cost lives, but Jalen's remained intact. Guilt flushed through him, and tears flooded his eyes. Of course, everything Kalee had told him was true. He shook as understanding tore through him, shredding every remaining piece of his soul. He had to let go. He rested his head on the floorboard below the window, allowed the tension in his muscles to fade, and then closed his eyes.

# 30

# The End of the Arrow

*Three years earlier*

Rain stained the horizon with sickness that day as a heavy fog obscured the mountains. Vertical streaks in the sky to the west indicated a band of heavier showers. Though he'd spend most of the day indoors, the weather induced a pervasive chill that could not erode the tension.

Jalen sat quietly in the den. The corners of his mouth drooped. At the end of it all, the fighting seemed trivial, the sort of spat couples had over the laundry not being done or dishes piling up too high. Still, the argument had been fierce. Had the love simply dissipated into nothing but mist so soon? He turned his ring over in his fingers for at least an hour, admiring the shine, but dreading an event that lied in the future.

Was it too much to ask that she listen? Jalen never experienced a shortage of advice he could dispense in any troubling time. When she had a bad day, he would drape his arm over her shoulder, nuzzle against her neck, and tell her to relax, for tomorrow would be another day and letting the care stack up day by day would assemble too much weight for her to handle. She'd always brushed it away. After a pleasant thank you, the tears would stop, and she'd go about her chores as if the conversation hadn't taken place at ll. But it did. And the remnant of the emotion lingered.

She departed late in the morning, just after the rain had started. The bus waited in the parking lot of a Christian church they should have been attending. She drove the car that two miles and called him to let him know the bus was ready to leave.

Forty miles never seemed that great a distance. Some kind of mountain retreat her boss had recommended, which could not be rescheduled no matter the weather. The day's activities were to include a fireside-styled pow-wow to motivate and inspire, a nature walk to appreciate the smaller things and to recommend breaks from stress, and some sort of trust and team building exercise. It would be over in a day and the bus would return near 8:00 pm.

The kiss goodbye had been bittersweet.

Pondering never came with so much weight. He turned his ring over again and again, staring at it, glancing out the window, and then returning the gaze as if it carried some new piece of information he hadn't noticed before.

His hear leapt when, after the sun had fallen below the horizon, the clock neared 8:00. He stared at his watch, rose from the table and laid back on the couch with the remote in his hand. It would be a great time to pretend to watch television. No, he didn't worry about her. The TV aired some kind of comedy show that somehow didn't make him laugh. Eight-thirty passed and she still had not returned. After another thirty minutes, Jalen dug out his phone and punched the button to dial her. After four rings, it went to her voice mail. "This is Beth, call me back, bye."

Instead of leaving a message, he redialed. This time, three rings sufficed and her voice mail picked up again. A third time yielded the same result. He clenched his teeth and rested his phone on the couch cushion, perfectly positioned should she call back. He'd chide her and let her know he missed her, no matter how passive-aggressive the tactic sounded.

She didn't call. He tried her again and again, and each time the pain grew. The next day, after experiencing little sleep, he phoned her boss.

"Where is she?" he asked quickly. "She didn't come home last night."

"Really? She seemed eager to see you, said she wanted to tell you something while we were taking the nature walk. She was on the bus home when we called roll."

"Can't be right," he said. "Her car is still at the parking lot. Just checked."

"Mabye she walked somewhere."

Jalen hung up the phone and dialed the police. They sent officers to the house, promising to look for her. The search ended with them combing through the mountains within a set perimeter should she just wander away. Four days passed. A week. Two weeks, a month, and then two. Then the call came. "The search came up empty and there hasn't been a sign of her. She hasn't used her credit cards or anything. I'm afraid at this point we're going to have to accept it. Your wife will never come home. Terribly sorry."

Jalen groaned and hung up the phone. Tears splattered his cheeks. The fight seemed meaningless two months later. And the way he'd let her leave gnawed his bones to powder. "Be careful." He knew the trek would be dangerous, given the weather. He might as well had signed her death warrant himself.

His sleep produced demons which cut his nights short. *I love you, please come home,* he pled. A sip of vodka would help to drown the sorrow. And then another. Soon, he drank for no reason and the memory of her name faded. The last of her became nothing but mist that poisoned his heart. Agony passed, but Beth never returned.

***

Jalen sunk into the couch in the lobby outside the security office, where his coworkers were busy installing a temporary system. He hadn't seen Kalee or Barry yet. The night before, after the carnage had fallen, Detective Lawrence didn't seem irate enough that Jalen had showed up. "Stupid decision," he'd said. Then he left to mourn his partner alone.

Doc sat by him and leaned forward with his elbows on his knees. He sighed and then turned to face Jalen. "Hell of a night, wasn't it?"

Jalen nodded against the cushions and closed his eyes.

"I met with the board this morning. The usual business meeting that ran too long, eating up half the day, only to universally agree that nothing will get done till next week. A couple of decisions relate to you, though."

Jalen struggled to lean forward and rubbed his eyes with his fists. His leg twitched.

"They want you to design a new system, you know given that the last one is shrapnel by now. One that will stand up against this type of hacking in the future. You've shown some merit in the past week, so they believe you can do it, if you are up to the challenge."

Jalen gaped at him. "So I'm not fired?"

The boss chuckled but didn't allow a grin to part his lips. He narrowed his eyes and let the expression droop. "Oh, you're fired alright. You destroyed company property and the board can't look past that. No. Think of this as a consulting position. You design the software, install all the firewalls, set up more physical security measures, ensure this type of thing doesn't happen again. Think you can handle that?"

"I don't come cheap," Jalen said.

"After I told them how much you were being paid, they kind of rolled their eyes. It's six figures, take it or leave it. You'll probably be spending a lot of time out here anyway, keeping stuff up to date, installing new stuff."

"What's the budget?"

"Undetermined, but early estimates run in the millions for new equipment, updated badge scanners, the works. They're going to be changing a bunch of protocols in the coming weeks."

"I don't know," Jalen said, knowing he was about to lie. "I think the university will offer me one twenty-five to do the same thing I was doing here."

"Make it one and three quarters," Doc said. "Keep in mind you won't be employed here, so there's a contract. We'll get lawyers drafting it up. I can't give you particulars, but I think five years is reasonable with a buyout clause and a bonus here and there based on effectiveness of the software."

"I'll have to consider it," Jalen said.

"Consider 'till the contract arrives at your house. Then come sign it and you'll start immediately."

Jalen could only nod. Still, he lowered his eyebrows and stared at the door. Barry emerged carrying a small stack of papers and stood in a corner to wait for him.

"Tell me Kalee got my job," Jalen said.

Doc swallowed and nodded. "Board agrees."

Silence stretched between them. Jalen adjusted his knees and leaned against the armrest before pushing himself forward and waiting for Doc to say more.

"She'll be making your salary with cost of living increases every year. So long as she doesn't make a virus that can wipe out every computer in there."

"I had to talk her into it," Jalen admitted. "Be sure that will never happen."

Another pause came and lingered. Doc stared at him until Jalen almost decided to get up and drive home.

"The board also has to thank you for exposing the Jakarta deal. Losses could have totaled in the billions and crippled this company. We're talking ten thousand layoffs minimum here.

"They didn't know that at first, of course, but a certain board member didn't really do the numbers all that well. Given his involvement with Taiki John Marinelle—you know him as Underscore John—Stanger resigned this morning. If not, they would have mauled the CFO over the whole deal, more bad business."

Barry pushed away from the wall and approached them. He sat down in the chair opposite a small end table and offered his knowledge. "According to the police, the fall killed Marinelle, after you tased him. Good shot. Seems to say something about the accuracy of the cops, doesn't it?"

"They lost people last night," Jalen said. He almost swallowed his heart. He gulped and let Barry continue.

"The tour guide, Kazinsky, they found more evidence tying him to Marinelle and Cambridge. Marinelle did most of his business in Singapore, but had an office in Indonesia. He went rogue figuring out how much Lynx could handle while getting paid millions under the table from some unscrupulous guys in Asia. Marinelle saw Kazinsky as an opportunity, but Kazinsky wasn't going to go along with it. So he sent Burton Cambridge in to get rid of him. Seems maybe the murder wasn't quite as tidy as Marinelle would have liked."

"Then what about Martez Williams?" Jalen asked.

"An engineer discovered his body early this morning fried to death up in an interstitial mechanical room next to one of the scrubbers. It was either an accident or suicide because they don't think he's been dead long enough for Marinelle to have killed him. Williams was the booby trap guy, Marinelle handled all the hacking."

Jalen shook his head.

"I'm sure they would have made it out of the country if you didn't go on the offensive last night," Barry added. "With all of the cash at their disposal, they'd be retiring on a beach in Belize or something and no one would ever find out."

"Two cops would still be alive," Jalen said.

"It's a hazard of the job," someone behind him said. Detective Lawrence wore a suit and a tie. He looked troubled but extended a hand for Jalen to shake instead of berating him.

Jalen hesitated, and then frowned as he shook the detective's hand. "I'd like to offer you a job."

"Already got one," Jalen said.

"Yeah?"

Jalen told him all about the offer from Doc and didn't leave out the salary.

"Well, good luck with that, my friend. Maybe I'll see you around. We'll get some drinks."

"Good plan," Jalen said. "But maybe they better be non-alcoholic drinks. Trying to cut back, you know."

"I was hoping I'd hear that," Lawrence said. "Take care and don't hesitate to call."

Barry stared at him. "Making friends with the fuzz already?"

Jalen smiled. "I didn't have anything to do with it."

After starting at him, Barry rose to his feet. He shook Jalen's hand, nodded at Doc, and then retreated into the office.

"Looks like you made it out of this okay after all," Doc said. He stood up, stretched his legs, and stared at Jalen for several seconds. He shook Jalen's hand. "I'll keep in touch."

Instead of getting up and driving home, Jalen leaned back on the couch and folded his hands across his stomach. He closed his eyes for what seemed like ten minutes when he sensed a presence. He opened his eyes and his heart leapt.

Kalee sat down next to him. Jalen leaned forward and looked away while biting his lip. He knew what she wanted to talk about but wasn't sure he wanted to discuss it. Instead of talking, he furrowed his eyebrows. She only stared at him.

"Congrats on the promotion," Jalen said.

"I don't know if it was worth it," she said quietly.

He nodded and then shifted his legs.

"So I guess this is goodbye. Maybe now you'll have some time to get your life in order, let Beth go."

"Maybe," Jalen said. "But it sounds like I'll be plenty busy building Lynx Technologies a new security system. I'll see you around."

She already knew about it. Instead of surprise, her face communicated some kind of comfort that she didn't often display. It took him a moment to realize what it meant.

"What about Beth?"

Jalen gulped. A tear touched his eye and trickled down his cheek while concern drifted across Kalee's face. She removed her glasses and set them on the coffee table.

"It's...It's over," Jalen said. "She won't come back. Hurts like a sonofabitch, but I always knew it. Thanks for helping me sort that out. Might take me a few more months or another year."

She leaned forward and slung her arm around his neck while touching his shoulder with her free hand. Her check felt warm against his ear. "I'll tell you what," she said. "If you let me read that diary of yours, I'll deal with it."

Jalen turned his head. Their eyes met and then wedged themselves closed. She moved her hands over his back. The moisture of her lips against his felt like bliss for a brief moment. He pulled away from her, opened his eyes, and stared.

"I'll think about it."

She pulled him in closer. Her embrace was warm. She kissed him and pressed her lips against his for a few seconds, which could never feel like long enough. He didn't want to let go of the warmth of her embrace, but she had work to do. She had to clean up her mess.

Releasing her felt like losing a wedge of his soul. He stood up and paced to the office door with her. "Maybe that's best," she said in reply to his last statement.

He smiled and studied her eyes as they stood next to the door. "I'm going to go get coffee and one of those health bars. Want one?"

Kalee grinned. "You owe me a hundred bucks for that soccer debacle, so I guess we'll have to call it even."

Jalen folded his arms around her and pressed his lips against hers one more time. He flashed a genuine smile and then strode away. He could feel her gaze as he walked out the front door, but forced himself not to look back.

Love had never felt so sudden or so sweet. As he drove home, Beth was the furthest thing from his mind.

The house lingered quiet. He found his stash of Vodka, opened the lid and sniffed it. The bottle had offered him both pleasure and relief at first, but now it mocked him. He frowned, carried it to the kitchen sink, and poured the remainder of it down the drain.

Entering the den, thoughts poured into his mind. He started the computer and stared at the keyboard for around ten minutes before he began to type. His heart hammered in his chest.

*Life can be like a freefall sometimes. Going through the motions, trying to forget, and hoping nobody will notice brings even more pain eventually. We all lose sometimes. All life is temporary while we do the best we can do. Humanity might be obsolete, but the heart will remain. You can reassemble the pieces of a shattered dish that has fallen from a shelf, but it will never be the same. From creation, the universe we know has ripped itself apart and expanded. No force can put it back together, for decay will last forever. Time is like an arrow. It can only move in one direction and along the way things fall apart. But what happens when matter has spread apart so much that it ceases to exist? What lies at the end of that arrow?*

*Peace can endure every tragedy that befalls us. Whether knowing that somehow everything will work out or exerting our faith in some God, we can glue the pieces back together and make the fragments even stronger than they were before. You can forget everything, but don't forget to grow. Fire makes us strong, and maybe that's what we deserve.*

# Acknowledgements

Writing this book brought me two months of joy. The original concept came in several distinct phases. As with most of my novels, I started by writing down some key details from one of my nightmares. From there I constructed the backbone of the plot, which is a rough outline that hits on the major points of emphasis. The second step consisted of building character flaws and relationships. I tinkered around with some ideas based on the direction involved with the first few paragraphs of the story, which I wrote around the same time as the outline.

My day job as a Building Information Modeling coordinator has taken me a lot of places and introduced me to some fantastic realms I never would have experienced without it. While all of the people and places mentioned in this novel are purely fictional, one job years ago caused my mind to wander. That project entailed travelling to the project location and exploring existing buildings on the campus of a large company to take measurements. What if, I wondered, a person was murdered here?

The third phase came several weeks after building the rough outline. Using all of my notes, I typed out a more detailed outline that guided the story to where I wanted it to go. Still, a lot of surprises came about, and these surprises make the writing a lot of fun.

Before I depart, a few thanks are in order.

First, I would like to thank Amanda Fitzpatrick for assisting with the detail editing and identifying areas where the structure could be improved. You do a great job.

As with the *Era Sinistra* books, Jeanine Henning designed the unbelievable cover art for this book. Jeanine, your professionalism and eye for detail are unmatched in the design world.

You may have noticed that a particular part of the plot for this book revolves around science. I enjoy reading about physics. Stephen Hawking wrote one of the best books about physics called *A Brief History of Time*. It is worth noting that I employed a concept Hawking calls "The Arrow of Time." Part of Jalen's struggle deals with thoughts that parallel this concept.

A few other people assisted by beta-reading and offering valuable insight. I send thanks to Jason Shirley and Bernard K. Finnigan, whose terrifying Halloween novel has been met with praise.

Last, I would like to express my gratitude for my wife Kristy, for her support and enthusiasm. Thank you for pulling no punches and giving me your honest opinion, but above all for encouraging me toward success. I love you.

-bm

# About the Author

Brad Mathews bends genre rules by creating dynamic, unorthodox characters thrust into criminal investigations.

He is known to use abstract imagery to construct striking realities that build into suspenseful mystery tales.

Mathews is Certified in Plumbing design, and his extensive Building Information Modeling experience gives him a unique ability to detail mechanical and industrial settings in his novels.

Mathews resides in Boise, Idaho with his family.